Book Five
of
The Gods of Space and Time

Sayonara Planet Earth

Vincent Gilvarry

eBook ISBN: 978-0-646-70270-4
Paperback ISBN: 978-0-646-70242-1

Contents

PREFACE

Addric Sharano is the main character in a series of epic and mostly light-hearted adventures called "The Gods of Space and Time," all of which are based on the belief that people are the most important things in life.

Addric is an eternal optimist, a young man who believes in the impossible. Officially, he is a Yumi Master, but he is also an intergalactic peacekeeper who works for an organisation known as the Intergalactic Alliance.

And unlike James Bond, who can do whatever he likes, Addric has to abide by a strict code of conduct, which means that he cannot take a life or use violence, and when he does encounter a problem, he deals with it using creative, non-violent methods.

Addric had his first taste of Planet Earth at the age of seventeen, and he couldn't wait to get back. Even though he is now a resident of this glorious planet, Addric originates from the Khavala, a galaxy on the outer perimeter of Alpha Centauri.

In this story, the inhabitants of Planet Earth have not only become obsessed with electronic devices; they have lost touch with the most important element of their being. According to the powers that be, this is a major problem, and if they want to survive, Earthlings have to change their ways or it's sayonara forever and ever.

Addric is assigned the task of dragging them back from the brink, and as the inhabitants of Planet Earth are about to find out, not all aliens have a bulbous head and big green eyes; some just happen to look like a Swedish version of Addric Sharano.

INTRODUCTION

Earthlings have battled just about everything, including members of their own species, but one of their most fearsome adversaries is also their great provider.

Mother Nature can be their best friend or their worst nightmare. She can take away in an instant everything they have done their best to create.

To those in the celestial realms, it comes as something of a surprise to discover that Planet Earth is destined for extinction. Word had passed around that its days were numbered.

A decision like that is not made lightly, and, in some cases, it is a directive from the highest echelons of power, but it's enough to bring thousands of celestial masters out of the woodwork.

They have been summoned to a conference, the like of which has never happened before. A new chapter of the Intergalactic Bible is about to be revealed, and any celestial master who has ever played a role in Earth's history is obliged to attend.

The Intergalactic Bible is the means by which messages of great import are conveyed by the divine logos. And on this occasion, it has a very concise message for those attending this conference. And when the Bible appears, it assumes the form of a sphere of golden light.

'Sisters and brothers, friends of old. We have known each other for an eternity, and it is only rarely that I have to intervene. And I do so on this occasion because of the events occurring in one of the most sacred of all territories.'

'Those of you who have had a close connection with Planet Earth will not be surprised to hear that issues have been developing in that domain for quite some time.'

'Unfortunately, Project Earth has been identified as a failure, primarily because the current inhabitants are a threat to its planned future.'

'They have become so obsessed with technology that it has taken over their lives.'

'This situation is counterproductive to the greater good, and as a result, their future now rests in your hands.'

'The people of Earth are no longer in control of their own lives. The internet has become the only god they recognize.'

'And to make things worse, they are no longer communicating with the most essential element of their being.'

'There are many amongst our ranks who have personal experience of these difficulties, but what are we to do - you might be asking?'

'This decision is not an easy one. The inhabitants of Earth must be made aware that their days are numbered.'

'You have one hour to make a decision as to what to do about Earth's future, and it will be up to you to find a solution to this problem.'

'However, if this situation is not resolved, that most glorious of all places will be terminated within ninety days.'

'The hearts of those that shine most brightly will be rewarded, but those who do not meet our standards will be reassigned, and the planet will be reprocessed for a future that is as yet unknown.'

CHAPTER 1

The spirits of the departed are not the only residents of graveyards, battlefields, abandoned houses, or places like Dead Man's Cove. As well as a few rats and mice scurrying through the debris, old doors with creaky hinges are just as common.

It is said that the deceased watch closely as you make your way through streets riddled with history. And apparently, there is an unwritten law that states that they can linger in the shadows for as long as they like.

You would probably find quite a few of them on an isolated promontory off the coast of Spain, loitering around the home of a Yumi Master called Addric Sharano.

From the moment he set eyes on that beautiful stretch of land, Addric knew that this was where he wanted to settle down. He first saw it while cruising around the Mediterranean many years before and decided to take a closer look.

The old monastery was once a retreat for a sect of monks, and when seen from the air, it resembles a dragon's head. Even though it probably had a different name, Addric decided to christen it Dragonshead.

It is as far from civilisation as you can get, and that was a bonus as far as Addric was concerned. Roads no longer went that way, and ships never gave it a second glance, but he saw its potential.

Perched on a gentle slope that overlooks the windswept shores of the Mediterranean, the view from his palatial villa is both spectacular and unforgettable.

Addric has always dreamed of having a house with a view of the ocean. And for a Yumi Master with the power to conjure up anything you can imagine, nothing could have been easier than to resurrect this relic of the past and bring it to life in the blink of an eye.

There was not much to see other than the crumbling remains of the abbey, a few wild goats that grazed on the hillside, and several acres of grapes withering on the vine.

The abbey is now a very different place and boasts a brand-new jetty and a boathouse, and even the little grotto on the beach, which was dedicated to the Holy Family, has had a 21st-century makeover.

This is the place that Addric and his wife Maya called home for the last thirty-five years. But she passed away over a year ago, and if he had not been a Yumi Master, Addric would have followed her into the next life.

Old age is a condition that afflicts just about everyone on Planet Earth, and unfortunately, it crept up on Maya much sooner than he would have liked. They never had children of their own but Addric adopted a little boy many years before. Jatoo is now a fifty years old man, and like Addric, he is also a Yumi Master.

He and his wife, Marina, are the proud parents of two beautiful children called Subandrah and Altheria, and they rarely need an excuse to visit their grandfather, but they have a pretty good one.

There is no such thing as an ocean where they come from, and they like to visit as often as possible. As Addric knows, there is nothing better than splashing around in the sparkling waters of the Mediterranean.

CHAPTER 2

The loss of a loved one is a condition that only time can heal, and other than the occasional visitor, Addric's only company has been a few passing spirits. And when his friends do make an appearance, some arrive by inter-dimensional portal while others just materialise out of the blue.

It is the morning of the 30th of March in the year 2048, and Addric is preparing his first coffee of the day when the front doorbell rings.

'Who could that be,' he says.

No one has ever rung that bell before, so he races down two flights of stairs and opens the door, only to discover that his visitor is the goddess Emphora.

'Emphora, please come in,' he says. 'I had a feeling that I would be seeing you sooner or later.'

'This is not just a social call, is it?'

'No, Addric, it's not. I am here for a reason.'

Emphora is typical of all Yumi women and is renowned for her grace and style. She usually wears her familiar silken gown and veil, but today she, is dressed in a very smart designer coat and hat. It is the sort of outfit that anyone with an ounce of common sense would wear on a blustery day at the beach.

'As usual, you look wonderful,' Addric says.

'Thank you, my boy. An old lady loves a compliment, especially from a handsome young man.'

The view from Addric's terrace is worth the effort, and even though she is here for a reason, Emphora is happy to catch up on the latest gossip. And after her second cup of coffee, she gets down to business.

'Addric, an issue of the utmost importance has arisen, and it's one that affects you more than anyone else.'

'It's not something I have done, is it?'

'No, Addric, it's what you hopefully will do, and as soon as you possibly can,' Emphora says somewhat cryptically.

'As the Head of the High Yumi Council, I was summoned to attend a meeting at the headquarters of the Intergalactic Alliance.'

The Alliance is an intergalactic body whose primary purpose is to monitor the evolutionary status of every inhabited system in the universe. They are also one of Addric's employers and he knows immediately that this means business.

'Now, and this is the difficult part,' Emphora says. 'They have been advised that Planet Earth has been found wanting.'

'The people of Earth are not meeting the standards expected of a race of developing beings. And unless they make radical changes in their lives, their future is in jeopardy.'

Earth has always had its problems, Addric knows that, but he is surprised to hear that a celestial body has decided to take punitive action just because the inhabitants are less than perfect.

'What does that mean?' he says.

'They have been designated for extinction, Addric.'

'No, they can't,' he cries. 'They wouldn't, would they?'

'Not if this problem can be rectified, but you Addric, have been identified as someone who could change the future of the people of this planet.'

'I have and why would that be?'

'If you want to find out more, you will have to accompany me to a meeting at Alliance headquarters, where you will be briefed in more detail.'

'I realise how distressing this must sound, Addric, but if you speak to some of the masters who have devoted their lives to the people of Earth, I am sure you could come up with a plan.'

'Why me?' he says.

'I believe that someone dobbed you in.'

'You,' he says.

'No, it wasn't, my boy, but think about it, Addric. You love this planet more than anyone, and you could not sit by and do nothing, not if there is something you could do.'

'That's true, Emphora.'

Addric takes a long deep breath and wanders over to the balcony; he is barely aware of the glistening waters of the Mediterranean, the numerous vessels in the distance, or that it's a beautiful day on which to be alive.

'Addric, you would rather die than let that happen, wouldn't you?'

'You know I would, Emphora.'

'Then, you will attend the meeting.'

'Of course, I will, as long as you are by my side.'

At the age of five, Addric was brave enough to stand up against the class bully and give him a taste of his own medicine. Ever since then, he has stood his ground against the occasional tyrant and even a psychopath with delusions of grandeur.

It wasn't because of any personal animosity; Addric cannot tolerate discrimination, and he has never been able to sit by and just let it happen.

'This has the smell of injustice written all over it,' he says

'I would be careful not to say that too loudly,' Emphora says.

'That decision came from the highest echelon of power, not just the Alliance itself if you get my drift.'

CHAPTER 3

Earth has been plagued by problems for as long as anyone can remember. Murder, war, and terrorism have featured on news bulletins for the last six decades, and they have never shown any sign of abating.

Most human beings are good people, but there are those who have always profited from violence, instability, and fear.

In days gone by, it was a controllable few, but ever since the advent of the internet and a mind-boggling array of electronic devices, things have degenerated to an all-time low.

The younger generation welcomed the electronic revolution with open arms, and their fascination for the latest product has never shown any sign of diminishing.

As the powers that be know, most people rarely communicate on a face-to-face basis anymore. They now live in a fabricated world called cyberspace.

'In other words,' Emphora says, 'they have sold their souls to a different master.'

******

If the corridors of the Intergalactic Alliance are anything to go by, the quality of life is obviously very important in the heavenly realms.

'So, who will be at this meeting,' Addric says.

'Four delegates from the conference, a celestial being called Lila Vectrona, an ascended master called Lord Roncardo, and two ambassadors from the Angelic realms, as far as I know.'

'You're not anxious, are you?'

'Have you heard that joke about the chicken that crossed the road?' Addric says somewhat cryptically.

'Ah yes, they are wonderfully inventive, aren't they? But God knows why the chicken decided to cross the road in the first place.'

'Because she had to get to the other side,' Addric says. 'And this little chicken is about to cross the very same road.'

'In that case, Addric, you are bound to have an interesting journey and meet a lot of wonderful people on the way.'

'But this little chicken has super-powers, Addric. It can fly through the air and do all sorts of things that a chicken can't do, which is why you are here, my boy.'

'Ah ha,' Emphora says, 'I see someone that I know.'

Heading towards them is a vision so unbelievable that it could be a supernova on two legs. Lila Vectrona is a sight for sore eyes as she sails down the hallway, followed by a cascade of long silken veils.

'Emphora, welcome back,' she says. 'I am so glad to see you again.'

'And I presume this is Addric.'

'Yes, it is,' Emphora says.

'Addric, allow me to introduce you to Lila Vectrona, a representative of the Celestial High Council.'

'Addric, I am delighted to meet you, and I am relieved to hear that you have decided to attend this meeting.'

Throw someone into an unfamiliar environment, along with a cluster of new faces, all of whom are eager to express their opinion, and you have a recipe as old as time.

Addric is not usually so reserved. He is simply trying to come to terms with a problem of titanic proportions.

He listens closely to what the Archangels Michael and Gabriel have to say, to the reasons why the people of Earth have fallen so low in the estimation of the Celestial Hierarchy.

'The primary issue is that they are no longer listening to their inner selves,' Michael says.

'Which means what?' Addric says.

'They are not listening to the very thing that connects them to the core and essence of all that is.'

On this occasion, Michael and Gabriel have chosen to assume human form, and if you didn't know any better, you would say they were in their early forties, but that is not the case at all.

They are of an indeterminate age and come from a world where time has no meaning and one in which no one has ever suffered the slings and arrows of misfortune.

'Every being in this universe is an intricate part of the greater whole,' Gabriel says. 'Unfortunately, the people of Earth have lost contact with the most essential part of their being.'

'And over the last fifty years, the problems have become even worse. They are surrounded by technology, which means that they are at the mercy of every possible electronic device that you can imagine.'

'But so do those from other planetary systems,' Addric says.

'Yes, but they use their equipment much more sensibly than the people of Earth,' Lila says. 'And that's the primary issue.'

'Technology has changed the psyche of the people over the last fifty years. And because of that, we have almost lost contact with the younger generations.'

'They don't even bother to make a personal decision about anything anymore,' Gabriel says.

'They are no longer aware of the rhythms of their body and choose to consult an electronic device instead.'

'In other words, they have relinquished their power as sentient beings and rely on a programmed device to run their lives.'

'As a consequence, the barometer that gauges the spiritual development of the people of Earth has fallen to an all-time low.'

'That was not the case at the beginning of the 21st century,' Lila says. 'They were doing brilliantly, and it did not go un-noticed.'

'Those of us in the celestial realms were ecstatic, so much so that a decision was made to make massive changes to the magnetics of the planet, one that would allow human beings to advance to the next level.'

'That is an integral element of the grand plan,' says Lord Roncardo, an ascended Master of some standing in the celestial community.

'As your wife once told you, Addric, Planet Earth was given a singular honour from the very start, one that many other planetary systems have also had.'

The Earth was designed as a garden in which non-souled beings, such as those from angelic families and beings from other star systems, could incarnate in human form.

'Earth is not just any old planet, Addric. The people of this planet have a grand future ahead. And one day soon, they will be very different to what they are now.'

'But they have no idea that they are participating in one of the most extraordinary endeavours in the known universe.'

'We could go on and on forever, but the question is, what is to be done?' Michael says.

'We are not permitted to interfere in this situation, which is why we have asked for your help.'

'Addric, are you interested in accepting this challenge?'

'Without a doubt, but I have no idea what I can do,' he says. 'As you know, a Yumi Master is not permitted to interfere in the lives of human beings.'

'I am sure that the head of the Yumi High Council will happily make an alteration to that rule,' Lord Roncardo says.

'Is that a possibility, Emphora?'

'It definitely is,' she says. 'It is a decision that I, as the Head of the Council, am entitled to make.'

'That is excellent, Emphora, but the most important thing you have to do Addric is increase the level of human consciousness.'

According to Kryon, a celestial being who has been transmitting information to the people of Earth since 1989, human consciousness is the combined thoughts and energies of every person on the planet.

'It's a vital component of the system necessary for the development of the human race,' Lord Roncardo says.

'In other words, it is the invisible engine that dictates the fortunes of the people and the planet.'

'Give me some time to think about this,' Addric says. 'And when I have formulated a plan of action, I will report back to you.'

'We are willing to assist in any way that we can,' Michael says, 'but there is one aspect of this situation that you must be aware of.'

'And what's that?' Addric says.

'If this problem cannot be resolved within ninety days, the worst of all possible scenarios will be activated.'

'I had a feeling that this was going to be an interesting day,' Addric says, 'but I did not expect it to be terrifying.'

'Perhaps a change of scenery would be a good idea,' Emphora says.

'Where do you have in mind?'

'One of my favourite places, a non-descript little restaurant overlooking the beach at Monte Carlo.'

'That sounds excellent.'

After several glasses of a particularly good vintage, Addric starts to relax.

'So, what are you thinking?' Emphora says.

'As you can imagine, my mind is like a rollercoaster, but I do have a couple of ideas.'

And what might they be?'

'Well, one option is to neutralise the electronic devices which have taken over people's lives.'

'Not everything, surely Addric?'

'No, not in places like hospitals and medical centers, but that's just one idea I have been thinking about.

'As Lila said, the most important changes have to occur at the level of human consciousness.'

'I can see why Adartha recommended you for this task.'

'He did,' says a surprised Addric. 'Why?'

Adartha, Prince of the Angelic realm of Ra-Silonay is a remarkable man in his own right and one who left an indelible impression on Addric's mind.

'He obviously believes that you are capable of handling this task. Who else could do it?'

'You could.'

'I will be stepping out of the picture unless you need my help, but you were about to tell me more about what you have in mind.'

'The solution has to be something that creeps up from behind. Something that will not only stop people in their tracks, but it must also have a powerful effect on their consciousness.'

'You are not thinking of some sort of natural disaster, are you?'

'Quite the opposite. In fact, subtlety is the way to go, something like a cat creeping up on a mouse.'

'I hear you, Addric. An idea like that will allow for a wide range of options.'

'Exactly, but I think it would be a good idea to call upon the assistance of a few old friends to help me nut this idea out.'

'Such as whom, for example.'

'Reuben Ali Shah comes to mind for one.'

'And why would that be.'

'Did I ever tell you how incredible he was in Lemuria?'

'No, you must have forgotten about that.'

'The way in which he handled the High Priest of the Temple of Lemuria was absolutely awesome.'

'In fact, I even got down on my knees and bowed to his inspired brilliance.'

'That's good to know. So, who else is on your hit list?'

'The one and only Countess of Farago, Lady Felicity Originalis. She is essential for a mission of this nature.'

'Good thinking, Addric. She has a wealth of experience and is a master of strategies to boot.'

'And then, of course, we cannot forget her sister, Countess Demetra, can we?'

Felicity and her sister Demetra are masters of the arcane arts, both of whom have a history of battling the dark side and the occasional psychopath as well.

'For a situation like this, their expertise will be very useful.'

'So, what are you going to do first?'

'Invite everyone to spend a few weeks at Dragonshead to start with. Things have been a bit on the quiet side lately.'

'I do understand, 'Emphora says.

She is not willing to say so, but she is all too aware of the depth of his pain.

'In that case, I think it would be a good idea to engage the services of a housemaid and a cook.'

'Are you offering your services,' he says hopefully.

'If you wish, but I was actually thinking of the Krugwah.'

'Ah, the ever-reliable Krugwah Catering and Cleaning Service. That's an excellent idea.'

'Eenah has never been to Earth before, and I know she would jump at the opportunity. Would you like me to mention it to her?'

'Why not? Someone has to keep us on our toes. But Jatoo and his family pop in every few days, so you can include him as well.'

'That's perfect. So, is that it?'

'I am also thinking about my old friends Yusef and Jolariel. They are good company and very useful in a crisis.'

'I live in a house with twenty-five unoccupied rooms, so we will have more than enough space for everyone, and we could make it a family affair as well.'

'We definitely could,' Emphora says. 'Okay, Addric, count me in.'

'I am in dire need of a change of scenery. And what could be better than to spend a few weeks in a villa on the coast of Spain.'

CHAPTER 5

Jolariel had to decline Addric's offer as he had to attend a series of book fairs in Europe. But his old friend, Yusef, a part-time pirate and man of leisure, is always available.

As the owner of a chain of antique shops in numerous European cities, free time is something that Yusef has to spare. And he not only jumps at the opportunity, he arrives several days before anyone else.

'I am so looking forward to seeing everyone again,' he says.

Yusef hasn't aged a day since Addric first met him in the lost continent of Lemuria. He still has his youthful looks, vibrant green eyes, and short-cropped hair. And if you didn't know any better, you would say that he is a thirty-year-old man.

Yusef has always been an incurable optimist. And as well as with a broad range of skills and talents, he has an excellent sense of humour, and he is looking forward to the next few weeks.

'The first contingent will be here soon,' Addric says. 'Brace yourself for more cuddles and kisses than you have had in ages.'

'I can deal with that, Addric, but will Elisabeth and Dheago be coming as well?'

'Yes, but they won't be staying for long.'

Addric's brother Dheago and his wife Elisabeth are now the parents of five teenage children, and their life is nothing if not busy. Dheago was an only child, but now he is a doting father, and his family means everything to him.

Most of Addric's friends are Yumi Masters and when they do travel, they use one form of portal or another.

One fine spring morning, almost a week to the day after Addric agreed to undertake one of the most difficult of all assignments, the first of his visitors arrived at his door.

'So, Addric, who can we expect first?'

'The Krugwah, of course, Eenah and her trusty companions, Peedie, Bootee, Malila, and Wimple. They should be here soon.'

'Ooh, has Eenah changed at all?' Yusef says.

He has every reason to ask, as Eenah is renowned for being both forthright and dictatorial. And as everyone knows, it is not advisable to get into her bad books.

'That would be impossible, Yusef, but the secret with Eenah is to look her in the eye and hope for the best.'

'That is not what I call good advice, Addric.'

'It has always worked for me.'

The arrival of a Krugwah portal is always accompanied by a glowing blue light and a colourful display of little golden sparks.

'She's here,' Addric says.

They step outside, only to be greeted by a sight that is a picture postcard classic. Eenah pokes her head through the door and peers around suspiciously.

'It's all good, Eenah. There's nothing to be afraid of, other than Yusef, of course.'

'That's not fair, Addric.'

The Krugwah are at the top of the list when it comes to Addric's favourite nature spirits. Their most defining features are big, soulful eyes, stumpy little legs, and a crop of ginger-coloured hair.

'I remember you,' Eenah says to Yusef. 'You're a good man. You'd have to be to be a friend of Addric's.'

'See, Yusef, I told you so.'

The kitchen is Eenah's domain and the preparation of food is something at which she excels. She has never seen an Earth kitchen before and inspects it closely.

'Perhaps we can get rid of this, this, and this. We have things to do, you know.'

'Whatever you like,' Addric says, 'but I do have a few requests.'

And what be that.'

'As you know, I am expecting guests, and I thought we could start with cakes and biscuits for afternoon tea,' Addric says hopefully.

'And then, for tonight, perhaps we could have a seafood banquet out on the terrace.'

Eenah wanders over to the door and looks out upon the Mediterranean. An ocean is something she has never seen before, and its very magnitude takes her by surprise.

'That looks dangerous.'

'That's an ocean, Eenah, and it can be dangerous sometimes, but you will be safe in here.'

'Maybe we will, maybe we won't,' she says. 'So, what sort of food you be wanting for tonight?'

'Seafood, of course.'

'And what's that?' she says in her usual straightforward style.

'Fish and prawns mostly, freshly caught from that very ocean out there.'

'So how we be getting these things.'

'Jatoo is an excellent fisherman. Ask him, and he will pop down and get some.'

'Okay, but what do I do with them?'

Eenah listens closely as Addric explains the fine art of cooking seafood to perfection.

'That be sounding very good. We can do that,' she says. 'Now, go away and leave me to my business.'

It's in everyone's interest to treat Eenah with the respect that she deserves. Addric learnt that lesson a long time ago. He is nothing if not diplomatic, especially where Eenah is concerned.

CHAPTER 6

When Felicity and Demetra arrive, they do so quietly, as might be expected. They are striking women in their own right and almost identical in appearance. They also have a vested interest in their appearance, and their long blonde hair is now a subtle shade of brown.

Emphora arrives not long after, accompanied by Jatoo, his wife Marina, and their two children. Altheria and Subandrah were named in honour of Jolariel's first son and daughter, two people that Jatoo remembers with affection.

The first time that Marina ever set eyes on Jatoo was at Elisabeth and Dheago's wedding, and it was love at first sight. They were only seven at the time, but as she told a nosey reporter, she knows a good man when she sees one.

The odd one out in this arrangement is an old friend of Addric's, a Yumi Master called Reuben Ali Shah.

Reuben had an interesting and varied life long before he became a Yumi Master. He was an employee of the National Security Organisation of Vela-Rishan and specialised in petty crime and part-time criminals.

It was a career path with limited prospects, but for a few unbelievable months he had a taste of what it meant to be a Yumi Master, but his final assignment was the one that changed his life.

Addric and Dheago had been accused of a crime that they didn't commit, and it was Reuben's job to follow their every move. But if it had not been for a Yumi Master called Lezula, they would never have become friends at all. Reuben is an exceptional human being and one that Addric is proud to call a friend.

Accompanied by their five children, Elisabeth and Dheago make an appearance just in time for afternoon tea. Elisabeth is now a middle-aged woman, and if she had not married Dheago, she would have lived the lifestyle of an itinerant archaeologist.

The most difficult thing she had to do was tell her parents that she was going to marry a man from the opposite side of the universe and make Vela-Rishan her permanent home.

As far as they were concerned, Dheago was a perfectly normal human being, but Elisabeth had no idea how to broach the subject that he was an alien.

Emphora came to the rescue and introduced herself as his grandmother. George and Helen were astounded to discover that she was an extremely wealthy woman and the matriarch of a very substantial family.

It's all true in one way, but it is normal for human beings to get a little suspicious when they hear things like that.

Emphora was not about to jeopardise their married life and decided to come clean. As a way of proving her point, she invited them to step into a Krugwah portal and explore the attractions of Vela-Rishan. And for a few glorious weeks, George and Helen had a mind-expanding holiday in a galaxy on the outer perimeter of Alpha Centauri.

They have long since passed on and their beautiful house in Bumpton is where Elisabeth and Dheago often spend a few relaxing days, especially when they are in need of a mental health break.

Their lives are so busy that Addric is mostly forgotten. And even though he has never said so, he misses his brother desperately. He and Dheago have a history that goes back a long way, but if it had not been for Addric, Dheago's life could have been different.

Not long after his tenth birthday, his parents passed away in tragic circumstances. Addric was not about to let a total stranger adopt his best friend, so he came to Dheago's rescue and offered him a home and a family.

Many years later, they discovered that they were actually the descendants of the ancient Rishani, the original inhabitants of Vela-Rishan, and nothing could ever change that.

After two long and lonely years, Addric's life is about to change in a way that he could never have imagined. He has accepted a challenge that many others would shy away from, and the fact that he has no idea what he is going to do is not unusual, but Addric always has a few tricks up his sleeve, and he is determined to succeed.

CHAPTER 7

The Krugwah may be small in stature, but that is not an indication of their talents and abilities. Amongst other things, they are masters of the culinary arts, and Eenah and her trusty companions deliver the goods in style. Their reputation is confirmed the moment they place several platters of baked fish and a mouth-watering dish of garlic prawns on the table.

Yusef is the first to get to his feet and offer Eenah a well-deserved round of applause. As he knows from experience, it is a good idea to ingratiate yourself as often as possible.

'Eenah, you have excelled yourself,' he says. 'The fish is cooked to perfection.'

'That be very nice, but if you be having any complaints, we be in the kitchen.'

The sight of the ocean was a bit of a shock at first, but once Eenah realised that it was a source of delicacies, she was not to be deterred.

She gave Jatoo strict instructions not to come back until he had six fish and several kilos of prawns, and the result of her efforts is a seafood banquet to remember.

Eenah happily accepts Yusef's praise, but it has been a very long day. After the table has been cleared, she announces that enough is enough and that she is going home.

'We be back tomorrow, bright and early, and breakfast be served at seven o'clock sharp.'

Addric is not about to let one of his favourite nature spirits disappear without saying goodbye.

'Thank you, Eenah,' he says as he blows her a farewell kiss. 'It was lovely to see you again.'

The ever-inscrutable Eenah has known Addric for a very long time, and even though she has a reputation as a tyrant of the first order, she cannot help but notice the sadness in his heart.

'Jatoo, you take care of your father, or I be having something to say about it.'

'I definitely will, you know that, Eenah.'

'He has a very big job ahead, and he needs all the help he can get.'

From the very first moment that Eenah ever set eyes on Jatoo, she has been his friend, his playmate, his companion, and his protector. And never once did she let him out of her sight. Very few people have ever seen the gentle side of Eenah, but Jatoo has.

'She never misses a thing, does she?'

It is in Eenah's interest to know what's going on, but she was listening closely to the discussions over the dinner table.

'I would not be surprised if she has a few ideas of her own,' Addric says. 'She has never been backward in coming forward.'

'And she would stand her ground to protect those that she loves. After all, it is her reason for being.'

'So very true,' Emphora says, 'but boys and girls, tomorrow will be a very big day.'

'And I think it's time to put the kids to bed and then sit down with a late-night sherry.'

'What a wonderful idea,' Yusef says.

'In that case, I will polish the glasses and maybe a few other things as well.'

It's the first week of April, and it's another beautiful day on Planet Earth. The sky is a cerulean blue, and a gentle breeze wafts in from the Mediterranean.

After a hearty Krugwah breakfast, Addric takes his grandchildren for a stroll along the beach. The kids are happy to amuse themselves but he is all too conscious of the task ahead. He only has ninety days to do the impossible, but as to what he will do, he has no idea.

His handsomely furnished den is the centre of operations with a collection of rare and valuable antiques which originated in the long-lost civilisation of Lemuria.

These are treasures that any museum would love to get their hands on. But if it had not been for the foresight of Jatoo's grandfather, they would not be here at all.

Addric stored them away until Jatoo had a home of his own, but there was far too much for one house, so Jatoo kept what he wanted and gave the rest to Addric.

A magnificent table now takes pride of place in the middle of the room, and it is here that they will brainstorm a few ideas over the next few weeks.

'The first item on the agenda is how we are going to do this,' Addric says as he stands before the team of people he has selected to assist in this venture.

'This campaign may test us to our limits, but if we do not succeed, the prospects for the people of Earth do not bear thinking on.'

Over the next few minutes, he brings them up to date on what he was told by Lila Vectrona and the Archangels Michael and Gabriel.

'Apparently, that information came from the highest of all sources,' he says. 'It was revealed to the minds of the delegates by the Intergalactic Bible.'

'And what's that,' Reuben says.

'Well, it's not a book at all, apparently.'

'The bible is the means by which a directive from on high is communicated to the mind,' Emphora says.

'And in this case, it was revealed to the minds of the celestial beings who were summoned to a special conference.'

'It stated that Earth's days are numbered unless someone can direct them down another path.'

'What a horrifying thought,' Yusef says. 'So, what are we doing wrong?'

'Well, you will be relieved to know that not everyone is at fault. The problem that we have to rectify is what is not happening and what should be happening.'

'And what is that?' Felicity says.

'People have become so obsessed with technology that it rules their lives. And unfortunately, they have lost that all-important connection to spirit.'

'And that's the thing we have to change,' Reuben says. 'Is that possible?'

'Yes, it is, or so I believe, and the most successful way to do that is to target human consciousness.'

'And just how are we going to do that?'

'Well, we are not going to use scare tactics and brute force. That would be counterproductive and alienate people even more. We will be using much more subtle methods of persuasion.'

'What sort of methods do you have in mind?' Felicity says.

'I don't know just yet, but it would be a good idea to consult Jatoo's mirror to start with.'

'Ah ha,' Yusef says, 'the old magic mirror trick.'

CHAPTER 9

Jatoo's mother died during childbirth, and he was raised by the priests of the Temple in Lemuria. At the age of seven, he was accused of stealing the most valuable item in the land. The key to the Sanctuary of Fire was vital to the continuation of all life in Lemuria.

Jatoo vowed and declared that he had never seen the key and had no idea where it was. Not knowing what else to do, he ran away, and in an effort to keep one step ahead of the law, he spent the next year on the run.

Jatoo lived the life of a beggar and slept in drains with half-starved dogs, but if he had not met Addric, he may have died. He had lost the will to live, and the only thing that kept him going was the thought that he would be seeing his mother again.

Addric had the inspired idea to give him a present, and when Jatoo looked into that little golden mirror, he saw the face of the mother he had never known.

On that day, his life changed in a way he could never have imagined, and not long after, he willingly embraced Addric as his father.

He was raised by Emphora, but the most formidable of all nature spirits prepared him for the day that he would become a Yumi Master.

'Jatoo's mirror has the ability to show the user exactly what they want to see,' Addric says. 'But the secret is to approach this task with a clear question in mind.'

'I believe that if we ask exactly the same question, then we will get the same answer.'

The mirror has been in Jatoo's possession ever since he was a boy and is rarely seen by anyone else.

'It showed me the face of the girl who proposed to me at the age of seven,' he says. 'And as you know, Marina is now my wife.'

Addric writes the question on a sheet of paper and passes it around for all to see.

'Read this before using the mirror, and when we have finished, we will see what we have got.'

'I will go first as the mirror has never given me false information,' Jatoo says.

He holds it up to his face and keeps that one thought in mind.

'You may not believe what I just saw, but I will wait to see what you have to say.'

'I see what you mean,' Yusef says. 'It really is a powerful tool.'

Addric watches closely as they pass the mirror around from one person to another.

'So, it's time to see what we have got,' he says. 'You go first, Jatoo.'

'I saw the face of not one Krugwah but thousands of them.'

'How amazing,' Felicity says. 'So did I.'

'As did I,' Yusef says.

They are baffled but none the less amazed that they all saw exactly the same thing.

'The Krugwah, the ever reliable and devoted Krugwah,' Addric says. 'The answer to our prayers.'

'But what could they do to change the consciousness of an entire planet,' Rueben says.

'Well, they have numerous skills and talents. And no doubt, they have a few that we don't know about,' Addric says.

'I have an idea for something they could do,' Demetra says. 'If a spaceship was seen by everyone on the planet, that would have an enormous impact on the minds of the population.'

'However, what if thousands of Krugwah just happened to appear above every city in the world, and it was broadcast across the network?

Then that would have exactly the same effect, wouldn't it?'

At that moment, Eenah appears at the door, and as everyone can see, she has business on her mind.

'Please come in,' Addric says. 'We have just been talking about you.'

'Why you be doing that?' says a suddenly hostile Eenah.

'It wasn't bad,' Emphora says reassuringly. 'We were just talking about all of the wonderful things that the Krugwah can do.'

As Emphora knows, it's how you deliver a message to Eenah that decreases the possibility of outright warfare. Eenah is not one to be slighted, and the mounting tension in her body disappears in an instant.

'Is there something we can do for you?'

'The Krugwah had a meeting last night.'

'And why was that?' Addric says.

'We hear what you be saying at the dinner table last night, that this planet is in terrible danger and you have to do something about it.'

'That's true, and it is.'

'You have ideas, but you not be sure if they be going to work. But one thing you mentioned, we did not know what that meant, so we had to ask the Krugwah elders.'

'And what was that,' Addric says.

'You be saying that you have to change human consciousness.'

'Yes, but how, that's the question.'

'Tell us what this thing is, Addric, and if it be what the elders said, we be thinking that we have a way to be helping you.'

Addric does his best to explain that it's the thoughts of every person on Planet Earth and that it's a powerful force for change, especially when everyone is of the same mindset.

'But Eenah, they aren't, and that's the reason for this situation.'

'Demetra, you be knowing those little children from Ditafarago, don't you?'

'The New Soul Children. Yes, Eenah, I know them very well.'

'They are very nice children because we have met them too, but they have a very special job.'

'That is true, is it not?

'Yes, it is Eenah. The New Soul Children creep into people's dreams and give them a helping hand, but they are not here to help us.'

'But the Krugwah are, and we could do the same thing.'

'You could,' says a surprised Addric.

'Of course, we can, silly. Krugwah can do many things, and if you want, we be happy to do that too.'

'We don't want something awful be to happening to this nice place.'

'Eenah, that is excellent news, and we will be happy to accept any help the Krugwah can offer.'

'But there are over seven billion people on this planet,' Yusef says. 'How many Krugwah are there?'

'Lots,' Eenah says. 'Lots and lots.'

'There are probably just as many Krugwah,' Emphora says, 'give or take a few million.'

'In that case, that's even better,' Addric says.

'Eenah, could you inform the Krugwah that we will be very grateful for their assistance?'

'So, when we be doing this dreaming thing?'

'Very soon Eenah. We will keep you informed.'

'Now, would you be liking some morning tea,' she says. 'We have made a chocolate slice, some cream cakes, and your very favourite cake Addric.'

'Yes, please,' he says.

'I have said it before, and I will say it again, the Krugwah are truly wonderful.'

'That being so very true,' Eenah says.

They are somewhat overwhelmed by the fact that they have got this far and in less than an hour. But, the next issue on the agenda is what the Krugwah should do.

'So, let me get this right,' Reuben says. 'The idea is for the Krugwah to enter the dream state of over seven billion people.'

'Yes, Reuben, that's what the New Soul Children do,' Demetra says. 'But that's more than enough to work with.'

'In that case, we will need a clearly defined strategy, a plan of action,' Felicity says.

'Like what.'

'The Krugwah should do something simple at first. And if it goes viral on the social network, then everyone will be talking about it.'

'Then we really will know if this idea is going to work,' Emphora says. 'That is an excellent idea.'

'What do you mean by simple?'

'Well, it's common knowledge that angels often appear in dreams,' Felicity says. 'But I don't think we should go down that path.'

'Perhaps the Krugwah could do something like offer everyone a flower, one that changes into something else.'

'Ah ha, I have it,' Yusef says. 'A child places a seed in the palm of their hand, and it turns into a beautiful flower.'

'That is an excellent suggestion,' Emphora says, 'and a timeless metaphor for the spirit within.'

'That idea has potential,' Addric says. 'So, let's test it out, shall we?'

In a dream about love, the sky is often a gentle shade of pink, but if it's an unusual shade of green, that may signify something else altogether.

A young woman called Francine Leclerc has been wandering around the Luxembourg Gardens, one of the most beautiful parks in Paris. She takes a seat on a bench, and not long after, she is approached by a little girl in a pale blue dress.

'Please hold out your hand.'

'Why?' Francine says.

'Because I have something for you.'

As to why she has been given a little brown seed, Francine has no idea, but before she has an opportunity to ask, the little girl vanishes into thin air.

To Francine's amazement, the seed starts to sprout, after which it opens to reveal a beautiful flower with delicate pink petals.

And when she wakes up the following morning, Francine has all but forgotten that dream because she has far too many things on her mind.

Stage one of her day is orchestrated by Stella, the voice of her Swizza Satellite phone. Stella becomes active at six o'clock on the dot and advises Francine on just about everything.

She even goes so far as to suggest the colour of lipstick that Francine should wear with a black suit, the standard uniform for employees of Cybernetics Inc.

If she's running late, Stella will tell her when the next bus is due, but that has only happened once in the last five years. For a woman with a high-powered job such as hers, it is essential that everything runs to schedule.

Stella advises Francine of her dietary needs, which, in most cases, is a vitamin-enriched beverage made from rehydrated fruit and vegetables. Francine always buys her fruit in tablet form, which she keeps on the second shelf of the refrigerator.

She makes it a rule not to speak to anyone at the bus stop. It is not recommended in a city like Paris, and if she did, she could lose a precious moment of her valuable time.

Francine's normal routine is to peruse The Telemetric Index, a bulletin that processes data related to the ever-changing cybernetics industry. This is vital information for anyone who works in the technology business.

If something looks important, Francine will request a visual report. And if it is related to the fluctuating state of the cybernetics economy, it will be assessed by the FACQ.

That is not the department of Frequently Asked Questions, but the department that analyses anomalies in the cybernetics quotient.

Any unexplained event that occurs in cyberspace is evidence of Philosophical Activity. In the business world, that's code for anyone who shares a program that has the capacity to go viral.

If that ever happens, it is monitored on a second-by-second basis. A report is placed in the hands of the Department for Cyberspace Information. An encoded program is deployed, and the offending program is modified or nullified.

A Red Alert is the worst of all possible scenarios, and an event of that nature has not happened since 2023. It appeared on every social media network around the world, but it was eventually downgraded to a prank.

A random hacker occasionally rears his head but so does another very vocal organisation. Multiplex usually attaches a message to one of the frequency bands by which the internet operates.

At that moment, however, Stella alerts Francine to a recent development in cyberspace.

'It appears that something unusual occurred last night, and it has been reported on every social media network in the world.'

'It seems that over four billion people have posted comments about the very same issue.'

'Stella, redirect me to Phillipe Nozac immediately,' Francine says.

At approximately two o'clock this morning, according to Monsieur Nozac, millions of people had the very same dream.

'They were given a seed by a little girl, one which grew into a plant and then sprouted into a flower.'

Francine does something that she has never done before. She turns off her phone and looks around, only to discover that everyone at the bus stop is talking about a dream they had the night before.

CHAPTER 11

Now that he has an idea with distinct possibilities, Addric reports back to Lila Vectrona at Intergalactic headquarters.

'That was inspired brilliance Addric, to call upon the services of the Krugwah.'

'It was their idea, not mine.'

'Of course, but from now on, you will require the assistance of experts in a rarefied field.'

'I think it would be a good idea if you made the acquaintance of two interesting women, Majura Krestovori and Seray Antropedes.'

'They are the Venusian Ambassadors to the Intergalactic Alliance and hold positions of responsibility as joint controllers of the celestial body known as The Department of Universal Intelligence.'

Addric has never met a Venusian before, and Majura and Seray are something of a surprise. They are at least seven feet tall and if they do have spherical heads and bulbous eyes, it's not obvious.

But they are very exotic creatures, nevertheless, adorned like ethereal spirits in gossamer pink gowns.

'We thought that rose was an appropriate colour for this occasion, considering the fact that over four billion Earthlings saw a flower in their dreams last night,' Seray says.

'And of course, every social media network is madly trying to analyse the meaning of that phenomenon,' Majura says.

'This department is an arm of the Intergalactic Alliance,' Majura says. 'And it's our job to monitor the level of activity in the consciousness of all life forms in the Solar System.'

'But in the case of Planet Earth, it's the decreasing level of activity.'

'Congratulations Addric, that really was a brilliant idea, and according to our data, it was a resounding success.'

'But Majura, did it have any effect on the consciousness of the people of Earth?'

'Yes, it appeared as a sharp spike on the graph, which means that it did not go un-noticed.'

'Unfortunately, over the last few hours, the people of Earth have reverted to type.'

'What does that mean?'

'Most Earthlings are so brainwashed by technology that to experience something of a non-electronic nature is almost un-natural.'

'So, they have forgotten about it?'

'Not yet, Addric, but anything is possible on Earth.'

'However, we have prepared a presentation that you might find interesting. It is freely available from the Quantum field, by the way.'

"And that means what,' he says.

'That is the means by which we judge the potential of human consciousness.'

'Potential is everything in a Quantum state, but it is also the barometer by which we assess what may or may not happen.'

'And quantum means what?' Addric says.

'Quantum, to quote our dear friend Kryon, the Magnetic Master, is a non-physical state, the soup of energy that surrounds everything in the known universe.'

'Human beings are programmed to think in a linear and logical fashion, but linearity does not exist in a Quantum state, and this is the problem.'

'Earthlings have become so used to linearity that they are baffled when something unusual happens.'

'When confronted by the idea that synchronicity, or magic, for want of a better word actually exists, frustration and disbelief rear their ugly heads.'

'This is the battle that you face Addric, how to break that spell and allow the people of Earth to understand that they are more than what they know.'

'But if we were to conduct another campaign like that, Majura, things could get even worse, even if it is harmless.'

'Anything you do is going to have an effect, Addric. But once something becomes a reality, it cannot be reversed. That is the nature of things.'

'Once they have experienced something new, the people of Earth cannot return to their old ways of thinking. And it is through your efforts that they will come to realise that.'

'But if I were you, I would not keep this campaign a secret for much longer. It would be a good idea to bring it out into the open as soon as possible.'

'If the Earth is to survive, it will only do so through the conscious intent of over seven billion people who receive the same message at the same time.

'Otherwise, theirs will be a fate too horrible to imagine. And if anyone can give them hope, it is you, Addric.'

'However, I am in possession of a vital piece of information, and one that you can use to your advantage.'

'And what is that Majura?'

'One of the leading players in the electronics industry is about to give you a helping hand.'

'Listen carefully, and I will tell you everything I know.'

The Krugwah campaign was a major success, and Addric's team is inspired to go to the next level.

'Now, let's toss a few ideas around to see what we could do next.'

'I think we should do something different,' Yusef says.

'Like what.'

'Well, maybe we could get a million people to do handstands, for example.'

'Handstands,' Addric says.

'Yes, or maybe we could get street musicians to play the same song at the same time.'

'I don't think a snake charmer in Mumbai would be familiar with The Star-Spangled Banner or God Save the King, Yusef.

'They could play their own national anthem, Addric.'

'The fallout from another global stunt would not go un-noticed, and in time, it would achieve the desired results.'

'That's the very thing we want to avoid,' Jatoo says. 'Isn't it?'

'Not anymore,' Addric says curiously.

'I was under the impression that we were not to do anything that smells of direct interference,' Felicity says.

'Didn't you say that this has to look authentic until you decide otherwise?'

'That's what I was led to believe,' Addric says. 'But I have an idea that I would like to share with you.'

'Like a game of tactics, perhaps.'

'In a manner of speaking, yes, Felicity.'

'What sort of tactics do you have in mind, Addric?'

'Sneaky tactics, of course.'

'My original idea was that we should disable the electronic equipment that has taken over people's lives.'

'Everything, all at once. That would be disastrous.'

'Let me get this right, Addric. Are you saying that we should infiltrate the corporations that create the equipment?'

'Or that we should sabotage the databases of multi-national companies?'

'That's the general idea,' Addric says.

'But that would look as if someone was orchestrating this thing from behind the scenes,' Reuben says.

'And that's what we are trying to avoid, aren't we?'

'There is absolutely no way that anyone could identify the perpetrators, Reuben.'

'I guess not.'

'Besides, no one, other than the Intergalactic Alliance, knows the identity of the crafty minds behind this charade.'

'But I agree, infiltration is an excellent idea,' Felicity says. 'Please explain how this sneaky idea will work.'

'We will not have to do anything at all, Felicity. Someone is about to do it for us.'

'Now, gather around folks and see what you think of this little gem of an idea.'

'I have been advised by my lady friends in the Department of Universal Intelligence that an electronics company called Swizzer Industries is about to get the ball rolling.'

The major players in cyberspace are the masters of the internet, and it's a very lucrative business. The internet has had top billing in the stock market for decades, and investors have profited from a stream of ideas from whiz kids and techno-savvy designers. They are always on the lookout for another niche market, and as a result, the IT Industry has made millions of people wealthy beyond their dreams.

For a teenager looking for a bit of extra cash, a sixty second video can be a pathway to untold wealth. The formula was there from the start. Simply upload a video and within twenty-four hours you will be raking in the cash.

Thousands of teenagers have stumbled onto fame and fortune simply because their quirky little idea went viral. A few became overnight celebrities, but most were never heard of again.

Computer nerds were the most identifiable kids on the block in the early 21st century. And when you have a geeky name like Milton Swizzer, you just have to be one. Milton made his first million by the age of fifteen and within two years he had his own business.

He endured one insult too many from the bullies at school, and the idea of calling his first game, *The Drop Kick Boys* was not just poetic justice; it was payback for years of psychological abuse.

Milton was a lot smarter than he looked, but behind those black-rimmed spectacles was a mind focused on bigger things. He developed a game that was designed to change the status quo.

And within two years, DKB was the primary tool used by every police department in the world as a means of monitoring and identifying a generation of cyber bullies.

Swizzer Industries soon morphed into Swizza and became one of the most recognisable brand names in the world. Milton was a billionaire by the time he was twenty-five, and his company had snaffled up a viable chunk of the market.

As a consequence, the Swizza Satellite phone is just one of many devices that control the lives of the people of Planet Earth.

Unfortunately, the Black Market is alive and well in cyberspace, and at one point, Milton's business was teetering on the brink of insolvency.

Intellectual property theft is a popular target, and a group of well-organised hackers infiltrated his database and made copies of his most profitable products.

Milton was not known as a whiz kid for nothing. In an effort to end this form of piracy, he locked himself away for five days. And when he re-emerged, he had devised a ground-breaking method of protecting his ideas.

Most companies use one form of psychological test or another when hiring new staff. But, the Swizza Test has nothing to do with intelligence, likeability, or any other compatibility factor.

In fact, it doesn't ask a potential employee anything much at all. If a new recruit has made it this far, they have to be as good as anyone else in the business. But as everyone now knows, if you want to work for Milton Swizzer, you have to play by his rules.

When entering or leaving the Swizzer complex, an employee must pass through a series of scanners. What they don't know is that their brains are being scanned, and any information related to company business is placed in a holding pattern.

It wasn't an original idea; Milton was a sci-fi addict from day one. He lapped up anything to do with particle beams and laser energy. As a child, he lived and breathed superheroes like Buck Rogers and Flash Gordon, but that was just the beginning.

The day that Star Trek hit the small screen, Milton was catapulted into light space. And along with millions of others, he willingly went where no human being had ever gone before.

But when it came to awesomeness, it did not get any better than the transporter on The Enterprise or that other fabulous idea, warp speed.

Captain Kirk's communicator was the inspiration for the mobile phone. And it wasn't long before products such as the sliding door and digital display monitors were available in the marketplace.

A popular cartoon show called The Jetsons may not have been at the top of the list when it came to awesomeness, but it paved the way for a host of new products, such as a robotic maid and robotic vacuum cleaner.

Their televiewer inspired the flat-screen television, video-conferencing, and wireless communication. The Jetsons not only zipped around in a family-sized spaceship, they lived in the upper echelons of the stratosphere. And their hi-tech residence was a freely floating space station where everything operated at the touch of a button.

But, it was the sci-fi movies of the early 21st-century that catapulted Milton into totally new territory, and two movies in particular took him even further.

In the cult classic, *Inception*, hired assassins use technology to infiltrate the subconscious in order to extract vital information during the dream state.

And in the conclusion to the movie *Artificial Intelligence*, human beings have disappeared off the scene, and the Earth is populated by highly evolved robots with the ability to manipulate consciousness by a form of mind control.

Telekinesis wasn't new territory, as the Russians have been experimenting with this idea for decades. But Milton's technological masterpiece may never have become a reality if he had not inherited a talent from his mother.

Shanala is a clairvoyant with the ability to see things that others cannot. As a child, she presumed that everyone could see elves and fairies and other unusual things. And when she realised that they couldn't, she decided to use her talents to make a decent living.

One night, Shanala had a dream in which an unfamiliar creature appeared in Milton's research laboratory. She had no idea what it meant, but she wanted to be there when Milton launched his latest project just in case something happened.

Milton's great dream has been to create a teleportation device that will allow a human being to travel through space and time.

And now, after years of preparation, that day has finally arrived. Swizzer Industries is about to test out a prototype for the world's first digital portal.

Other than Shanala and a bunch of technicians, no one else will be a witness to what they hope will be a very memorable day.

The tenth floor of Swizzer Industries looks more like the control deck of a spaceship, a hi-tech laboratory in which several prototypes have already been developed.

The Trans-Portal Device, or TPD as it is commonly known, has the potential to revolutionise the world of transportation. And it's in Milton's interests to refine his creation so that it is a marketable product.

His ultimate plan is to develop a bracelet that can be activated at the touch of a button, but that day is still a long way off. The TPD is no longer a work in progress, as a series of experiments have so far proved.

His research department tested his idea out on a batch of mannequins, all of which were dispatched through a digital gateway. The first one reappeared on the other side of the laboratory, and the second one ended up on the other side of town.

Today, however, the plan is somewhat different. Milton will become the first human being in history to physically relocate from San Francisco to the front lawn of the White House in Washington D.C.

CHAPTER 14

Addric doesn't understand as much about human consciousness as he would like and decides to visit Majura Krestovori and Seray Antropedes.

'Any event related to human development registers in the human consciousness, which means that what humanity decides is what will happen,' Majura says.

'At the beginning of the 21st century, the people of Earth decided that they were ready to move to the next level.'

'The magnetics of the planet were adjusted to cope with what was expected to be the great leap forward.'

'We were hoping to see the end of poverty and the end of warfare, and everything else that has plagued human beings for the last 6000 years, but unfortunately, it didn't happen.'

'The path they followed took us all by surprise,' Seray says. 'The people of the Earth did an unexpected detour and chose to travel the path of technology instead.'

'And in the process, they lost contact with the very thing that they are.'

'However, Addric, and this is the secret.'

'A serious or life-threatening illness can change the consciousness of an individual. But a natural or man-made disaster can change the consciousness of the entire planet.'

'But it has to be something as powerful as a tsunami, something that affects everyone at an emotional level.'

'But that isn't all, Addric, and this is an idea you might be able to use to your advantage.'

'Normally, we would not be permitted to share this information, but this is an exceptional situation. The future of Earth hangs in the balance, and we are going to do so nevertheless.'

'Your idea to disable electronic equipment is a good one, but you will not have to do it yourself. There's a young entrepreneur who is about to do that for you.'

'Milton Swizzer's company is about to test out a prototype for a digital teleportation device. But what Milton doesn't know is that this is not the time for such an invention.'

'For one thing, the magnetics of the planet will not allow for it. Every device in the world will simply cease to operate as soon as he has activated his portal.'

'And that will be equivalent to a tsunami in every way.'

'But what can I do?' Addric says.

'Firstly, you have to make sure that you are present at Milton's launch. Apparently, he is planning to make an appearance on the front lawn of the White House.'

'And if I was you, Addric, I would accompany him on that journey as he will need a saviour and a companion.'

'However, the hi-tech equipment in his laboratory will fail, and so too will every electronic device in the world.'

'If Milton is not incinerated, he will, at the very least, be stranded in the middle of nowhere. And that's when things will start to get interesting.'

'Everyone on the planet will be overwhelmed because the very thing that gives them a reason for being will not work anymore.'

'The outpouring of grief, disbelief, and distress will accelerate to such a point that it will have exactly the same effect as a tsunami.'

'And that, Addric, is the secret of generating a turbo-boosted spike in human consciousness.'

'Everyone will have the same response to that disaster.'

'However, make sure that your team is ready for the fallout as it will be of global proportions.'

'But beware, there is a powerbase of big players in the background, all of whom have a major stake in the electronics industry.'

'If they realise that this is going to destabilise the status quo, they will do their utmost to get the upper hand, and that will not be good.'

'But Addric, this will be the perfect opportunity to step in and do your thing.'

'And it will also be the perfect time for the Krugwah to engage in a little Krugwah magic of one form or another.'

'If anyone can generate a floodtide of emotion, it's the Krugwah.'

CHAPTER 15

Numerous things went wrong in Milton's early experiments, and on one occasion, a mannequin simply disappeared off the radar and was never seen again.

If his device malfunctions, it will cause all sorts of problems, especially if a traveler doesn't arrive at their destination in one piece.

As a consequence, the technicians have programmed the TPD to respond to a number of possible problems.

The most vital program of all is a holographic facsimile of the user's body, a capsule designed as a safeguard in case anything goes wrong.

The worst of all possible scenarios is that they could be consumed by a high-speed blast as they are catapulted into light space. To end up as a random display of molecules orbiting in hyperspace would not be good for business.

And as a precautionary measure, everyone is dressed in protective clothing. This is a day of excitement in the research department of Swizzer Industries. They are about to do what no human being has ever done before, and the digital clock is counting down to zero.

'Twenty minutes to go before initiation,' says Tom Denwright.

Major Tom, as he is commonly known, is half-human and half-android by nature. Tom became a convert on the day that he picked up his first iPad. And from that moment, every cell in his body surrendered to the allure of technology.

After that, there was no going back, but Tom is just one of many in Swizzer Industries who have been diagnosed with a condition similar to Asperger's Syndrome.

Tom had a very strange dream recently, one in which he was wallowing in an ocean of tears, so he decided to consult an App on his Swizza Satellite phone.

Tom has never been interested in the prophecies of fortune tellers, but he asked a question about the program known as *Mystic Mentality* and was surprised at what it had to say.

'Water represents the emotional self, but an ocean of water is very significant, it means that you are drowning in a pool of uncertainty.'

'You have lost touch with your feelings, and if you continue to block them out, they will find a way to reconnect with you.'

'Emotional self,' Tom says half-jokingly.

Like anyone diagnosed with Non-Articulated Response Syndrome, programming is the only thing that Tom understands.

Dozens of technicians are waiting for Milton to make an appearance. It is now 10.26 AM on the morning of Tuesday the 11th of April, and they are about to make history.

The only other witness to what is about to happen is Shanala, Milton's mother. On most occasions, she wears a garment of satin or silk, but on this occasion, she is dressed in a muted grey suit.

With her shoulder-length hair tied back in a loose but elegant bun, she sits quietly behind a glass wall and watches closely as the technicians prepare for the latest version of the TPD to be activated.

The pivotal moment is almost at hand, but something else is happening behind the scenes, and the last thing that Shanala expected to see is the very same creature that she saw in her dream.

She could never forget those overly large eyes or that little pot belly with short, stumpy legs, and she is desperately hoping that it's harmless.

Wimple is not about to sabotage Milton's ground-breaking invention. He is here for another reason. This is not the time for the people of Earth to make a leap of such a magnitude. If and when the time comes, it will be with the consent of the Intergalactic Alliance.

If Earthlings harness this form of travel, they will be travelling beyond the limits of the Solar System, places they are not allowed to go.

Before they do anything else, they have a major test to pass, and it doesn't involve a portal that can travel to other worlds.

Milton is Shanala's only son, and the last thing she wants is for someone to sabotage his work. When he finally makes an appearance, he is dressed in a heat-resistant flight suit.

The moment of truth has arrived, and on Major Tom's command, he takes his place in front of the digital gateway.

At that very moment, another man takes his place at Milton's side. As to why he is wearing a flight suit, Shanala has no idea, but she knows instinctively that something is wrong.

The very moment Milton steps through the gateway, Addric follows along behind. And before Shanala can sound the alarm, Milton has gone, and the only thing she can do is hope and pray that everything will be alright.

CHAPTER 16

The last thing that Milton expected is that he would come to a dead halt in the middle of nowhere. He scrambles to his feet, only to discover that this is not Washington DC at all.

What went wrong? Other than what he had seen on the simulator, he had no idea what a high-speed flight through space and time would be like.

Milton always knew that he would do something like this. He knew it on the day that he saw Doctor Who travelling through space and time in the TARDIS.

But when he saw Mr. Spock and Captain Kirk step into the transporter on Star Trek, he knew that this was what he was going to do. And for the last ten years, it has been the driving force in his life.

Over a period of time, he pieced together a mental model of the code structure of a transportal machine. He studied physics and everything that scientists believe to be the foundation of a vast and complex system.

He consumed masses of information on the properties of matter and the fundamental forces of nature. But there were so many factors which could affect the space-time continuum.

He devised a program that would account for the fact that energy travels at the speed of light, that space curves and folds, that the planet is rotating at a mind-boggling speed, and that the force of gravity varies from one place to another.

He factored in countless sub-routines in case of an emergency, all of which are accessed from a digital device on his wrist.

One function monitors biological features such as heart rate, and others, yet again, are designed to indicate his telemetry and location. But for all of his efforts, something went horribly wrong, and Milton doesn't understand why.

He scrolls through every application, searching for anything at all, but to his horror, not one single function is working. He is hopelessly lost and surrounded by electromagnetic waves for mile after endless cosmic mile.

Milton was once diagnosed with a neurological condition similar to that of a high-functioning autistic savant. Unlike his parents, who have a rich and varied inner life, Milton does not.

He didn't understand fairytales and had no interest in anything but science, facts, and logic but all that is about to change, Milton is about to have his first brush with fame, and not for the reason that he might have imagined.

When he sees a barely visible figure making its way through a minefield of fluctuating electromagnetic waves, he starts to panic.

A few moments later, he is followed by another creature, something that is less than half his size, but this thing is obviously not a homosapien at all.

If Addric were to ask Milton how many grains of sand there are in the world, he would probably come up with a close approximation.

'Then what about stars in the sky?' Addric would have said.

'That could never be known,' would have been Milton's reply.

'You might be surprised to find that there are more stars in the sky than there are grains of sand on the beach.'

To anyone with Non-Articulated Response Syndrome, social customs are an enigma. People like that live in a world of their own, and when they do say anything at all, they usually launch into a one-sided conversation about their primary topic of interest.

And that is exactly what Milton would have done if it had not been for Shanala. She went out of her way to ensure that her son was as normal as possible.

When it first appeared in the 1950s, autism was considered to be an abnormality, and ever since then the statistics have zoomed out of all proportions, but now it is not considered an abnormal condition at all.

The advent of the personal computer changed everything, and even infants know what to do by the age of two.

The children of the early 21st century were different and child prodigies were popping up everywhere. They were gifted, they were talented, they were highly intelligent, and they had an in-built drive to succeed.

They were exhibiting skills and talents that adults of previous generations took years to perfect. Children from all over the world were showing their elders that things have changed, that there really are new kids on the block, and Milton Swizzer was no exception.

'It appears that you have lost your way,' Addric says.

'I have come to a standstill, but I have not yet worked out why,' Milton says. 'Perhaps it's the electromagnetic fields of the planet. I didn't factor them into my equation.'

'And it will not be possible to do so, not for a very long time,' Addric says.

Under normal circumstances, Milton would not engage in a casual conversation with a stranger, but this is an exceptional situation. His idea has been a miserable failure, and he needs answers to questions.

'But I don't understand,' he says. 'Who are you, and how did you get here?'

'Well, for one thing, I followed you,' Addric said.

'From where?'

'From your laboratory in San Francisco, of course.'

'But how is that possible. I see no evidence of a device that allows you to travel through space and time.'

'I don't need one, and neither does Wimple. We are hot-wired to do things like this. But this is not the place to discuss science or anything else, is it?'

'Perhaps you would like to accompany us on a short journey and I will explain everything.'

'So, where are we going?' Milton says.

'I believe it would be a good idea to see things from a somewhat different perspective.'

'What sort of perspective do you mean?'

'A much bigger perspective, you could say.'

Milton is in no position to argue, but he is somewhat hesitant about this idea.

'My name is Addric Sharano, and I am a human being. My friend Wimple is not a creepy little alien in disguise. He is a nature spirit of sorts, but we are here to save you nevertheless.'

'You can stay here if you wish, Milton, but you won't survive for much longer.'

'It's your choice. What do you say?'

'I'll go with you, but only if you take me home.'

'I will, eventually, but as I said, there are issues to be considered and you need to understand exactly what they are.'

'I guess I have no other choice, do I?'

'Not really. None at all, in fact.'

'So, Milton, take my hand and get ready for the fastest ride of your life.'

Zephyrus Two was originally a space station on the outer edge of the Milky Way, but it was abandoned many years ago. An enterprising entrepreneur saw its potential as an intergalactic hotel, and to attract passing traffic, it was relocated to the Solar System.

Zephyrus Two is now known as The Callisto Intergalactic, primarily because it has a view of three of the nine moons of Jupiter.

It now boasts a state-of-the-art hotel and an inter-dimensional transit centre. And as Addric knows, it is also the location of the incomparable Cosmic Café.

This is not your everyday coffee shop, but The Cosmic Café is renowned for its excellent service. This grand establishment is situated at the very top of the hotel, and it has a spectacular view of three of the moons of Jupiter, Europa, Callisto, and Ganymede.

The Callisto caters to guests from numerous planetary systems, and unless they are planning to go on a sightseeing tour, they have no need for a breathing apparatus. Amongst other things, it is not recommended, and everyone knows why.

Most visitors arrive by one form of interstellar vessel or another, after which they are free to do whatever takes their fancy.

Self-propelled visitors like Addric can go directly to the outer door of the Cosmic Café, take a leisurely stroll along a long glass corridor, and then take a seat at a table of their choice.

And it is from here that they have a view of stupendous proportions. Most visitors do not come to the Cosmic Cafe to engage in frivolous conversation, and if they do, it soon fades into insignificance.

The mighty planet Jupiter is surrounded by bands of cloud that generate a powerhouse of atmospheric activity.

That alone is enough to quell any interest in conversation, but this is where Addric brings Milton, and the scenery will play a part in his well-thought-out routine.

'I have brought you here for a reason,' Addric says. 'But before we get into that, Milton, a light lunch would be a good idea.'

'What do you say to that?'

Milton is completely overwhelmed and has no idea what to say. The view is captivating, but the clientele are obviously aliens of one form or another, especially the exotic creatures waiting on tables.

As a regular visitor, Addric is familiar with the routine. He registered with the Maître D, an elegant woman with a pale green complexion and lustrous yellow eyes.

'Addric, it's lovely to see you again,' she said. 'Zubia will no doubt want to serve you personally.'

'In that case, I will escort my friends to my usual table.'

Wimple follows along behind and takes a seat with a classic view of the Bubble Nebula.

'Very pretty,' he says.

'Milton, I should warn you in advance that our host, Zubia Lembossa, is, how shall I say, a little different.'

'Like, what does that mean, Addric?'

'Well, for one thing, she's from Kaziopea.'

'That means nothing to me,' Milton says.

'Kaziopea is a planet in the Darvelian Sector of the Exora Five galaxy.'

It's essential to keep Milton grounded if not informed. As Addric can see, he really is out of his depth.

When Zubia makes an appearance, she glides across the floor like a breeze across a pond, and it's enough to take Milton's breath away.

Zubia is swathed in long flowing veils wearing a headpiece fit for a queen, and she looks as exotic as her infamous establishment.

'Greetings Addric,' she says. 'It is so wonderful to see you again. I was so sorry to hear of Maya's passing. She was a lovely woman and a beautiful human being. Please accept my condolences.'

'Thank you, Zubia, I appreciate that.'

'But I see that you have brought a few friends along as well. I presume this is a business lunch and not a sightseeing tour.'

'It is Zubia, in a fashion, yes.'

'Perhaps you would like to try our latest sensation.'

'And what is that?'

'An interstellar cocktail, of course.'

'Sounds good to me,' Addric says.

'But I won't bore you with our in-house reading material. I have a feeling that your friend knows all about universal energy, teleportation, the human energy field, and a particular favourite of yours, Addric, energy manipulation.'

Milton is completely flabbergasted and is about to say that he is definitely interested, but Addric cuts him off at the pass.

'Perhaps we should leave that until later.'

'Whatever you wish,' Zubia says. 'I shall be back in a few minutes.'

Milton's head is spinning, and he has no idea what to think.

'So, Addric, are you from Earth or somewhere else?'

'Earth is my second home.'

'It is, so where is your other home?'

'I am sure that you have heard of the star system Alpha Centauri.'

'Of course, I have, but that's light years away from here. So how did you get here?'

'Wimple arrived by portal but I can physically relocate to anywhere I wish, as long as I have been there before.'

Part one of Addric's plan is working out beautifully. To bring Milton to the Cosmic Café was a brilliant idea. Discussing matters of such significance anywhere else may not have had the same effect.

Zubia reappears a few minutes later, and in her hands, she carries a tray with three exotic cocktails in long-stemmed glasses.

'Oh Zubia, they look absolutely incredible,' Addric says. 'But what are they?'

'This is my latest creation, the granddaddy of all cocktails, an el supremo that I call a Lightning Conductor.'

'That sounds very enervating,' he says.

'It is actually a lime green liqueur with a smattering of fluorescent pink bubbles.'

'I like to tell my customers that it's riddled with distilled cosmic energy, static electricity and high voltage electrons.'

'It sounds so much more interesting than the usual thing, doesn't it? And it is guaranteed to put a little oomph in your engine as well.'

Addric takes a tentative sip and gives Zubia the nod of approval.

'Um, it's absolutely delicious,' he says. 'This could propel a rocket ship to Mars and back.'

'I believe that some desperado tried that a few years ago, but we never heard from him again.'

Before she wanders off to attend to a few of her faithful customers, Zubia offers Milton the use of Zilmo tag.

'Perhaps you would find this useful,' she says.

'What is it?' Milton says as he inspects a thin sliver of plastic that looks like a false fingernail.

'This is the Zilmo Tag, a knowledge base of information on everything in the known universe.'

'It's essential reading for anyone with a busy life and little time to catch up on the latest news.'

'This version of the Tag is the latest in hi-tech communication, and it even comes with a comprehensive menu.'

'And after you have chosen your area of interest, a holographic screen offers you a series of options.'

'However, you can participate in the experience in different ways, or you can fast-track an inquiry by simply touching the item of interest.'

'I think that will come in very useful,' Addric says as he slips it into his pocket.

'Perhaps it would be better if we left it until later, as we have things of an urgent nature to discuss.'

'Of course, Addric, I shall leave it in your safekeeping,' Zubia says.

CHAPTER 18

Addric selects a dish from the classic Earth menu, fresh pasta with a spicy sauce, accompanied by a glass of chilled wine. After which, he is ready to launch Milton into the ionosphere.

'So, Addric, what is this all about?'

'It's about what you can and cannot do, Milton.

'What you don't know is that there is a rule by which everyone in the universe must abide, and a few others that it's essential to know about.'

'Rule Number One is known as the Prime Directive, a rule which states that all life is sacrosanct.'

'It exists everywhere, Milton, especially on Earth, and the penalty for breaking the Prime Directive is either death or incarceration.'

'Depending on where you live, of course.'

'That rule comes from the very highest level if you follow my meaning, a directive enforced by the Intergalactic Alliance.'

'And who are they?' Milton says.

'An organisation whose sole purpose is to monitor the evolution of every life-form in the universe.'

'But they have a particular interest in the evolutionary status of Planet Earth.'

Addric is keeping a close eye on Milton just to make sure he understands the importance of what he is saying.

'Rule number two is that Planet Earth is out of bounds to everyone. In other words, no alien life-form must ever interfere in its development.'

'To some extent, that explains why aliens have never made themselves known.'

As Milton can clearly see, he is surrounded by alien life forms, all of whom are obviously very sophisticated and highly developed beings in their own right.

'But you're an alien, aren't you?'

'I am Milton, but I am also a human being, and a Yumi Master. That's what I do for a living, and on the odd occasion, I have to abide by the same equally stringent rules.'

'You don't look old enough to be a master of anything.'

'I am a Yumi Master nevertheless, Milton. I have a fifty-year-old son, and I am old enough to be your grandfather.'

'However, I have been assigned by the Intergalactic Alliance to do two things, one of which is to prevent a global catastrophe.'

'And what sort of catastrophe would that be?'

'The extinction of all life on Planet Earth,' Addric says with deliberate intent.

It's obvious that Addric is serious, but Milton is somewhat surprised to hear what else he has to say.

'If you had made it all the way to Washington DC, you would have triggered an event of global proportions.'

'Not only that, you would have disrupted the electromagnetic field of the planet.'

'Just in case you are not aware, Milton, they function as a deflector shield diverting charged particles from the Sun so that the planet is not incinerated.'

'If I had not come along, Milton, you may have gone down in history as the first human being to be incinerated by electromagnetic energy.'

'And if you had made it to Washington DC at all, it would have been as a little pile of ash and cinders.'

'Not only that, every electronic device in the world would cease to function, and at this point in time, they probably have.'

Milton's head is spinning as he tries to come to grips with the enormity of what Addric is saying.

'I had no idea.'

'However, Milton, there's more,' Addric says.

'Do you remember that incident from last week, the one where everyone on social media sites commented on the fact that they had exactly the same dream?'

'Did you have something to do with that?'

'Of course I did, Milton, but I am not working alone.'

'That extraordinary experience was the inspired idea of Wimple's extended family.'

'Is true,' Wimple says.

'And what did you hope to achieve by pulling such a stunt?'

'That was no stunt, Milton. Saving the human race from annihilation is not what I would describe as a stunt. That was an attempt to reverse the problem.'

'By invading our dreams, what would that prove?'

'Milton, this issue is a lot more serious than a global power outage or the loss of your life.'

'We have been advised by our contacts in the Intergalactic Alliance that if the people of Planet Earth are to survive, two things must change.'

'And what are they?'

'Have you ever heard of a concept called human consciousness?'

'Yes, but I have no idea what it is.'

'It's the combined thoughts and energies of every person on the planet. And it is a vital component of the system necessary for the development of the human race.'

'It has plummeted to an all-time low, primarily because people are no longer communicating at an inner level. By that, I mean the guidance system that comes from within.'

'In other words, Milton, the people of Earth have chosen a form of enslavement. They have chosen to be controlled by electronic devices such as those made by your company.'

'If this situation cannot be rectified, then the worst of all possible scenarios will be set in motion. Civilisation as you know it will be eliminated, and the Earth will be reprocessed.'

'And if you remember the story of Noah's Ark, you will understand exactly what I mean.'

According to the way that Addric sees things, Milton is in the perfect position to do something about this situation.

He has created some of the most popular devices on the market, and if he puts his mind to it, he could come up with an idea to reverse the problem.

'We have to do something to change this situation,' Addric says. 'And more importantly, we have to wean people off their addiction to electronic devices.'

'We chose to invade your dreams for a reason, Milton. The results were positive, and everyone noticed.'

'The statistics went through the roof, and according to my contacts in the Intergalactic Alliance, it also had an effect on human consciousness.'

'And that's what we have to reinvigorate, the power of people to create their own potential and their own future.'

'In other words, we have to find a way to save them from extinction.'

'What could I do?' Milton says.

'We will consider all possible options, and maybe we will even get a bit of help from the Zilmo Tag.'

'We will not be catching up with the latest news, but we will do a bit of useful research.'

'Under normal circumstances, Earthlings do not have access to any outside information, and that's for a very good reason.'

'And why is that?'

'That is also a directive from the highest of all levels, Milton.'

'The people of Planet Earth are participating in one of the most extraordinary endeavours in the known universe.'

'In a time long gone, this planet was inhabited by a race of highly advanced beings whose task was to prepare the planet for long-term habitation.'

'That took many thousands of years as the Earth was a very different place then. It was to have a singular honour and one that only a few heavenly bodies have ever had.'

'The Earth was designed as a place in which non-souled beings could have an experience in physical form.'

'That process started a very long time ago, but the original inhabitants have long since disappeared off the scene.'

'Earth is now the home of people like you. But if they want to survive, they have to change their ways.'

'And if they do survive, they will pave the way for the most glorious era in human history.'

'In other words, they will become sovereign beings in their own right. And that, in my books, is something worth fighting for.'

Milton is thoroughly overwhelmed by this revelation.

'So, I presume that you have a master plan,' he says.

'No, Milton, just a few ideas, but if we want to succeed, we have to do whatever we can.'

'We will explore a few of those options after I have taken you home, of course.'

'Unfortunately, once you re-enter Earth's atmosphere, the electromagnetic fields will erase any memory of this experience.'

'They may do a bit of damage as well, but they will be there in some form.'

'And in what form will that be?'

'Everyone strives to create something that has never existed before. And to do so, they download ideas from a higher source, from their own selves in fact.'

'You do exactly the same thing, Milton, just in case you didn't know. Your inspiration comes from yourself.'

'After this, I will take you to a place that is sometimes referred to as Station 51. It's a repository in an alternate universe where ideas are given form and substance.'

'And hopefully, you might come up with a few ideas that could be useful to our cause.'

'And after that, several things must happen.'

'That sounds a bit ominous,' Milton says.

'The first thing I intend to do, Milton, is follow you around like a shadow. Secondly, it's essential that we meet in person.'

'And the best way for that to happen is for you to have an accident of some kind. Not a life-threatening accident, but a carefully orchestrated one.'

'Thirdly, I would like you to meet my backup team to make sure that you are on the right track.'

'You will not be aware of my identity, not unless I decide otherwise, but it's an arrangement that will be mutually beneficial to everyone.'

'What do you think of that idea?' Addric says in all hopefulness.

'Well, put it this way, Addric, I, for one, do not want to be responsible for the extinction of life on Earth.'

'And it's apparent that a lot of people have gone to a great deal of effort to prevent a catastrophe.'

''And if I can help in any way, I definitely will.'

'Count me in.'

'That's excellent,' Addric says.

'So now, it's time for a quick tour of Station 51 so that you can explore a few of its options.'

'You never know what you might come up with.'

A few hours later, Milton is found in an unconscious state not far from the Golden Gate Bridge. There wasn't much left of his flight suit; his arms had been singed, and he had suffered burns to his lower legs. But if it had not been for a passing stranger, his condition may have been a lot worse.

If Milton had arrived at his destination, his team would have hailed their experiment as a success. Unfortunately, the result of his efforts was a massive power crisis.

For the first time in history, every electronic device in the world stopped working for three and a half agonising days.

Every city in the world came to a standstill, and people were forced to do something they had not done in ages. They stepped out onto the streets and spoke to a complete stranger.

Essential services were spared, but everyone else had to suffer the indignity of a cold shower and food rations, but Tuesday the 11th of April would never be forgotten.

That was the day on which every vehicle powered by a digitally enhanced engine came to a dead stop on every street and highway in the world.

No one had any idea what was going on, and they were not happy about it at all. To Addric's amazement, this disruption really did cause a sharp spike in Majura Krestovori's graph.

'As a means of raising human consciousness to an all-time high, that idea worked beautifully Addric, but it's a pointless exercise unless someone tells them what's going on.'

'Do you have any ideas on how you might accomplish that on a global scale?'

'Actually, ladies, I do. Do you know that old saying, if you can't beat them, join them?'

'Of course, we do Addric.'

'Well, I have had one of my old-fashioned, brilliant ideas.'

'Please, don't keep us in suspense any longer,' Seray says. 'What is it Addric?'

'Firstly, I was thinking that it would be a good idea to send everyone a message at the same time.'

'That will be the moment that every communication device on Earth comes back online.'

'I like where you're going,' Seray says. 'But how do you propose to accomplish such a thing, and what sort of message will it be?'

'That, I have not yet decided, but our new friend Milton Swizzer will play a part, as will his mother and Wimple.'

'Ah ha, I presume that you mean a combination of old-fashioned telepathy with a touch of Krugwah magic thrown in for good measure.'

'Absolutely, Milton's mother is the perfect conduit. And as you know, she is accustomed to receiving messages from the spirit world.'

'As a means of delivering a global message, that's a brilliant idea, Addric, but it could just as easily backfire.'

'I am aware of that, but perhaps you would like to help me to draft out a few ideas, just to start with.'

'Oh yes indeed, Addric, there is nothing better than a creative writing class to get the juices flowing.'

'And the end product is bound to be a best seller.'

'I was only thinking of a few lines of text, Seray, not a full-blown manuscript.'

'That was not lost on me at all, Addric. And neither is the fact that we have a readymade market.'

'Unfortunately, they come from different cultures with different languages, different mindsets, and in most cases, different traditions.'

'In that case, Google Translator will be running hot for the first time in its long and illustrious career,' Addric says.

'Ah yes, of course. This is definitely a situation in which one should never underestimate the wonders of modern technology.'

According to his doctor, Milton's concussion was a result of a fall from a great height. That was mystery number one.

As to the origin of his burns, he had absolutely no idea, and Shanala was not about to reveal what he had been up to.

Milton was bedridden for a few days, and as she sat by his side in the hospital, Shanala was very conscious of the company that she kept.

She rarely bothered about them, but they were there all the same. Sometimes, it was a few glittering orbs radiating a soft but gentle light, and at other times, it was numerous overactive fairies. But the last thing she expected to see was the man in the black leather flight suit.

To Shanala's surprise, he is accompanied by the very same creature that she saw a few days before. As to what it is, she cannot decide, but it has a lovely face and beautiful eyes and a delightful tuft of ginger-coloured hair.

Wimple has been assigned the task of communicating with Shanala, and after an intensive rehearsal, he is ready to play his part. He rises into the air, cocks his head from one side to the other, does a very slow backspin, spreads his arms, and pretends to be a bird in flight.

Visitors from the non-physical realms have never done anything out of the ordinary before, but this creature is a little different for some reason.

Using one finger, Wimple taps out a message on his hand and indicates with gestures that he wants her to watch closely.

'I think he is trying to communicate in sign language,' she says.

Wimple repeats the routine several times over and encourages Shanala to do the same. It takes a while before she works out what he is saying, and when she does, Wimple gives her a hearty round of applause.

'But I don't understand. What do you want me to do with this?'

Milton has been watching this performance closely, and it's enough to rouse him from his slumbers.

'Mother,' he says. 'Get me to my office immediately.'

'And whatever you do, don't forget that message.'

After three and a half days of enforced silence, the satellites languishing idly around the Earth are suddenly reactivated. Most people had given up hope of ever being able to use their devices again. But when they hear that familiar ringtone, they can barely believe their luck. And at that moment, everyone on Earth receives exactly the same text, voice, and email message.

'Be the one that you know to be true. Listen within and listen to you.'

Milton was under the impression that he had activated the satellites, but as he would come to learn, it was Addric's intergalactic friends who were responsible for that little coup.

'Addric, please accept my congratulations.' Reuben says. 'The social media sites have gone psycho, and everyone is posting about that mysterious message.'

The excitement in Addric's den is infectious and Emphora has no idea whether to laugh or cry.

'You never cease to amaze me,' she says.

'I cannot accept any responsibility for that,' Addric said. 'I had a lot of help from two very wonderful aliens, Majura Krestovori and Seray Antropedes.'

'And who are they? Felicity says.

'The Venusian ambassadors to the Intergalactic Alliance, and I can assure you, Felicity, that they are like-minded souls.'

'But I think Wimple deserves a round of applause because he delivered an Oscar-winning performance.'

The ever-bashful Wimple cannot help but laugh out loud, but Eenah, as usual, has something to say.

'This be deserving of a special celebration,' she says.

'I will drink to that,' Yusef says. 'What do you have in mind, Eenah?'

'I am thinking that a party would be good, but we must invite our new friends.'

'And which friends would they be.'

'Milton Swizzer and his mother, of course. Who else would I be talking about?'

'Why?' Addric says.

'Because they must know who they be dealing with.'

'If we want to get Milton on our side, it would be a good idea if he be having the bigger picture in his head.'

'But I told Milton that I wasn't going to reveal my identity for a while.'

'Forget about that, Addric. He just has to know.'

'It can't hurt,' Emphora says. 'But how do we make ourselves known.'

'Well, I told Milton that would be the result of a highly orchestrated accident.'

'And that be it,' Eenah says. 'So how you be doing this, I am thinking.'

There's an old Earth saying that things happen in threes. Three has always been the favourite choice of the numerically inclined, the eternally hopeful and even the local soothsayer.

But before anything else happens, little Mr. Milton will have to suffer the indignity of a life-threatening accident, but he will survive to tell the tale.

Milton's daily routine is nothing if not regulated; after all, he is the head of a major corporation.

What he doesn't know is that Addric has been following him around for the last few days, and at one point, he even took a close look at his diary.

Up until the day of his accident, Milton's life ran like clockwork. He is usually up at five-thirty and follows the same routine every day.

His chauffeur, Cedric, collects him at seven on the dot, and they travel the same route through the streets of San Francisco every day of the week.

Milton's routine is nothing if not consistent. This, as Addric realises, is yet another reason why the people of the 21st century have lost their way.

He follows Milton from one meeting to another, but the language of choice of high-level technocrats is dreadfully uninspiring.

'How do these people ever find the time to have an original thought?' Addric says. 'If the people of Earth are to achieve anything at all, this has to change.'

Milton is one of the prime offenders because he and his kind have imposed an all-encompassing spell on the minds of at least half of the people in the world.

Milton's work ethic is based on robotic determination. And from the moment that a meeting starts, he is involved with one group of designers or another. But by day four, his mind is elsewhere, and it is definitely not on the job.

'His recent experiences are starting to take on a life of their own,' Addric says.

The celestial realm, fondly referred to as Station 51, is an inspired wonderland with ideas that are just waiting to be brought to life. It's a magnet to creative people from all walks of life, and for a few passing hours, Milton had an opportunity to soak up the atmosphere.

He wandered around, gazing in awe and wonder as someone, somewhere, connected with a divinely inspired thought and then brought it to life. It was only a short visit, but it left an indelible imprint on his mind.

'And it had the desired effect,' Addric says.

By the end of the week, Milton has had enough. He grabs his briefcase, cancels all other meetings for the day, and leaves the office just before lunch.

'Cedric,' he says. 'Please take me to Golden Gate Park.'

Milton has always been mesmerised by the Golden Gate Bridge, especially when a fog drifts in from the ocean. He wanders around aimlessly for a while and then decides to visit the Institute of Fine Art.

Shanala was determined that he would have a cultural education whether he wanted one or not. But Milton was on a totally different wavelength, and he had no interest in a recorded voice that regaled him with the details of the history of portraiture in North America.

The Institute is a renowned cultural icon that exhibits the treasures of American history, and like all money-making institutions, it has to appeal to the masses.

On that afternoon, Milton decides to take a look at an exhibition called *Revelations of a Soul Master*. Under normal circumstances, something as vague as the inner life of a mystically inspired artist would not be on his radar. And the moment that he steps across the threshold, he has another life-changing experience.

As he contemplates one of the massive paintings that dominate the gallery, a surge of energy ripples up his spine, and Milton leaps three feet into the air.

'What was that,' he cries.

There isn't another soul in sight and Milton has no idea what just happened, but he doesn't know what to think when he hears a voice whispering in his ear.

'Concentrate on the painting,' Addric says.

The canvas is at least six meters high by eight meters wide, and the subject matter is a vast and mystical world of astounding beauty.

Milton knows that he has seen that place before, but his heart is beating so loudly that it is reverberating in his ears.

'I think I am going to have a heart attack,' he cries. He races out the door and takes a few very deep breaths.

He is a million miles away and staring out into space, but there is something about the Bridge that attracts his attention.

Cedric has been waiting patiently for the last two hours, but Milton has a very strange look on his face. Cedric has no idea what to think when he asks to be taken to the Bridge. He is all too aware of its reputation as a final destination for the depressed, the lost, and the hopeless.

'If that is what you wish, Sir, I will be happy to oblige.'

Milton created an empire on pure skill and talent and he has everything that a man could ask for. And not once in the last ten years has Cedric had a reason to complain, but this is an unusual request. Milton's decision to leave work earlier than usual is way out of character, and Cedric has every reason to be concerned.

'Pick me up on the other side,' Milton says.

It is almost five thirty, and the pedestrian pass will only be open for another thirty minutes. At this time of day, the bridge is a busy place with hundreds of people moving along at a rapid pace.

Signs have been posted at regular intervals as one of many initiatives to prevent a potential suicide. A permanent barrier was erected twenty years before but it has since been removed.

The fate of would-be jumpers is now in the hands of plain-clothed patrol officers and overhead cameras who keep a close eye on anyone who is planning to leap off the bridge. Not everyone succeeds, but the determined always find a way.

Unbeknownst to Milton, Addric is following along behind, and he is only seconds away from enacting his one-off plan.

Milton is about to have an experience that should, in theory, elevate him off the ground and catapult him high into the air.

The Kundalini is a reservoir of energy at the base of the spine, and once activated, it flows up to the brain and blends with the cerebral cortex. If that ever happens, the sensory system of the recipient operates at full power, and in some cases, it is said, they can even walk on water.

'Okay, it's time to do this,' Addric says.

He taps Milton on the base of the spine, and to his amazement, it works. Milton leaps into the air and over the side of the Bridge, and a few seconds later, he is plummeting at a rate of knots and is about to have a face-first impact with San Francisco Bay.

According to the experts, anyone who falls from a height of 245 feet will collide with the water at a rate of 120 kilometers per hour. Their rib cage will be demolished, their internal organs will be lacerated, and they will drown immediately.

This is the scenario that Addric has set in place. He told Milton that their first meeting would be the result of a potentially life-threatening accident, but he did say that it would not be fatal.

Hundreds of pedestrians stop in their tracks, and just before Milton collides with the watery barrier that separates this life from the next, Addric leaps over the side and saves him from a fate worse than death.

If he had waited a few seconds more, every bone in Milton's body would have shattered into a hundred little pieces.

CHAPTER 21

Milton is the biggest news story of the day and the media are onto it immediately. According to one intrepid reporter, Milton tried to commit suicide, while another said that he was kidnapped.

No one would have taken any interest in this story if it had not been for a snap-happy pedestrian. The result of his lightning-sharp reflexes was a twenty-second video that told a very different tale.

What the authorities don't know is that Milton is in safe hands. He passed out in Addric's arms, but that was only to be expected. He leapt off the Golden Gate Bridge and almost had an encounter with life on the other side.

For the next eighteen hours, Milton is dead to the world, and while he has time on his hands, Addric decides to collect some driftwood for the BBQ, but before he does so, he leaves a note on Milton's bedside table.

Milton's first thought on waking up is that he has been abducted, but this is obviously not a prison cell. It is a room of substantial proportions, decorated with a style of furniture that he has never seen before.

He wanders around, only to discover that someone has left a towel, a toothbrush, a pair of jeans, and a casual shirt on a table in the middle of the room.

'They even know my size,' he says. 'What else do they know about my anatomy?'

Milton never goes anywhere without his personal communicator, but he is relieved to see that it's still there.

'And there's a note as well,' he says.

'Dear Milton. Do not be concerned, you have not been kidnapped as the media are saying. In fact, it's just the opposite. I am the mysterious man who came to your rescue.

You will find a fresh set of clothes and a few other things on the table. You suit has been laundered and your shoes have been polished to within an inch of their life.

If you wake up any time in the next hour, I will either be in the living room or down at the beach. And I am looking forward to meeting you.

Regards

Marcus.

'That's a relief. At least he doesn't sound like an axe murderer.'

Milton activates his communicator and is expecting to see at least thirty messages, but the only working functions are the clock and the date.

'What's wrong with this thing?' he says. 'A communicator only drops out if there is a problem.'

'But look at the time. It's three o'clock in the afternoon. That means a whole day is missing from my life.'

'What happened to yesterday?'

He wanders over to the window, only to discover that it's a beautiful day. The Sun is shining, and seagulls are gliding along on a cushion of air. And other than a man wandering along the beach, the place is deserted.

'That must be Marcus,' he says.

'I have to find out what this is all about, but not until I have had a shower.'

Addric decided to disguise himself as a fictitious character called Marcus, and he now has wavy black hair and dark brown eyes. And for the first time in his life, he has the sort of tan that you only get by lazing around on a secluded beach on the coast of Spain.

'So, who are you and what's your story?' Milton says.

'My name is Marcus Grunewald, and I inherited a fortune from my father,' Addric says.

'And I now live a life of luxury in this beautiful villa on the coast of Spain.'

'And you are the guy who saved me.'

'Yes, I am,' Addric says.

To Milton's surprise, he is all over the television and is the news story of the day.

'Milton Swizzer managed to leap over the barrier of the Golden Gate Bridge,' the news reporter says. 'Hundreds of people can verify it, but one man even got his last few seconds on video.'

'The part that baffles everyone is that Milton was saved by a mysterious Superman who came out of nowhere at the last moment. He scooped him up and then disappeared over the horizon.'

'Yet another story that will have an effect on human consciousness,' Addric says to himself.

'You don't look like the guy who came to my rescue,' Milton says. That's a different person altogether.'

'That's not you, is it?'

'Yes and no,' Addric says, 'I am actually in disguise at the moment.'

'Well, it's a pretty good one if you ask me.'

'You obviously have special powers of some sort.'

'More or less,' Addric says. 'You could say that I was lucky to inherit several special gifts as well.'

'So, what else can you do apart from fly?'

'You name it, Milton, and I can do it.'

'Such as,' Milton says.

'Well, I can appear and disappear at will. I can fly, and I can conjure up anything you can imagine.'

'But the part that might make you a little green with envy, Milton, is that I can physically relocate to anywhere I like.'

'That does make me green with envy.'

'I nearly lost my life in an effort to travel a couple of thousand miles in a portal.'

'I know,' Addric says.

Under normal circumstances, he would not reveal his identity to anyone, but this is different and Addric is enjoying this little subterfuge.

'How do you know that?' Milton says. 'I didn't release that information to the press. And the only person who does know is my mother.'

'Shanala the clairvoyant. Yes, that's true, but I just happen to know that as well because I was the one who alerted her to your accident.'

Addric is being purposefully all-knowing and hoping to get Milton on side, but he still has a few rickety bridges to cross before that happens.

'So, what am I doing here,' Milton says. 'And why did you save me?'

'You, Milton, have the power to save the world from extinction,' Addric says with a knowing look in his eye.

'You're joking, aren't you. That's your line of work.'

'Under normal circumstances, it is, but I need your help.'

'You're serious, aren't you?'

'Why would I joke about something like that?'

It turns out to be a long and interesting afternoon, but Milton is in dire need of an update on a few things that he has forgotten about since their little chat at the Cosmic Café.

'Why don't we sit out on the terrace and discuss this situation in a little more detail.'

'I need a good stiff drink,' Milton says. 'And I wouldn't mind a bite to eat as well.'

'Just say what you want, Milton, and I will conjure it up out of thin air.'

'I am famished, actually.'

'Easily done,' Addric says.

Milton has never been a big drinker, but he does imbibe on the odd occasion. He listens closely as Addric explains the situation in detail, the imminent fate of the people of Earth, and what their future could be.

'We will not fail as I am quite fond of this planet. And if it was to disappear in a puff of smoke, well, that would be a disaster of cosmic proportions, wouldn't it?'

'It certainly would, but what can I do.'

'The thing we have to do is wean people off contraptions like yours and give them back their dignity.'

'Those devices rule their lives, Milton. They alienate people from a vital connection to spirit, and that is the primary issue.'

'I have been assigned the task of changing the status quo. You see, we have to find a way to amplify the very thing that threatens the future of this planet.'

'And what is that?' Milton says.

'I know that you have heard of human consciousness as we have had this conversation before.'

'We have,' says a surprised Milton.

'Yes, we have. I was the one who came to your rescue when you were about to be incinerated on the way to Washington DC.'

'I whisked you away to the planet Jupiter, where we spent several hours discussing the very same things that we are discussing now.'

'As I explained then, human consciousness is a powerful force. It's a result of the thoughts and feelings of every person on the planet and it is vital to all life, but it's disappearing down the plug hole.'

'If it gets any lower, the powers that be have been advised from the highest of all levels that the inhabitants of Earth are to be reprocessed.'

'And the planet is to be terraformed without its current inhabitants.'

'Do you want that to happen?' Addric says as he zooms in a little too closely.

'I certainly do not, Marcus. What do you take me for? 'What exactly do you want me to do.'

'I want you to become a part of my team. And between us all, we will figure something out, one idea at a time.'

'What do you have in mind, Marcus?'

'Well, we were the brains behind that dream incursion incident and the message that you sent last week. Anything that attracts the attention of everyone on the planet is the solution to this problem.'

'But the main thing we have to do is reduce their reliance on electronic devices and allow them to think for themselves.'

'That sounds like a job and a half if ever there was one,' Milton says. 'If I haven't said so before, count me in, Marcus.'

'You did, Milton, after which I returned you to Earth and then sent one of my offsiders to visit you in hospital.'

'If I was to say that I am thoroughly overwhelmed, would you believe that as well, Marcus?'

'Of course, Milton, especially after what you have been through.'

'I think it's time to waddle off to bed, or you are going to pass out on the spot.'

'Very true,' he says.

CHAPTER 22

Addric is starting to get the hang of this idea, but the secret is to make every performance count. As to how he will return Milton back to the real world is something he hasn't worked out as yet.

Milton is fast sleep, so he decides to make a quick visit to his old friends Majura Krestovori and Seray Antropedes.

'Addric, if I was to say that you are the brightest wizard of the age, what would you say?'

'I would say what Hermione Grainger probably wanted to say, Majura, but JK Rowling never put the words in her mouth.'

'That was a compliment, my friend.'

'I realise that, Majura, and I appreciate it, but I am here to grill you intensively once again.'

'Ooh, we love being grilled, Addric. After all, we were once witches of some distinction.'

'Unfortunately, we were promoted to positions of power. Now, what can we do for you?'

As you know, I have little Mister Milton on a short leash, and before I return him to the world of the living, I thought it would be a good idea to do so in such a way that everyone noticed.'

'Ah, I love a good challenge,' Majura says. 'However, could we interest you in a drink before we get down to business?'

'That depends on what it is.'

'Vosomor, Addric. What else do highly advanced beings drink.'

'I know it well, ladies, and I will be happy to indulge.'

Vosomor is the beverage of the gods, a honey-flavoured elixir that opens a pathway to the unknown and the unseen.

'The secrets of the universe often need a little lubrication before they become apparent,'

Majura says. 'But two or three tiny little glasses is more than enough for anyone.'

It only takes a few seconds before Vosomor finds its target, and when it does, the vague and the obscure become as clear as a bell.

'Hold on, I am receiving something of an unusual nature,' Majura says.

'Clarity would be good, my sister,' Seray says. 'Spit it out.'

'Does Milton have a brother?'

'Not that I am aware of, but I can check it out. Just give me a few minutes.'

Seray approaches the celestial equivalent of a computer screen, and Addric takes an immediate interest. It is not a screen in the usual sense of the word, but it does resemble a ripple in time and space.

'This is our version of Google and it never lies.'

'Ooh, you are correct. Little Mister Milton does have a brother, a twin brother in fact, and he is masquerading as a she.'

'Connor Burnett, aka Constance Brunette, was adopted at birth by Milton's mother, but get this Addric; she even works for Swizzer Industries.'

'Ah ha, that might explain a few things.'

'Like what, for example?'

'Like the fact that some of Milton's programs have been tampered with.'

'What else does Mega-Google have to reveal?'

'The Almighty Mouth knows all, Addric.'

'Constance has a problem and an interest of a specific kind.'

'Is he an autistic savant, as well?'

'No, Addric, he is not, but Constance is engaged in espionage and supplies other companies with information about any new ideas developed by Swizzer Industries.'

'The cheeky little rascal,' Majura says. 'That boy needs a good lesson in etiquette.'

'That would be a waste of time, Majura. After all, this is the 21st century and people don't have a clue about etiquette.'

'But we do Addric. We come from the old world, and we would love to ease our way into his organisation and give things a bit of a rustle up.'

'You could reincarnate as a human being?' Addric says.

'If only. That's just wishful thinking on my part, Addric, but it would be so much fun to be flesh and blood again.'

'Unfortunately, we are bound by convention. And the only thing we can do is evaporate and un-evaporate at will if you know what I mean.'

That, as Addric realises, is probably the standard fantasy of most celestial beings.

'But ladies, how will I return Milton back to life. That's what I want to know.'

'It doesn't matter what you do or how you do it, Addric. Pick a time and pick a place.'

'Just make sure that the television cameras are rolling.'

'And if he becomes prime-time news, the reincarnation of Mr. Milton Swizzer will be the only thing that people will be talking about for the next six weeks.'

'And that's what we want, total and unequivocal interest.'

'Indeed, it is ladies. It is indeed.'

Every television network in the world is obsessed with what happened to Milton Swizzer, but they really want to know the identity of the anonymous Superman. And if Milton ever resurfaces, he will become the celebrity of the decade.

'Of course,' Addric says, as another brilliant idea reveals itself in all of its glory. 'Little Mister Milton is about to get the makeover of all makeovers.'

When Milton resurfaces the next morning, he is a little worse for wear. Addric sits him down and serves up the sort of breakfast recommended for a recovering alcoholic.

To ensure that Milton knows exactly what is going on, he pumps up the volume on the television.

'Milton, you really are famous now.'

'It looks like it, doesn't it?'

'And I think we should take advantage of that idea and mine it for everything thing it's got.'

'We will get a lot of mileage out of this now that you are the news item of the day.'

'How do you mean?'

'I have been up all night planning out what we are going to do.'

'We will take advantage of the idea that your saviour is a Superman and that he has a message for the people of Earth.'

'You have?' Milton says.

'Absolutely, and I will even ask a few friends to put on a show that no one will ever forget.'

'Who do you have in mind?'

'A few old mates and maybe six thousand nature spirits as well, the usual line-up.'

'Are they like you, perhaps?'

'If you mean, do they have the same gifts and talents as me? The answer to that is yes, they do, Milton.'

'The Krugwah are not human, but everyone else is.'

'So how will they get here?'

'They will probably arrive by some form of portal. They have several options to choose from.'

'They do, what sort of portals?'

'Primarily energetic, voice-activated, of course. Is there any other type?'

'Do you have access to a portal as well?' Milton says hopefully.

'Of course I do, I just snap my fingers and there it is.'

'I would love to travel in a portal. Please take me somewhere that no one has ever been before, Marcus.'

'Well, I am going home for a quick visit. You are welcome to come along if you wish?'

'Where's home Marcus?'

'I know that you have heard of Alpha Centauri because you told me so.'

'But Vela-Rishan is just a bit further than a few light years away. In fact, it's over 10 million light years away.'

Milton's breakfast has gone stone cold, but being the good host that he is, Addric quietly passes his hand over the plate so that he doesn't complain about the service.

'And how long does it take to get there?'

'About thirty seconds or so.'

'How long before we leave.'

'Twenty minutes, but don't rush. We have plenty of time.'

Now that Milton is on side, Addric decides to come clean and reveal his real identity.

'It was just a precaution. This is not what I normally look like. I made a few cosmetic changes to my appearance.'

'You're not a creepy little alien in disguise. Are you?'

'No, not at all. I changed the style of my hair and the colour of my eyes, but I also changed my name.'

'That's a relief,' Milton says.

'I actually have blond hair and blue eyes, like all aliens, of course. Just joking, Milton, and my name is not Marcus but Addric.'

'Okay, so how long will this makeover take?'

'About one second approximately.'

'I will turn around and when you see me again, I will be back to my normal self.'

'There, what do you think of that?' he says.

'Pretty good, actually.'

'Nothing fazes me, Addric. After all, I live in San Francisco, the gay capital of the world.'

'Almost everyone changes their appearance on a daily basis, but not for the same reason, of course.'

Over the next few minutes, Addric provides Milton with a few items of information related to their destination.

'I come from a place called Vela-Rishan, and it can be quite cool, so we will have to dress accordingly.'

'You will be relieved to hear that the inhabitants are human beings as well, normal human beings, not unlike some that I could mention.'

'Now, we have a variety of portals to choose from, but the most efficient is a Krugwah portal.'

'But be warned, Milton, it doesn't look anything like a portal. It looks more like a flesh-eating monster with a big blue eye.'

'However, it's perfectly harmless, and it doesn't have a taste for human flesh, as far as I know.'

It has been Milton's life-long dream to travel through time and space and he is beside himself with anticipation.

'Where exactly is Alpha Centauri?'

'Well, you take the second star to the right and keep going until morning,' Addric says.

'Peter Pan, I loved that story,' Milton says. 'Well, I loved the idea that Peter could fly more than anything?'

'It is exhilarating, believe me,' Addric says. 'I dreamt of flying as a boy, but little did I know that it would ever happen.'

'Tell me your story, Addric, I want to know everything.'

'That will have to wait until later, Milton, as our taxi has arrived.'

Like all Krugwah portals, this one resembles a luminescent mouth with a long, deep throat, but it's a doorway that wins Milton over. It glows like blue fire and radiates little sparks of golden light.

'Pretty impressive, isn't it?'

'It sure is Addric.

As a mode of transport, energetic portals have no equal. They can accommodate any number of passengers and the transference process is instantaneous.

'Follow me, Milton, and prepare to be pampered by a few nurturing universal energies. They are so much nicer than the electromagnetic fields of the planet. Of that, I can assure you.'

And a few minutes later, Milton is overwhelmed by what he sees. The Serinada Gardens is their first port of call, a magnificent park surrounded by beautifully kept gardens. At one end is the awe-inspiring Temple of Emphora, and at the other, is the equally impressive Serinada Hotel.

'That building over there is our cultural centre,' Addric says. 'But if you look up there, you will see the highest mountain in the realm.'

'That's the Askadera, and it just happens to be surrounded by one of the most impressive cities in the known universe, the Imperial City of Vela-Rishan.'

'Wow, this is unbelievable Addric. I had no idea it would look like this.'

'Now Milton, you can say you have travelled through space and time, and you have even been to another world.

'But I would be very careful who I told. The people of Earth can be, well, you know, a bit strange about things like that.'

'It will have to be my very own secret then, won't it?'

'Yes, that's a good idea, Milton.'

'Now, can you see the uppermost point of the Askadera?'

'Almost, there's too much cloud. Why?'

'Well, that's where we are going next. That is the primary residence of the Goddess Emphora, and the reason why we are here.'

'We are here to see a Goddess!'

'Indeed, she is one of my partners in crime. And they are all waiting for an update on what I plan to do next.'

'But how do we get there, Addric?'

'We will take a portal, of course, and be there in a jiffy.'

Far too many things have been happening and Milton's head is spinning, and when he steps out of the portal, it is only to discover that he really is on the top of a mountain.

'And the view is one of a kind, as you can see,' Addric says. 'Vela-Rishan is an inter-dimensional realm suspended in a perpetual ocean of nothingness.'

'This is not a planet, and there is no such thing as an ocean,' Addric says. 'But whether we like it or not, we are surrounded by a domain called the Abyss.

'It's a no-go zone. Apparently, it's inhabited by phantoms and lost souls, but you will be pleased to hear that it is not on our itinerary.'

'That is a relief, Addric.'

'But this beautiful house definitely is.'

Milton is in another galaxy with a man who can do just about anything, and the next thing on this rollercoaster ride is to meet a real live goddess who lives in a palatial villa on the top of a sacred mountain.

'This place is a palace and you will be very impressed.'

Emphora's private residence is surrounded by freshwater pools that trickle down the mountainside and tumble over the edge in lacy waterfalls and rivulets.

Milton looks up, only to see a woman dressed in a long flowing gown. Emphora has eyes that sparkle like crystal and a distinctive but classically timeless face. As he is about to find out, she has a sense of humour and a heart of gold.

'That is none other than the Goddess Emphora,' Addric says, 'a legendary figure in her own right, as you will soon discover.

'Addric, how lovely to see you,' she says. 'And it appears that we have company as well.'

'Yes, we do. Allow me to introduce you to the future saviour of Planet Earth, Mr. Milton Swizzer.'

'It is lovely to meet you, Milton, but please come inside and meet everyone else.'

'It's a little too chilly at this time of year, but I can assure you that it's as warm as toast inside.'

Milton's dream to travel through space and time came and went far too quickly, but now that he has met Addric's team, his enthusiasm for this campaign has increased tenfold.

He never wanted to be a celebrity but there's not much that he can do about it. He is about to become one, whether he likes it or not.

'I will manage somehow, I am not without skills as a public speaker,' he says. 'After all, I do spend my time inspiring others to greater heights, if that counts for anything.'

'You will do brilliantly, Milton. Besides, I will be at your side whispering sweet little nothings in your ear,' Addric says.

'And maybe make a few unusual things happen.'

'That is reassuring, Addric. I could never have done this alone.'

Public interest in the identity of the mysterious Superman has not abated over the last few days, and it is this element that Addric is about to use to his advantage.

He sends a message to a television station and informs them that Milton will arrive at work at 7.30 the following morning.

Word soon gets around, and hundreds of reporters, accompanied by camera crews, set themselves up in front of Swizzer Plaza.

Milton is the man of the moment, but they really want to know the identity of the superman who came to his rescue.

As a consequence, Addric is about to take his mission to the next level. The media can be a Godsend in some situations, and they will be the perfect vehicle to accelerate his cause.

Swizzer Industries is a purpose-built structure in the shape of the letter S, and over the last few years, it has become a major tourist attraction for hot air balloon enthusiasts in particular.

At seven o'clock on Monday, the 29th of April, the sky is a leaden grey and the public is out in force. They are not about to miss out on an opportunity like this.

The life of a reporter can be both tough and hectic, especially if they do not deliver the goods. As a result, things can get a little uncomfortable at head office.

The moment that Milton makes an appearance, he will be steamrolled by the media, and that would not be a productive exercise at all, so Addric came up with a different plan.

Milton is up bright and early on his big day and spends his time wandering along the terrace rehearsing his speech.

'It's almost time to go,' Addric says. 'So, how are you feeling Milton?'

'Uncommonly good, considering what I am about to do. But I have had an amazing few days, Addric, and I really could stay here for a lot longer.'

'All you have to do is ask Milton, and I will appear out of the blue and escort you to my island of serenity.'

Before anything else happens, Milton has to catch up with his parents. Shanala hasn't heard from him for days and she will be worried sick. He does the right thing and sends her a secure message on his communicator.

'I am fine, Mother, and I am in good hands. But before I face the press this morning, I am going to make a quick visit to see you and Dad. Meet me at the back door at 6.30 sharp. Love Milton.'

When Shanala sees a strange blue light in the back garden she doesn't know what to think, not until she hears someone knocking on the door.

'Mum, it's me,' Milton says. 'Please let me in before anyone sees us.'

Shanala has been beside herself with worry. Milton is her only son and she had no idea what had happened to him.

'Milton,' she cries as she plasters him with kisses. 'It's so good to see you.'

'It's okay, Mum, I have been in good hands.'

Once she and Hector have come to terms with the fact that he is still alive, Shanala gives Addric the once over in the way that only a psychic can do.

'I remember you,' she says. 'You're the man who saved Milton's life, aren't you?'

'The one and the same,' Addric says.

'Please accept my heartfelt gratitude. You have no idea what it means to have Milton back.'

'I have a son and two grandchildren, and I would be devastated if anything happened to them.'

'You have no idea how happy I am to hear that,' Shanala says. 'But you don't look like a Superman at all. You look perfectly normal to me.'

'Well, I am, except for a few modifications here and there.'

'How am I ever going to repay you for saving Milton's life?'

'You don't have to Shanala. That's what I do.'

Shanala and Hector listen closely as Addric provides them with a condensed version of what's about to happen.

'But don't worry about Milton. He really is in good hands.'

'You have an honest face, Addric, of that I am certain.'

'Thank you Shanala, but the best place to be this morning will be in front of the television.'

'But don't forget the tissues. You never know, you just might need them.'

It's almost twenty past seven, and the paparazzi are on tenterhooks. If Milton is to arrive at all, it will be in the next few minutes, but the last thing they expect is to see a beam of light streaming down from the heavens

For all they know, it could be an alien invasion. They have seen every sci-fi movie of the last three decades, and even though they are Hollywood fantasies, this could be the real thing.

Hundreds of curious sightseers are not about to miss out on the story of the century. But the moment they see a beam of light streaming down from above, they make a very speedy retreat.

'It could be a light from the Mothership,' one nervous reporter says. 'But I know as much as you do.'

The prospect of an alien invasion has been the most popular theory over the last two days. And when the networks ran out of things to say, they decided to replay some of the sci-fi classics of yesteryear.

Movies like *Independence Day* have been playing non-stop, and everyone knows the outcome if this really is the Mothership.

The clock is ticking and they watch closely as a beam of light from an unknown source inches its way to the ground, and at exactly 7.30 on the dot, it reaches its target.

The atmosphere shimmers back and forth, and the glowing blue doorway of a Krugwah portal appears, radiating little sparks of golden light.

'I have a strange feeling about this,' one reporter says.

His suspicions are confirmed a moment later when a vision appears in the plaza of Swizzer Industries.

It's an idyllic scene of Grecian women in long silken veils wandering through an apple orchard. And when they reach the line that separates one world from another, they step aside, and Milton makes an appearance.

The moment that he steps across the threshold, this will be history in the making, and one single photograph will be worth a king's ransom.

And when he does so, the air is alive with flashing lights and reporters asking one question after another.

Milton simply raises his hand and refuses to say anything, not until he has absolute silence.

'Ladies and gentlemen, I am not an apparition. It is me, Milton Swizzer of Swizzer Industries.'

'Before I say anything at all, I must alert you to the fact that this is not an alien invasion. I repeat, this is not an alien invasion.'

'I will not be answering questions, but I am here to tell you what happened the other day.'

'As you know, I came close to death last Friday afternoon, and I almost lost my life in San Francisco Bay.'

'I did not plan to jump off the Bridge but somehow or another, I did. As you know, a mystery man appeared at the last moment and saved me from a potentially fatal accident.'

'You have seen that footage numerous times over the last few days and I am here to tell you why.'

'I do not have a death wish, but I was saved by someone that I am honoured to call a friend. This man has gone out of his way to show me nothing but honesty and friendship.'

'He is the Superman that you have been talking about, but he is a man. Of that, there is no doubt at all.'

'He is an honest and intelligent man who has assured me that he will make himself known when the time is right. And he will, but before that happens, there are other things that you must know.'

'In a few moments, you will hear an important message from a representative of the celestial hierarchy.'

'This woman is a goddess in her own right, and like many of her kind, she has done whatever she can to give us a helping hand over the years.'

'However, before I introduce this esteemed lady, please respect the fact that she is here to share a message of great importance.'

'Ladies and gentlemen, boys and girls of Planet Earth, it is my pleasure to introduce a most serene and gracious lady.'

'As I have said, she is a goddess in her own right, and she has agreed to be here on this day for one reason and one alone.'

Milton clasps his hands together in an attitude of prayer and bows respectfully.

'Please welcome her serene highness, Emphora, the Goddess of Wisdom.'

Everyone watches with bated breath as a gracious-looking woman steps through the portal. She has a commanding presence and clear blue eyes. Her veil is held in place by a simple golden band, and she is dressed in a long flowing gown of blue silk and satin.

'Greetings to you, one and all, people of Planet Earth. As Milton has said, I am the Goddess of Wisdom, and I am here on this day to deliver a message of some importance.'

'I beg of you my brothers and sisters, please listen closely to what I have to say, but listen with your hearts and not your mind.'

'Planet Earth is one of the most beautiful of all planets in the universe. And it has been my home for longer than any of you can possibly imagine.'

'I love this planet for the very same reasons that you do, but your future as custodians is no longer assured, and there is a very good reason for that.'

'Over the last five decades, the people of Earth have chosen to ignore the voice of the spirit within.'

'And that is the primary problem. You have relinquished the power to make independent decisions in your life.'

'Unfortunately, you have chosen to allow your lives to be controlled by technology.'

'The people of Earth have the potential for greatness, but many have chosen to ignore that in favour of electronic devices that do the thinking for them.'

'I am not saying that you should discard your equipment, but if you want to survive, you have to find an acceptable balance.'

'This is the problem which must be resolved. If you do not reconnect with the spirit within, your future as inhabitants of this planet will be discontinued.'

'This directive is not of my making. It comes from the highest of all possible places, and I am sure that you know exactly where I mean.'

'But if you want to change your future, you also have to change your habits. If you can do that, your salvation will be assured.'

'Your progress will be monitored by a device known as an implant, a spiritual barometer which we will plant in every major city across the globe.'

'This barometer has its roots in the grid system of the planet, and if it changes from black to white, it will be a clear indication of what you have chosen.'

'One of my associates, the young man who saved Milton's life, will make himself known in a few weeks' time.'

'It is his task to evaluate the results of the implants and keep me updated on your progress.'

'If the readings are negative, then the message is clear. You have chosen to relinquish your right to be custodians of this planet.'

'However, you can change your lives and your future much sooner than you realise.'

'If you choose not to heed this message, then the worst of all possible scenarios will be set in place.'

'However, before I bring this transmission to a close, I must tell you that I am not the only one who will be monitoring your progress.'

'There are many other, far more powerful beings who are also watching you closely.'

'I hope and pray that you, my beloved friends, will do what is best for yourselves and what is best for this glorious planet that you call home.'

'I must leave now, but you will be seeing me again. Good luck and may God bless you.'

Emphora bows gracefully, fades away into the background and the Krugwah portal vanishes from view.

And over the next hour, a blue light is seen in thousands of places across the globe and a black implant now stands in its place.

CHAPTER 26

Several days have passed, and as far as the ratings are concerned, the event in Swizzer Plaza was liquid gold, and it's the only thing that people are talking about. Even the Catholic Church is begging their followers to do what the Goddess has asked.

'That's good news,' Addric says.

'That might have something to do with the fact that Emphora looked a lot like Mother Mary,' Felicity says.

'And who is that?' Jatoo says.

'The mother of Jesus Christ. I thought you knew that. She is loved and revered by Catholics everywhere.'

'Well, maybe I did, once upon a time.'

'I think it was the way which Emphora delivered the message,' Shanala says. 'It was both graceful and heartfelt.'

'I thought I did a pretty good job in my first starring role,' Emphora says, 'but thank you for the compliment, my dear.'

Shanala and Hector were happy to accept Addric's offer to spend a few days at Dragonshead. Their only alternative was to be bombarded by the paparazzi, and they were not looking forward to that at all.

Shanala absolutely adores Wimple, but she is not so sure about Eenah. She runs hot and cold and can be quite abrasive. Shanala sensibly takes Yusef's advice and hopes for the best.

This is the story of the century, and the importance of the message is not lost on the networks. They go out of their way to do whatever they can to encourage people to heed the advice of the Goddess.

'I don't know whether any of you have noticed,' Yusef says, 'but they haven't mentioned any of the people who are struggling with the idea of changing their ways.'

'Most of the offenders are probably the younger generation,' Felicity says. 'And I would not be surprised if technocrats are leaping out of fifty-storey buildings.'

'They're worried sick,' Milton says. 'Based on what I have heard from the people at my office.'

'Your company creates most of these products,' Jatoo says.

'Only twenty percent. Besides, I have given instructions to make alterations to all of our products.'

'That's good to hear. Like what, for instance?'

'It's a feature of applications that most users will find absolutely annoying,' Milton says.

'Most programs are designed to make our lives easier, but the revised version will do the opposite.'

'So, what is this radical new idea?'

'At crucial intervals, a program will ask a user if they can complete this task in some other way.'

'That's pretty good,' Jatoo says.

'If those features were included in a game, it would drive a player absolutely nuts, wouldn't it?'

'Of course, it would, and you'd just forget about it.'

'It is also an issue for my staff because they have the same problem as everyone else.'

'But I believe that some of my competitors are playing the waiting game.'

'Perhaps we should investigate their facilities and see for ourselves,' Reuben says.

'It's time to rustle a few feathers. Why don't we make a whirlwind tour of Silicon Valley?'

'That would be a waste of time,' Milton says. 'Most companies enforce high-level security measures designed to prevent their ideas from being pirated by other companies.'

'Technicians wear optical implants, and all we would be able to see is a blank screen.'

'And it wouldn't help much as the programs are written in a secure code. Even the staff cannot talk about their work.'

Hundreds of electronic companies are located in the Santa Clara Valley in Southern California, and it would take months to check them all out. On Reuben's suggestion, they decide to investigate one of them, nevertheless.

'Parchek Max is a company that produces applications for the education market,' Milton says, 'but they also have a seriously big stake in personal guidance modules.'

'And that's code for what?' Felicity says.

'It's industry jargon, which refers to anything that makes life easier.'

'Such as, for example.'

'Anything at all, really, self-management is a big money spinner, especially an application that can think for you. They give advice on what to do in just about any situation.'

'Some programs are designed to read your metabolism, while others give advice on dietary issues.'

'Many users have implants to maintain their vital organs in a state of health. That's good for those with liver and kidney problems and heavy drinkers, of course.'

'And there are literally hundreds of programs like that.'

'I now understand why the human consciousness index has dropped to an all-time low,' Felicity says.

'Well, I think we should make a discrete but fleeting visit to Parchek Max,' Addric says.

One of the advantages of being a Yumi Master is that they can choose to be invisible. As Milton is not in that category, Emphora is happy to provide him with the ability to slip behind the visible field.

'This is so cool,' he says. 'What fun you could have.'

'I am afraid that's a no-no,' Addric says. 'That is just one of the rules by which Yumi Masters have to abide, I am sorry to say.'

'Party poopers aren't we,' Emphora says.

'It's a good thing that this isn't available to the general public,' Milton says, 'otherwise the criminally inclined would rule the world.'

'They're the ones we are after,' Felicity says, 'those with an itching desire not to conform.'

'Can you believe that,' Jatoo says. 'They know that their days are numbered, but some companies are still determined to go their own way.'

'Yes, but at what cost,' Emphora says. 'They could hold out for as long as they want.'

'But we will track them down one way or another,' Addric says, 'and the implants will identify the naughty boys in particular.'

'That I did not know,' Emphora says.

'It wasn't what I had in mind when I came up with the idea, but in their wisdom, the ever-resourceful Majura and Seray thought otherwise.'

'You came up with the idea of the implant,' Felicity says. 'You are a clever boy Addric.'

'Thanks for the vote of confidence, your Ladyship.'

A few moments later, they step through the doors of the Parchek Max building, only to see programmers in secure cubicles who are staring at a blank screen. There is nothing much to see and they are just about to leave when Milton sees a young woman that he recognises.

'What is she doing here?'

'Who is she?' Jatoo says.

'Constance Brunette.'

'Oh dear,' Addric thought, 'I had forgotten about her.'

This is Milton's twin brother and the brother that he knows nothing about.

'And she is selling Swizza secrets to the opposition.'

'She deserves a good talking to,' Felicity says. 'Why don't we do just that?'

'Folks,' Addric says somewhat hesitantly. 'I don't think we should go down that path just yet?'

'And why is that?' Felicity says.

'For one thing, I am in possession of very delicate information about that young lady.'

'You think she's a cross-dresser too,' Milton says.

'I know for a fact that she is.'

'You can pick them a mile away. They're everywhere in San Francisco, but why should that stop us?'

'Because Constance Brunette is also known as Connor Burnett,' Addric says.

'And there's more, Addric, isn't there?'

'Yes, Milton, there is.'

Well, spit it out,' Felicity says. 'We haven't got all day.'

'She, or rather he, is actually your twin brother, Milton.'

'How do you know that?' he says.

'The all-knowing Seray Antropedes told me, of course. She can suss out information on anything.'

This is a bombshell that almost knocks Milton off his feet.

'But my mother never said anything about him.'

It's apparent that Milton is confused by this revelation, but no matter how he tries, he cannot take his eyes off Constance.

'Perhaps we should leave Miss Brunette to her own devices,' Emphora says, 'so that Milton can have a quiet chat with his mother.'

Their plan to engage in a little underhanded espionage lasted less than thirty minutes. And when they get back to Dragonshead, it's obvious to Shanala that something is terribly wrong.

'What happened?' she says

'Perhaps it would be better if you spoke about this privately,' Addric says. 'Please feel free to do so in my den.'

'Mother, I just found out something that I never knew before.'

'You met Connor, didn't you?'

'Yes, why didn't you tell me I have a brother?'

'I tried so many times, Milton, believe me, I did, but I just couldn't do it, or the time wasn't right.'

'How did you find out?'

Shanala is not surprised to find that Connor is one of Milton's employees. But she is surprised to hear that he dresses as a woman, and that he also has a part-time interest in industrial espionage.

'Why did you give him away, Mother?'

'I was young and un-married, Milton, and I wasn't making enough money for myself, let alone two little infants.'

'It was a difficult pregnancy, and I had to have a Caesarean, or you both would have died, but there were complications, and I nearly died.'

'Doctor Burnett was my physician, and if it had not been for her support, God knows what would have happened.'

'She adopted Connor, didn't she?'

'Yes, my darling, she did, and he had a very loving mother, as you have had.'

'But what are you going do about this, Milton?'

'Well, we were about to interrogate Connor when Addric spilled the beans. After that, we decided to forget the whole thing and come back here.'

'However, and this is just an idea and one that I would never have contemplated if it wasn't for the fact that we have the support of these wonderful people.'

'What are you going to do, Milton?'

'I have a brother, Mum, and I would like to get to know him.'

'I am thinking that we should kidnap Connor and bring him back here.'

'Oh Milton, this is happening so quickly.'

'If we did, I wouldn't have to report him to the authorities.'

'After all, he is involved in industrial espionage and the penalty for that is jail. And I don't want to send my only brother to jail, not if I can help it.'

Once Shanala has come to terms with this life-changing situation, Milton approaches Addric and Felicity with another idea.

'How would you like to help me kidnap my brother?'

'Of course we would,' Felicity says. 'I see no reason why we can't.'

'Thank you, Felicity. You're always upfront, aren't you?'

'Why not Milton. Subterfuge and lies only lead to pain and anguish in the end.'

'So, when do you want to do this?'

'Tonight, perhaps,' he says.

CHAPTER 27

San Francisco has changed radically over the years, and people have invested billions in transforming downtrodden areas into high-class neighbourhoods.

Apparently, Connor frequents a nightclub on a regular basis, but Addric has to prepare himself for the idea that he is about to make his first foray into unknown territory.

'So, we are going to a gay bar.'

'They are called social clubs now,' Felicity says. 'Keep up with the times, Addric.'

'And they are seriously impressive,' Milton says. 'They're more like five-star hotels with all mod cons.'

'I don't want to know anything else other than the overall plan.'

'Okay, so this will be our story. We are Europeans travellers on an overseas holiday,' Felicity says. 'We will disguise ourselves as someone or another, as most people will be out for a good time on a Saturday night.'

'It will be so much fun, Reuben, but the boys will absolutely love you, Jatoo.'

'I am not going, Felicity. I am a married man.'

'This is business. It's not personal, Jatoo, and you are more than capable of taking care of a few muscle-bound men.'

'Nah, Felicity, I'm not interested.'

'I will deal with you later, young man.'

'Now Milton, this is your turf. What's the dress code?'

'Well, the men don't wear much at all and the women vary. Some are positively beautiful and a few are a bit on the rugged side, but the cross-dressers can be very deceptive.'

'How do you know all this?' Shanala says.

'I am a wealthy tycoon, Mum. I take my clients out on the town, ply them with alcohol, and get them to sign on the dotted line.'

'Milton Swizzer, I thought you were a good boy.'

'I am Mum. I just pretend a lot, that's all.'

'You do, since when?'

'That's how you do things in the San Francisco business world. You pretend to be something you're not. I have become very good at that.'

'And so obviously has your brother.'

'Worry not,' Emphora says, 'I have no doubt that they will return with the goods.'

The lights of the establishment, commonly referred to as The Cat's Meow, and officially known as the Sonata Meridian are dimmed for effect, and the dance floor is alive with half-crazed night owls dancing to the beat of a different drum.

A member must present their ID before they can enter, but Milton's entourage doesn't have to worry about that. Invisibility is one thing that a Yumi Master can do with ease, so they slip past the security guards and their presence doesn't even register as a tinkle.

'Phase One has been accomplished,' Felicity says. 'We are in and it's a fancy-dress party as well.'

Glitz and glitter are the order of the day, and just about every second person is dressed as a cinematic heroine of days gone by.

Cleopatra is a popular choice, but so too are several Disney characters, especially the evil queens from Maleficent and Snow White, both of whom have been a cult favourite for decades.

And they are the perfect opportunity for the most timid of men to dress up, sharpen their claws, and practice the fine art of spicy repartee.

'Before we appear in all of our glory, you boys will have to choose a costume,' Felicity says.

'Well, what's it going to be, a Roman gladiator, an Apache Indian, a half-naked cowboy, Tarzan or some other muscle-bound creature.'

'I am going for classy,' she says, 'Morticia Addams from the Addams Family.'

With a speed that takes Milton by surprise, Felicity whips up a body-hugging black velvet dress. With a flick of the wrist, she transforms herself into the spitting image of Morticia Addams, and in one hand, she holds the stem of a headless rose.

'Wow, you look awesome,' Milton says. 'You really could be Morticia Addams.'

Addric is not as keen on this idea as Felicity. In fact, he is not comfortable at all.

'What's the problem?' Felicity says.

'Most of these men are almost naked and I have a lily-white complexion.'

'Do something about it, Addric. Go for broke. Disguise yourself as one of the 300 Spartans with a deep brown tan.'

'Do I know this woman?' he whispers to Reuben.

'She has had a few drinks.'

Felicity was so excited about a night on the town that she polished off two bottles of champagne before they even left.

'Now, Milton, how would you like to dress?'

'In clothes, preferably.'

'Yes, of course, but what sort?'

'I was thinking to emulate Connor and wear what he is wearing.'

'A good plan and curiously conceived,' Felicity says. 'But where is he, and what is he wearing.'

'If I am correct, that's him over there, disguised as a creepy version of little Miss Muffett.'

'He does have an interesting wardrobe, doesn't he? And he knows how to hold his own.'

Connor looks decidedly gaudy in a fairytale sort of way, but he has attracted the interest of two sturdy young cowboys.

'How apt, a man with a plan. I think Connor has been here once or twice before,' Felicity says.

'Okay boys, choose your poison. Let's shuffle these cowboys out of the way and wine and dine Connor with our sort of magic.'

The very instant that Felicity makes an appearance on the dance floor she is the centre of attention.

'I never want to go to a place like this ever again,' Addric says. 'And if one more man pinches me on the backside, I will have to do something about it.'

Knowing that he would definitely be off the radar as a potential conquest, Reuben decided to impersonate Frankenstein. With bloodshot eyes, a flat head, and a rusty old bolt through his neck, he is a dead ringer for little old Frankie.

Unfortunately, Addric's choice of costume was not so well thought out.

'If you were not dressed as the most recognisable Egyptian Pharaoh of all time, you would be perfectly safe,' Reuben says.

With the physique of a Spartan soldier, Addric looks positively electric as Tutankhamen, and a gaggle of scantily dressed men obviously think so as well.

To the clientele of The Cat's Meow, he is like iron filings to a magnet, but these would-be contenders are not to be deterred. Word soon passes around that Tutankhamen is the catch of the day.

Felicity's plan is to maneuver Connor over to the exit door and whisk him away before anyone notices.

She does her best to edge her way through the crowd, but hundreds of night owls are just dying to make her acquaintance.

Felicity is deflected from her course at every turn, but she is having a gay old time in more ways than one. Everyone wants to meet this fetching she-cat in a black velvet dress, and they are all lining up for a bit of lighthearted chit-chat.

Milton eventually makes it to the bar on the opposite side of the room, but Connor is away with the fairies and doesn't even notice his fairytale sister in several meters of fluffy pink tulle.

He is having a highly inebriated chat with Hansel of Hansel and Gretel fame, a young man called Carlos in microscopic leather tights.

'Yet another member of the fairytale community,' Reuben says.

'I think it's time to rustle a few feathers, Addric or we will never get out of this place alive.'

Addric has had enough of being poked and prodded by a bunch of over-excited gladiators and decides to do something about it.

'I have to get rid of these guys, Reuben. I am going to change into something less attractive. I'll be back in a minute.'

He does his best to keep three muscle men at bay, so he disappears through the exit door, but when he steps back inside, his would-be admirers are a little baffled, to say the least. The last person they expected to see is Quasimodo, the Hunchback of Notre Dame.

'Bon soir, messieurs,' Addric says in a modulated French accent. 'A most enchanting evening, is it not?'

'Bon appetite and excusez-moi, s'il vous plait.'

His devoted fans are mystified, but the gladiator is not to be deterred. He dashes out the door and down the corridor, only to discover that the man of his dreams has simply vanished.

'That's a much better idea,' Reuben says. 'No one will bother you again, of that you can be assured.'

'Come on, let's get Connor and get out of here.'

Everyone on the dance floor steps aside when Frankenstein and Quasimodo force their way through the crowd. After which, they sidle casually up to Milton and do their best to attract his attention.

He is a little peeved that someone is trying to muscle in on his turf and Reuben has no choice but to whisper quietly in his ear.

'In that case,' he says to Connor, 'I would like you to meet two friends of mine, Quasimodo and Frankenstein.'

Connor has a glazed look in his eyes and languidly holds out a pink-gloved hand.

'Charmed, I am sure,' he says. 'Such handsome creatures you are.'

Not long after they whisked Connor away, he doubled up in pain and was diagnosed with an acute case of liver poisoning. Luckily, Demetra's knowledge of potions was more than sufficient for a problem of this nature.

As a consequence, he has spent the last few days in a bedroom that was hastily remodeled to look like a private room in a private hospital.

As to what they should do next has been the primary topic of conversation for the last few hours.

'Before he returns to the world of the living,' Felicity says, 'he needs a teensy-weensy bit of reprogramming or something like that.'

'You can download programs for just that purpose.' Milton says.

'No, you can't do something like that,' Shanala says. 'That's what got us into this situation in the first place.'

'I agree,' Emphora says, 'but I think I know the perfect solution to this problem, and it is not entirely unethical.'

'And what might that be?' Felicity says.

'Dream incursion, of course. We get our dear friends, the Krugwah, to ease their way into Connor's dreams and whisper sweet little nothings in his ear.'

'Ah yes, of course. Why didn't I think of that?'

'Eenah, you can do that, can't you?'

'What you be wanting us to do?' she says.

She has been working away in the kitchen preparing yet another delicious lunch, but Eenah's antenna is always fully active.

'Well, something normal would be good,' Addric says, 'but it should be as real as possible so that you don't freak him out.'

'Okay, let's plot and plan and test it out while we have the opportunity,' Felicity says.

As a one-off idea, it works like a charm, and Eenah is happy with her first-ever performance as the star of a reality dream sequence.

'This plan be working out very nicely,' she says. 'We just popped in to have a little chat with Connor.

'He is doing very good. In fact, he be wondering where he is.'

'And what did you tell him?' Addric says.

'We be saying that he is at the beach and that a few old friends are waiting to see him.'

'Well done, Eenah. In which case, Milton, this is the perfect time to visit your brother while he is recuperating in hospital.'

'He's still asleep,' Demetra says, 'but it won't be long before the medication wears off.'

'Well, that's even better, and you Milton, should be at his side when he wakes up.'

Armed with motherly advice, Milton places a bunch of flowers on the bedside table and then takes a seat at Connor's side.

When it came to the issue of what he would say, Emphora suggested that he tell him the truth, a little at a time, of course.

This is a special moment for Milton; he is about to meet a brother he never knew he had, and he is a little apprehensive. Connor is his spitting image with brown hair and eyes, and he even has a dimple on his chin.

When he eventually comes around, Connor has a vacant look on his face and it's some time before he says anything.

'I can hear waves breaking on the shore,' he says drowsily. 'Where am I?'

'You're at the beach Connor, but you're in very good hands. My friends went to a lot of trouble to save your life.'

'Why, was I dying or something?'

'If it hadn't been for their skills, yes, Connor, you probably would have.'

Connor gives that idea some thought, but memories are rising to the surface. Some of them are real and others are the result of a few friendly visitors in his dream state.

'Is this a hospital?'

'Sort of,' Milton says.

'Who's paying for it?'

Connor has every reason to be worried, as a few days in a private hospital in America is not inexpensive.

'Officially, I am Connor, but this is not a hospital. It's a room in a mansion on the coast of Spain.'

'How did I get here?'

'That's a long story.'

'So then, who are you?'

'I am your twin brother, Milton, and your employer?'

'Ah, so we meet at long last.'

Milton is not about to sabotage his relationship with Connor for anything in the world. He has always wanted a sibling, but it takes a few moments for Connor to come to terms with that revelation.

'So, you know everything, don't you?'

'That you have been leading a double life and engaging in industrial espionage, I do. But I went to a lot of effort to get you as far away from that world as possible.'

'Why? Connor says.

'Because I have no intention of allowing my one and only brother to drink himself to death or go to jail, that's why.'

'If I remember correctly, something strange happened to you at the Golden Gate Bridge.'

'That's true, Connor, but there has been another world-shattering event since then. And as you can clearly see, everyone is talking about it.'

The event that sparked worldwide interest is still prime-time news on television, and the footage of the Goddess of Wisdom has been replayed at least a thousand times over the last week.

'Were you really saved by some Superman, by some guy who could fly? Was that for real?'

'In every way and his name is Addric.'

'Addric, so what else does he do?'

'He and his friends can do things that mere mortals only dream about,' Milton says. 'And if you would like to meet them, they are waiting outside.'

'But so is your mother if you are interested.'

'That would be your mother,' Connor says.

'That's our mother, Connor, and her name is Shanala.'

'And she and my father are two special people that you should get to know.'

The day that a mother finally meets a long-lost child is likely to be one filled with sadness and tears, but it's an equally difficult time for Connor.

He is still a little fragile and doing his best to come to terms with the fact that he is about to meet his birth mother.

While he showers, Milton has a few moments in which to alert everyone to the success of his mission.

'In that case, we will head down to the grotto, as we are going to have a BBQ on the beach tonight,' Addric says.

'It is compulsory to have a BBQ on the beach, both before and after a catastrophe. Isn't that right, Jatoo?'

'You haven't lived, Milton, not until you have had your fill of prawns marinated in garlic sauce, homemade bread, oven-fried fish, chilled wine, and a performance by the Krugwah Choir.'

'That sounds excellent. Thank you, my friends, for everything you have done.'

'Think nothing of it,' Addric says. 'We will be seeing you soon, Milton.'

'You definitely will be Addric.'

Connor's story is not unlike that of Milton. They both lived solitary lives, but after his parents died in a car accident, Connor found comfort in the arms of strangers.

And even though that hasn't changed, his other interests have. As Connor Burnett, he was a reluctant traveller, but as Constance Brunette, he was a very different person altogether.

One of the most important moments of his life is only minutes away, and he prepares himself for what will be an emotionally difficult situation.

'Mum is so looking forward to meeting you,' Milton says.

'Believe it or not, I am looking forward to meeting her as well.'

'My parents gave me everything you could ask for, Milton, but they were rarely ever there. And as you can see, that didn't turn out so well in the end.'

'From now on, Connor, everything will be different.'

'I hope so, Milton.'

This is an equally difficult moment for Shanala, as she is about to meet a child she thought she would never see again. She has been pacing back and forth for the last three days but she is not alone and never has been.

Shanala has always had the support and companionship of a very faithful husband. Hector has been by her side ever since the day they met at a meditation group in downtown San Francisco twenty-five years ago.

Baby Milton approved of him from the very first moment, and from that day on, they settled down to a good life. Together, they had the strength to succeed, and once they were on their feet, they never looked back.

Raising a boy with special abilities was a challenge, and they did everything in their power to give Milton as normal a life as possible.

And after the things that have happened over the last few days, they know they have succeeded. Milton is not only a successful businessman, he is famous for other reasons, and they are proud to be a part of his life.

A chapter that closed many years ago is about to open once again. And they are all standing side-by-side, waiting for the moment when Connor steps out of the darkness and into the light. And hopefully, he will be by their side to see them through what might be troubled times.

CHAPTER 30

When you are the sole proprietor of a prime piece of real estate on the southern coast of Spain, and no one even knows that you are there, you can do whatever you like.

A house with a view of the ocean was Addric's long-held dream, and he knew immediately that this is where he wanted to live.

It features a grand and rambling home with established gardens, and the best part of all is that it has a commanding view of the Mediterranean as well.

Scattered throughout the grounds are numerous old buildings, including a windmill, a woodshed, and a storage barn. And on the beach, down below is a boathouse and a jetty. But the most interesting place of all is the grotto, a relic of the past that had suffered from the ravages of time.

It was not the work of a master craftsman, and in times gone by it would have housed a statue of the Holy Family, but Addric saw its potential as something very different.

And now, it is a place to sit and contemplate the ocean, or when friends and family come to visit, it's the perfect place for a BBQ on the beach.

Addric's pride and joy is a wood-fired oven inspired by one that he saw in Lemuria. Waldo was a cattleman who loved nothing better than to cook, and his pride and joy was a smoking volcano on four huge legs.

A fire smoldered away in a chamber down below; it had an oven on one side and a sizzling hotplate as well, but the best part of all was the rotisserie. And on that night, Addric had his first-ever taste of spit-roasted pig.

Eenah has prepared the dough for three loaves of bread, a huge bowl of marinated prawns and several freshly caught fish. The driftwood that litters the beach is the kindling for the fire, and now that the Sun has set, it's time to light the first match of the day.

The tables are awash with a selection of Krugwah nibbles. The wine is chilled to perfection, and the moment that Yusef places the bread in the oven, Connor and his family appear on the steps below the house.

'Ah,' Emphora sighs. 'Just what I was hoping to see.'

Tears fill her eyes as they walk arm in arm along the beach. After many years of unexpressed heartache, Shanala is once again reunited with her long-lost son.

'It is lovely to meet you at last,' she says as she steps forward and gives Connor a kiss on the cheek.

'You must be Emphora,' he says. 'I have seen your performance about fifty times now.'

'My first Oscar is in the wings from what I have heard, but you are very welcome Connor, and I, for one, am delighted to meet you.'

'So many new faces,' he says as Emphora introduces him to everyone in turn. 'I will do my best to remember your names, but if I forget, just give me a gentle reminder.'

'I certainly will,' Eenah says in her typically straightforward style.

'And you, I remember you from my dreams. I believe that you are a nature spirit.'

'Dat being so very true, but you can call me Eenah. I hope you are hungry, Connor.'

'I am famished, Eenah.'

'Good, then sit down and eat something. You need fattening up.'

Connor has every reason to feel a little out of sorts. He is on a beach in a foreign land and has just met his first nature spirit, but his life could have been a lot worse if it had not been for Milton.

On that day, Connor Burnett discovered that not everyone lives like ravaged night owls on the streets of San Francisco.

These people obviously live very different lives, and they are not only gracious enough to welcome a stranger into their lives, they do so without reservations.

They might be the inhabitants of another world, but they were willing to step up and do what they could to protect a place they knew and loved. And when it's all over they will ask for nothing in return.

Connor's education is about to start all over again. He owes his life to these people. They might have saved him from a potentially life-threatening illness, but they did rescue him from a sort of self-induced madness, and more importantly, from a life of perpetual loneliness.

As far as he is concerned, that life no longer exists, but this one does. He now has a family to call his own and this time, it is real. And from what he can see, if the company is anything to go by, life can only get better.

The news that some people couldn't care less about the future of the Earth had to rise to the surface eventually and it does so the following morning. The networks have been focusing on the positives, but another issue has been brewing away in the background.

According to the latest report, users of electronic devices have slumped to an all-time low. But according to an unrevealed source, a few of the big players in the technology industry have plans to rectify that problem.

'How could they be so thick-headed?' Reuben says.

'I have a suspicion that this is the brainchild of two moguls of the technology industry,' Milton says.

'One of those is Pradak Vengali, and the other is Zagra Scherle. They have been involved in some very dicey deals over the years.'

'Their main claim to fame is that they managed to wriggle out of one court case after another, simply because of the wealth they have at their disposal.'

'They are famous for foolishly choosing to believe that they could dispose of a generation of online warriors using their own methods,' Connor says.

According to Milton, Vengali, and Scherle were trashed every step of the way by a group of on-liners called the Disrupticons, and they were better organised than they had bargained for.

'They are not fanatics or hackers,' Connor says. 'They are a worldwide collective with a mission.'

'Over the years, they have used every trick in the book to keep the internet in the hands of the common man and as far from the politicians and technocrats as possible.'

That battle has been raging for several decades now because the internet means freedom such as people have never known before, and the Disrupticons have millions of supporters who want to keep it that way.

Vengali and Scherle were not prepared for the backlash that followed. As they discovered, the Disrupticons were masters of strategy and made sure that the public was kept in the informational loop at all times.

'That was one occasion in which the agents of industrial espionage came in very useful,' Connor said.

'And if it had not been for them, Vengali and Scherle may have succeeded, and things would be very different.'

'But that's all history now, the Disrupticons are still out there, and they are not likely to go away.'

In a week from now, Addric will assess the results of the implants scattered around the world. In their zeal to support his quest, the media have made sure that the message of the Goddess is still front-page news.

The question as to whether the people of Planet Earth will survive has finally been asked, and it was not by the media but by a mother of three children.

'What will happen if the results are negative?' she said.

That has been the question on everyone's mind, and this young woman was the first to put it into words.

'I would not be surprised if the heartless army is just waiting for a chance to bring us all down.'

It was on that day that a new phrase was coined. The concept of the Heartless Army was imprinted onto the minds of the global population and the media took it up with a vengeance.

'Who is she talking about,' Jatoo says.

'The mean-spirited, the secretly angry, those who take pleasure in making someone's life a misery,' Felicity says.

'In other words, sociopaths, but today we can definitely include a few technocrats in that category, but this could work to our advantage.'

Felicity has a reputation for pinpointing the weakness of an opponent, and she is not about to let the Heartless Army get the upper hand, not if she has anything to say about it.

'But how do we identify them.'

'I know just the thing,' Connor says. 'It's a program used by multi-national corporations to isolate their target audience, and it feeds into every resource on the internet.'

'But we would need access to a supercomputer to do that,' Milton says.

'Well, do you have one?' Felicity says.

'We don't, but banks and just about every major government organisation does. They use high-performance machines designed for high-volume processing.'

The advantage of having two computer whiz kids at their disposal could come in very useful, as Felicity realises.

'So, would they be able to identify the mean-spirited and the nasty?

'I would say no to a question like that, Felicity.'

'Then what are we to do?'

'There are two possible solutions,' Addric says.

'And what are they?' Felicity says.

'Jatoo's mirror, for one thing, but that's not all. I just happen to be in possession of a very useful device called the Zilmo Tag.'

'What is it and what does it do?'

'It's a bit like Jatoo's mirror, but its range is far more extensive. And it can provide information on just about anything in the known universe.'

'And where does this magic thing come from, Addric?'

'I obtained it from a rather interesting woman called Zubia Lembossa, an inhabitant of Kaziopea.'

'And who is she and where is that?'

'It's a planet in the Darvelian Sector of the Exora Five galaxy. Zubia owns a popular restaurant that orbits Callisto, one of the nine moons of Jupiter.'

'Ah yes, The Callisto Intergalactic Hotel. I know it well,' Emphora said. 'I haven't been there for ages.'

'That's where I took Milton just before he became the biggest news item in the world, but you will love it, Felicity.'

'That is so unbelievable,' Connor says. 'Are you saying that there are other life forms out there?'

'This isn't the only inhabited planet in the universe,' Emphora says. 'It's just one of millions.'

'But why haven't we seen anyone else?'

'It's the law,' Addric says. 'No one gets to interfere in this territory, not even your neighbours from Mars, Venus, or any other planet in the Solar System.'

'What law and who made that decision, Addric?'

'It is a divine decree which has been in place from the very beginning, Connor, long before this civilisation ever existed.'

'It was a decree from the very highest level if you follow my meaning.'

'Like God, for instance.'

'Yes, for want of a name.'

'This is no ordinary situation, Connor. I was asked if I wanted this job and I accepted.'

'In this case, we have been given a special dispensation. In other words, we have the freedom to do whatever we can. Otherwise, the inhabitants of Earth will not have a future.'

Connor's head is spinning. He knows what they are doing and why. He knows a little about them but not a lot, but he has questions.

'So, that means you are aliens. You are extra-terrestrials, aren't you?'

'Yes, but not the type that you see in movies. As Milton knows, the world that we come from is as normal as this one.'

'You have been there,' he says.

'I sure have Connor, and not only that, I have even travelled in an inter-dimensional portal,' Milton says proudly.

'That is so unbelievable. I know that you can fly Addric. Everyone knows that. However, let me get this straight.'

'Emphora. Are you really the Goddess of Wisdom?'

'No, I am not, but I am a goddess of sorts.'

'Okay, so what about the rest of you.'

'Well, Jatoo, Reuben, and I are Yumi Masters,' Addric says.

'And that means what?'

'That's our job. We are officially Peacekeepers of the Universe.'

'Okay, I can understand that idea, but what about you, Felicity and you, Demetra?'

'We are masters of the arcane arts, or as some people refer to us, sorcerers, magicians, wizards, or witches. Take it as you will.'

'Holee,' Connor says. 'Does that mean that you have powers and can do things.'

'Of course we can, Connor. You name it and we can do it.'

'We couldn't leave you in the dark for too much longer, now could we,' Addric says. 'After all, you are now officially a part of our team, whether you like it or not.'

'In that case, we should have a name,' Jatoo says, 'like, well, come on, help me out.'

'That's an excellent idea,' Reuben says. 'How about the Magnetic Masters.'

'No, that doesn't say anything,' Felicity says. 'Besides, Kryon requisitioned that one ages ago.'

'Hmm, okay, how about, Live Long and Prosper,' Milton says hopefully.

'No, but you're getting the idea.'

'Star Trek fans will get over excited if they think that Captain Kirk and Mr. Spock are about to be reincarnated for the 26th time.'

'Come on boys. Where is that old-fashioned brilliance that you are noted for?'

'I've got it,' Jatoo says, 'May the force be with you.'

'Hmm, it will be and sooner than you think Jatoo. This was your idea, so get with the program for heaven's sake.'

'Lubrication,' Felicity says with an inspired glint in her eye.

'What sort of name is that?' says a horrified Addric.

'It's not a name but a suggestion that we discuss this like civilised human beings over a glass or two of chilled wine.'

'After all, it is a well-known fact that chemicals have an effect on the creative process. Artists have known that for centuries.'

'Okay,' Addric says, 'I should have realised that.'

They will soon have to make an appearance on the world stage. And if the public knows that they have a bunch of real live superheroes working in their interests, that will be so much better, but a name is absolutely necessary. Several bottles of Dom Perignon helps to some degree, but not with the creative process.

'We will get there,' Felicity says. 'We will find a name for this group of odd-minded souls, eventually.'

'In the meantime, Addric, you were going to tell us about the implants, if I remember correctly.'

'Ah yes, I had forgotten about that Felicity. The implants are designed to monitor the consciousness of the population. And if they change from black to white, it's a clear sign that the people of one place or another have understood the importance of our message.'

'Hopefully, we should get a lot more than just a bunch of fuzzy statistics, but this is the good part. We should be able to put names to faces for those who are actively rejecting the idea of global salvation.'

'That is truly brilliant,' Felicity says. 'Global salvation. What a thought.'

'So, that means we should be able to identify the Heartless Army,' Connor says. 'And we should be able to nail a few of the companies that are trying to undermine the routine.'

'That's it in a nutshell,' Addric says. 'And that is where you and Milton will come in useful.'

'We have no idea what the implants will reveal until next week, but in the meantime, we should go out there and make ourselves known.'

'That means we will definitely need a name,' Jatoo says, 'because people will want to know who we are.'

'Agreed, a name would do it,' Felicity says. 'But what sort of appearance do you have in mind Addric?'

'We just go out there and be seen, of course.'

'If you don't mind, I have a few things to say about this situation,' Connor says. 'I am an inhabitant of this planet and I have been to the edge and seen what lies beyond.'

'These are my people, give or take a few million lost souls but they are. I wouldn't recommend most of them for a life-saving certificate, but for better or worse, they are not so different to me.'

'We are a vulnerable species. We have suffered for thousands of years and we have never been told one single thing about who we are or where we fit into the grand scheme of things.'

'However, if people did know, they would be on side in an instant.'

'Emphora told them just about everything,' Jatoo says. 'Didn't she?'

'Not everything,' Connor says. 'You didn't tell me that you are extra-terrestrials or that other planets are inhabited.'

'If we had known a long time ago that we are not alone in the universe or that someone has been keeping a close eye on everything we did, we would have done things very differently.'

'In other words, give us a reason for being. Alert people to the fact that they belong to a universal community, but don't leave them to stew in their own juices any longer.'

'That's the primary reason why everyone has turned away from their inner selves.'

'Electronic devices get us through the daily grind, and for one thing, they even answer back.'

As can be expected, they are deep in thought, feeling a little guilty perhaps, all too aware that Connor is speaking the truth. Their moment of introspection is interrupted by a gentle tapping on the door. Emphora stepped out of the room a few minutes earlier to attend to another problem.

'If I may intrude,' she says.

'Emphora, you don't have to knock, you know that.'

'Thank you, Addric, but I could not help but hear your heartfelt thoughts, from a distance, of course.'

'That's my way and that's what I do Connor. I am always listening to the prayers of my people and I do whatever I can.'

'But I agree with what you said, because something like that got me into trouble a long time ago.'

'I argued for the very thing that you are arguing for. I did not want the people of Vela-Rishan to live in a world where they had no connection to the very thing that is so necessary for their lives.'

'And I did not like the idea of a society in which people knew nothing of their origins, and I said what I had to.'

'In the end, the powers that be gave me permission to maintain a presence in the lives of the people of Vela-Rishan.'

'And to some extent, that explains why we are here today. And why Addric is doing what he is doing.'

'I went out on a limb to create a special group of people who would be there in one place or another when things got difficult for people like you, Connor.'

'I presume you know that Addric is a Yumi Master?'

'I do, but I have no idea what he does.'

'Addric is just one of many special angels whose sole purpose is to attend to problems that require a sensitive touch, shall we say.'

'A Yumi Master rarely works alone, as that would be far too difficult. They need the clear voice of reason by their side, as we all do.'

'And that includes friends like Felicity, Demetra, Reuben and Yusef and even the Krugwah.'

'And as of today, two members of the very species that we are trying to save, which is you and Milton, of course.'

'And I for one think it's a good idea to have two Earthlings on the team.'

'Milton has left an indelible impression on the minds of the population. And if they saw him standing side-by-side with his brother; that could work to our advantage.'

'For one thing, the gay community represents ten percent of the population, and like you, Connor, they are highly intelligent and very perceptive people.'

'And I have no doubt that they will stand up and be counted if and when the time comes.'

'Believe me, we will need all the support we can get, especially if it comes to a showdown with the Heartless Army.'

'A healthy percentage of people have already made a decision, but we will need even more on side if they are to survive.'

'And that means it would be a good idea to have a visible presence so that we can get even more people on side.'

'By all means, visit as many places as possible, and make yourselves as popular as the Royal Family.'

'In other words, now is the time to become world-class celebrities, but it would be a good idea to give yourself a name.'

'We haven't been able to decide on one yet,' Jatoo says.

'I believe that Connor has mentioned a perfectly good name at least twice in the last twenty minutes, and no one has even noticed.'

'What could be better than The Extra-Terrestrials.'

'That is absolutely perfect,' Felicity says. 'Thank you, Emphora, and thank you, Connor, of course. But that means we have to be working on the same page.'

'What do you mean by that?' Addric says.

'Milton's saviour has to make an appearance as he promised, but people will have questions.'

'And you, Addric, will have to tell them what they want to know, but it would be even better if you looked the part.'

'As Superman, I don't think so.'

'No, not as Superman, but as Super-Addric, so to speak. However, you must appear in a suitable costume as well. That's mandatory for a superhero.'

'So, not the black leather flight suit then.'

'No, not this time, something different, but whatever you choose, it must make a statement. And that means it must also have a visible logo of Planet Earth on the lapel or somewhere like that.'

'What do you think of that idea?'

'That sounds excellent, but when the Extra-Terrestrials make an appearance, they should all look the same, shouldn't they?'

'Of course, we will, when the time comes.'

So, perhaps we should take a walk along the beach and plot and plan what we are going to do. The fresh air will do us all the world of good for one thing,' Felicity says. 'And when we get back, it will be time for a glass or two of chilled wine, just to start with.'

Alerting the media to the fact that Milton will soon be making an appearance alongside his new friend and saviour only requires one message to the offices of every major network in the world.

'Addric has agreed to appear at a place and time that is yet to be arranged.'

'That will take off like wildfire,' Milton says. 'And it's all we will hear about for the next few days.'

'That's exactly what we want,' Felicity says. 'But where will you appear, Addric, that's the big question?'

'Obviously, somewhere that's big enough for thousands of reporters and just as many paparazzi,' Connor says, 'like St Peter's Square in Rome, for example.'

'You are a genius,' Felicity says.

'Pope Nicholas is one of our biggest supporters. And I have a feeling that if we ask nicely, he will be more than happy to introduce Addric on his famous balcony.'

'Milton, can you send a message to the Pope?'

'I certainly can,' he said.

Felicity has probably had one too many wines, but she is definitely onto a winner.

'Now, about the issue of your outfit, Addric. It should send a clear message as to your status and purpose. You have to look classy and approachable, that's for certain.'

'I have an idea,' Addric says. 'Do you remember the outfits that Dheago and I wore at his wedding?'

'Ah, yes, but I think we should go to the next level. In which case, we should do a bit of research.'

'Google will be perfect in that case,' Milton says.

The fashions of the 18th century have potential, but Addric happens to notice an outfit that takes his fancy.

'That one there. What's that?'

'That's the military uniform of the Hussars,' Milton says. 'They were soldiers of some description.'

'According to this, they were dashing in appearance, and reckless in every way, serious drinkers, womanisers and swashbucklers.'

'Bad boys, in other words.'

'That is interesting,' Addric says, 'but I like the look of the jacket in particular, a short-waist with gold buttons.'

'So, what do you think Felicity?'

'I think you would look very distinguished, but who's that guy there.'

'That's an actor called Kenneth Brannagh who played the part of Hamlet in the 1996 movie of the same name.'

'That's a very smart look. Is that more like it, Addric?'

'Definitely, the jacket's a good length, and I like the standup collar and knee-length boots.'

'But it has to be white leather with gold accessories,' Felicity says. 'That will not send a message that you are an alien.'

'You will be the pin-up boy of the century,' Jatoo says.

'Thanks for your vote of support, Jatoo, but this is what we will all have to wear.'

'What do you think of that idea?'

'That's great,' Connor says, 'and I for one am looking forward to it.'

At that moment Milton receives a message on his communicator.

'Wow, you won't believe this, but it's from the Vatican.'

'What does it say?' Felicity says.

'On behalf of His Holiness, Pope Nicholas the 6th, the Vatican would be honoured to introduce Milton Swizzer and his friends to the world at a special event to be celebrated at 11 am on Tuesday the 13th of May. If these arrangements are suitable, please contact the Offices of the Holy See. Thank you. And kind regards. Monsignor Roberto Della Grazia.

'That's the coolest message I have ever got.'

'It sure is, but I think that all seven members of the Extra-Terrestrials, accompanied by the Goddess of Wisdom should make their debut next Tuesday. Don't you?'

'Absolutely,' he says.

A few hours later, Milton receives yet another message from Monsignor Roberto Della Grazia.

'His Holiness is wondering if he could meet Addric and his friends in advance to discuss a few of the operational details. He will be available on Sunday night in his private apartment.'

'Can we do that, Addric?'

'Of course, we can, Milton. 'We will take a Krugwah portal.'

'Wow, did you hear that, Connor? You are not only going to meet the Pope; you are about to have your first-ever experience of travelling through space and time.'

'What is this Krugwah portal thing?' he says.

'It's like the transporter from Star Trek, and you can travel absolutely anywhere in seconds.'

'Wow, that's what you call mind-blowing.'

'In that case, Milton, please advise His Holiness that we will be there,' Addric says.

'After which, we will find a nice little restaurant with a classic view of Rome and spend the remainder of the evening in a state of unadulterated bliss.'

'What do you think of that?'

Everyone is over the Moon but Shanala's primary concern is protocol.

'What do you wear to a private audience with the Pope?'

'The Italians are renowned for their class and style,' Emphora says. 'However, we will probably have to wear a veil for the audience.'

Shanala is not the only one whose feet barely touch the ground over the next few hours and even Eenah is excited.

'Addric, do you think Him Holy Person would like to meet the Krugwah?'

'Not this time, Eenah, but on the big day, and that's Tuesday, I believe that a Krugwah spectacular would be in order.'

'And when you have finished, you could waft on down, have a chat with Him Holy Person and wow 80,000 spectators, not to mention seven billion online viewers.'

'Ooh, we can be doing that Addric. How big of a spectacular are you thinking?'

'The Krugwah at their very best, of course.'

'We be getting onto that idea right now Addric, and we be letting you know what we be planning to do.'

'This will be good Eenah, this will be really good.'

'Okay everyone, I have an announcement,' Addric says. 'There will be an emergency meeting in my den in ten minutes and that includes you, Shanala and Hector.'

Felicity has already had three glasses of wine and hardly knows what to think.

'We are going to have a private audience with the Pope,' she swoons. 'Can you believe that Demetra?'

'Get a grip,' Demetra says. 'One of your best friends is a goddess, just in case you have forgotten.

She can do things that Pope Nicholas would give his eye teeth to do.'

'He's African,' Felicity says. 'He may not have any of his original teeth left. After all, he was raised in Soweto.'

'And you have lost your marbles, my sister.'

Felicity usually sees to it that everyone has a drink, but she is adrift in her very own wonderland.

'If I may have your attention, please, the meeting is about to begin,' Addric says. 'I would like to start by expressing my heartfelt thanks for your unwavering support.'

'We are onto a winner,' says a very wobbly Felicity, 'and you Addric are our leader.'

'Thank you for your support, my dear and beloved friend, and I hope and pray that we are, but you may be wondering why I have called this meeting.'

'As you know, we have scored the big one, a private meeting with Pope Nicholas. And not even the President of the United States has done that on such short notice.'

'Well, we have edged our way up the ladder, thanks to Milton,' Reuben says.

'We have indeed, and we are about to mine it for all it's worth.'

Over the next few minutes, Addric fills them in on his big plan.

'Pope Nicholas is a very open-minded man, inspired of course, by one of his predecessors, the late and great Francis the First.'

'He dragged the Catholic Church into the light and they have never looked back.'

'But you could not ask for a better stroke of luck than a one-off performance at Vatican Square.'

'So, what have you got in mind?' Yusef says.

'Just about everything I can imagine, a performance by the Krugwah, an appearance by the

Goddess of Wisdom, followed by the ET's of course, and hopefully a message from the Pope.'

'However, the Krugwah Choir will also make an appearance, and for the finale, we will need a few soul-stirring songs.'

'And I am thinking that you, Milton and Connor could, maybe, hopefully, sort of work closely with lovely little Eenah and come up with something, perhaps.'

'That shouldn't be too difficult,' Connor says.

'In that case, make sure that you are wearing your battle armour,' Yusef says. 'This is Eenah that we are talking about.'

CHAPTER 34

Breakfast on the beach is the perfect way to start a new day and everyone is excited, but the women are madly trying to work out what they will wear.

'But what about us,' Connor says. 'What are we going to wear?'

'How about a shopping spree,' Milton says. 'I know where we can get Italian suits of the finest quality.'

'Milton, we are a hundred miles from anywhere. How do you propose to get there?'

'By a Krugwah portal, of course, if that's okay, Addric.'

'Why not? We want to look our best, don't we boys?'

After a whirlwind tour of New York, they arrive home several hours later with a lot more baggage than a couple of classy Italian suits.

'Boys,' Felicity says. 'Whose credit card did you annihilate this time?'

'Mine, of course,' Milton says. 'It hasn't had a workout like that in years. But once you see the finished product, you will be green with envy.'

'And once you see what we will be wearing, Milton, so will you,' she says. 'We have just returned from a shopping spree with Emphora.'

'To where,' he said.

'Paris and Milan of course. 'Where else do women shop?'

'And just how did you pay for the goods?' Jatoo said.

'Emphora, of course. She is the only woman I know who has a Swiss bank account and owns an island in the Caribbean as well.'

'Hmm, there are names for people like you,' he thought, 'and St Felicity the Kindhearted isn't one of them.'

A passing stranger would have made a fortune if they had been lucky enough to spot the ET's trawling their way through one exclusive shop after another. And if they had taken at least one photo, they could have retired off the royalties and lived a life of luxury.

When they emerge from their bedrooms at 7.30 on the dot, everyone gathers in the lounge room.

'Ladies,' Addric says. 'You look positively glamorous.'

'We are indeed,' says an uncommonly sober Felicity. 'But you boys don't look too bad either.'

'Thank you, your Ladyship. However, I think it's time to get out of here as we have an appointment with the Pope.'

'Please follow me. Our taxi is this way.'

'It's not every day that you have a private appointment with the Supreme Pontiff of the Roman Catholic Church, but for us, today is that day,' Felicity says.

Monsignor Roberto Della Grazia is a handsome young man with a gentle disposition and short black hair, but he is also a Master of Diplomacy and fluent in five European languages.

He knows that his guests will be arriving at 7.48 on the dot, but it's fortunate that he didn't get a glimpse of their mode of transport. To see such distinguished visitors disembarking from a Krugwah portal would have been the last straw.

Prior to their arrival, Roberto spent a few reflective minutes preparing himself, simply because he has never had to deal with anyone like this before.

'I am sure that I will not need your support, good Jesus, but please be by my side, just in case.'

Roberto moves to the door on hearing a light but distinctive knocking sound, and opens it tentatively, only to see ten of the most beautifully dressed people that he has ever seen in his life.

'Greetings and welcome to the Vatican,' he says.

Roberto has trained himself to remember the names of one important dignitary after another. He knows that one of these young men is Milton Swizzer, but which one. He holds out his hand and hopes for the best.

'Milton,' he says.

'It's Connor, actually, your eminence. This is Milton.'

'My apologies,' he says. 'His Holiness is eager to meet you, my friends. Please come in.'

They follow Roberto into the Holy Father's private rooms, only to see a beautiful smiling face with a full set of teeth.

'See, I told you so, didn't I,' Demetra whispers to Felicity.

Nicholas is a solidly built man with broad shoulders and piercing black eyes, and Felicity is instantly bewitched by this magnificent specimen of African manhood.

'And you must be Milton,' Pope Nicholas says.

'I am your Holiness and it's a great honour to meet you.'

'Forget about protocol Milton. That's only for special occasions.'

'Now let me see if I can work out who's who.'

'I was brought up by three different faiths, a bunch of witchdoctors, the Catholic church and the secret world of the women of Soweto.'

'They infused a different ideology into my head and it has served me well over the years.'

'And if I am correct, you, my beautiful lady are the Goddess of Wisdom.'

'Well spotted, your Holiness,' Emphora says. 'Even in disguise it seems that I am recognisable.'

'It's that face. It's all we see on television lately, something for which I am very thankful.'

'You have single-handedly reignited the faith of every lapsed Catholic in the world. And believe me, that is no easy task. Congratulations, my dear.'

'We are doing our best, your Holiness.'

'I know that for a fact, and I want to hear all about it. You have no idea how much I have been looking forward to this moment.'

'Now that Monsignor Roberto is out of the way, why don't we sit down and talk turkey.'

'Please take a seat,' he says as he escorts them into a sumptuously furnished lounge room.

'I am accustomed to having a drink and I have plenty to offer. This is the Vatican after all.'

When they leave his apartment two hours later, their feet barely even touch the ground.

'I can see why they elected him Pope,' Felicity says. 'He is absolutely normal. Is it normal for a Pope to be normal?'

'It is from his point of view,' Emphora says. 'But that's what you get in the modern church, a glorious human being doing his best to beat the odds.'

'Emphora,' Jatoo says. We should invite him to dinner.'

'I agree, let's go back and get him.'

The following morning, the news of the day is that the Goddess of Wisdom will be making an appearance in St Peter's Square in Rome. She has chosen their city and the Roman people could not be happier.

'Emphora, I think you have won a few hearts,' Shanala says.

'Like sixty million in Italy alone,' Addric says. 'That should do a lot for the stats.'

They spend the remainder of the day planning their spectacular, and to Eenah's delight, the Krugwah will play a major role at the end.

'But what if some disgruntled member of the Heartless Army decides to take a potshot at us?' Connor says.

'I have a few tricks up my sleeve for situations like that. Do not be concerned, Connor. All Yumi Masters are capable of handling such things with ease.'

'That's a relief Addric. Is there anything else I should know?'

'We will keep you posted. This is only the beginning.'

'Will we get to see any UFO's as well,' he says.

'Other than the ET's, absolutely not. However, if you include a few thousand Krugwah as mini flying saucers, then, yes, you will,'

'So, what are they,' Connor says.

'They are the most adorable nature spirits you could ever wish to meet,' Addric says. 'They are like visible angels in a way.'

'However, a piece of advice Connor. It's not a good idea to mess with the Krugwah, because those cute little critters are very powerful.'

'They are also the most loving and generous creatures you will ever encounter and they are very talented as well.'

'But when it comes to aerial acrobatics and high-class aerodynamics, the Krugwah have no equal,' Jatoo says. 'They make the birds of the world look like second class paper planes.'

'Like all Krugwah, Eenah has an in-built sensory system that can detect danger before it even happens,' Reuben says. 'We have stood by their side in a military campaign, and they can be positively lethal.'

'I feel a lot better knowing that, but a terrorist could use this as an opportunity to make a point for the Heartless Army,' Connor says.

'Let them try and they will soon see why they should not have bothered,' Emphora says.

'Hmm,' he sighs, 'we Earthlings have a long way to go, don't we?'

'You will get there as long as we can get you through this situation,' Emphora says. 'After that, the future planned for the human race will kick in, and you will never look back.'

'So, are you saying that we will be like you one day?'

'From what I understand, the people of this planet have unlimited potential,' Emphora says. 'Something like that doesn't happen overnight, but it will happen eventually.'

'I am so looking forward to that day, and I hope to be around to see it.'

'You will be, if you want to be,' Emphora says cryptically.

Up until Tuesday, the 13th of May, a few people in remote areas of the world may not have heard of the Vatican, but all that is about to change.

Vatican City covers 44 hectares or 110 acres and is the smallest sovereign country in the world, but it's not the only one. There are several others, one of which is the Principality of Monaco at 2.2 square kilometers.

But the Vatican is definitely the most spectacular. And it is here that you will find three of the most famous buildings in the world, the Basilica of St Peter's, the Sistine Chapel, and the Papal Palace, also known as the Castel Gandolfo.

The Piazza San Pietro, or St. Peter's Square as it's also known, was built in the 17th century, a vast open space on a grand scale, designed by the architect Bernini.

The piazza was conceived as a place in which thousands of people could gather together to see the Pope as he gave his blessings from the balcony of the Vatican Palace.

The Basilica of St. Peter's is the focal point of the piazza, and the square is surrounded by an imposing colonnade of colossal Tuscan columns, all of which are designed to embrace the faithful in the arms of the church.

It is here that thousands of people gather for liturgical functions, masses, burials, and papal coronations. And it all happens under the watchful gaze of one hundred and forty saints who take pride of place on the colonnade above the plaza.

St Peter's Square is probably the most visited place in all of Italy. As to how many people will gather in the plaza is impossible to say, but word has passed around that it's compulsory to wear something white.

By mid-morning, over 80,000 people are waiting for the moment that the Goddess of Wisdom makes an appearance.

As to whether she will appear on the famous balcony is not yet known, but most people are hoping that she will appear in a beam of silver light.

Addric is prepared for several possibilities, one of which is that a terrorist could use this as the perfect opportunity to do what they do best.

The possession of arms is now a thing of the past, and military hardware has long since been superseded by numerous hi-tech alternatives.

A sharpshooter could operate from a distance. As a consequence, Addric has devised a number of failsafe options. And one of those is to use the skills and cunning of his close friends the Krugwah.

Eenah and Wimple will be peering into every dark corner, but they will also be scrutinising the contents of every pocket and purse.

The Krugwah have an in-built scanning system, and when it comes to the fine art of espionage, they are second to none.

They will simply dissolve into the background, somewhere above the plaza, from where they will be able to see every little thing. If someone even removes a tissue from their pocket, Eenah will know, but that's not all she has to do.

The Krugwah intelligence network is always active, and in this situation, it will be on red alert. If they do identify anything of an unusual nature, they are to warn Addric immediately.

This is the electronic age and a terrorist could operate from anywhere at all, but as Emphora said, they will regret it if they try.

CHAPTER 36

On a lavishly decorated podium under the famous Vatican balcony, Milton appears dressed in a suit of white leather, and to the sound of applause, he steps up to the microphone.

'Saluto alla poplazione di Roma e al mondo,' he says.

'That's all the Italian I know, but translated into English, it means greetings to the people of Rome and to the people of the world.'

'My friends, as you probably know, I am Milton Swizzer and it is my pleasure to welcome you to this very special event.'

'First of all, we have gathered here for the most important of all reasons. Our survival as a race is at risk, but we would never have known anything about it if it had not been for a representative of the celestial alliance.'

'That most serene and gracious lady, the Goddess of Wisdom has agreed to make an appearance once again. And she will stand by our side and support us in any way that she can, but she will not be the only guest of the day.'

'Because of the urgency of this situation, His Holiness Pope Nicholas will also be joining us on this stage.

'As you know, Pope Nicholas is a man of insight, but he is also a man of hope. And at this time in our lives, we need as much of that as we can get.'

'But that's not all. We will also be treated to a spectacular display of aerodynamics by a special group of nature spirits called the Krugwah. That will be a performance you will never forget.'

'But I know for a fact that you are all looking forward to seeing the face of Addric Sharano, the young man who saved my life several weeks ago.'

'Addric will be making an appearance accompanied by his support team, the Extra-

Terrestrials. These are a special group of people selected by Addric to assist in this time of need.'

'But before anything else happens, I suggest that you look to the sky where you will see a pinpoint of light.'

'That is the doorway to an inter-dimensional portal, and it is through that door that our illustrious guest will make an entrance.'

'Ladies and gentlemen, please put your hands together and welcome that most serene and gracious lady, the Goddess of Wisdom.'

A beam of light appears in the highest point of the heavens and inches its way to the ground, and when it reaches the stage, it glows like blue fire. Emphora appears dressed in her blue silken veils, opens her arms, and bows respectfully.

This is a magic moment for the people of Rome, but it has not gone un-noticed that she looks just like Mary, the mother of Jesus. As every Catholic knows, she has been a tireless crusader for world peace.

She is revered and loved by people the world over, and in an attempt to get her message across, Mary has made an appearance in many regions of the world.

Before Emphora gets anywhere near the microphone, she raises her arms and a cascade of rose petals fall like snowflakes onto the heads of the people gathered in the plaza.

'Greetings, ladies and gentlemen, boys and girls of Rome,' she says. 'Please keep those petals close to your heart as they are infused with the power of love.'

'It is a great honour to support you in this most vital of all causes, as I, for one, do not want to see this beautiful planet disappear off the radar, never to be seen again.'

'It could happen but that will not be its fate if you are doing as I have asked.'

'I know that many of you are doing your best to make changes in your life, but there are others yet again who are not interested in the least.'

'People of Planet Earth, please be assured that you will have a future and you will survive.'

'But for those we now refer to as the Heartless Army, I have a message. If you choose not to support this cause, then you can expect to suffer the consequences.'

'I know for a fact that Addric and his team will happily take you out of the equation. That is not a threat but a warning as this is a very serious situation.'

'Addric and his son, Jatoo, were here 50,000 years ago when a deluge of cosmic proportions wiped this planet clean.'

'And I can assure you that you do not want to see a repeat performance of something like that again.'

'However, before I take my leave, I want to assure you that most of you are on target and that you are winning this battle. And you can rest assured that your future will not be jepoardised by the minority.'

'I can see from your faces that I have caused far more distress than I was planning to, but I can remedy that problem far more easily than you might imagine.'

'Please hold out your hands, because I have a gift for each and every one of you.'

Eighty thousand people cannot believe their eyes when an energetic replica of the Earth suddenly appears in the palm of their hands.

'I am not finished yet,' Emphora says. 'Now, close your eyes and infuse it with a wish.'

Everyone does so, and a ball of pure energy is suddenly transformed into a ball of solid glass. This miracle is streaming live across the world and into the hearts and minds of seven billion people, wherever they may be.

Milton returns to the microphone, holds his sphere high above his head and bows to Emphora.

'This, my friends, is a memento that you will treasure until the end of time. And believe me, we will get there.'

'On your behalf, I would like to thank the Goddess of Wisdom for honouring us with her presence and for giving us this extraordinary and beautiful present.'

'I think it's only fitting that you show your thanks in the way that only the people of Rome can do.'

The applause that follows is thunderous, and when it eventually dies down, Milton bows respectfully to Emphora once again.

'People of Rome, this extraordinary event would not have been possible if we did not have the support of His Holiness, Pope Nicholas.'

'Please put your hands together and welcome the Supreme Pontiff of the Holy Catholic Church.'

Dressed in a white Papal cassock, Nicholas steps up to the microphone, raises his snow dome into the air and waits patiently for the applause to subside.

'We are so fortunate, my friends. We are truly blessed to be in the presence of such a gracious Lady as the Goddess of Wisdom.'

'She has come from afar to shine a light into our lives. As you no doubt agree, she has already achieved that with most of us. And like you, I was overwhelmed by what she had to say.'

'Hers was a message of such profound importance that it cannot and must not be ignored. It touched the hearts and souls of people around the world. Unfortunately, it has not found its way into the hearts of everyone on the planet.'

'Hopefully, it will in time, but as she said, it is imperative that we make fundamental changes in our lives, or sadly, our tenure of this world will come to a very abrupt end.'

'In other words, this beautiful planet that has nurtured one civilisation after another will be terminated.'

'That is a frightening thing to have to say, but it could happen. The inhabitants of this planet have been judged and found wanting.'

'If there is anyone out there who cannot change the habits of a lifetime, then we are doomed. To survive, we must do this together, and we must support each other in any way that we can.'

'That is why I have agreed to stand side-by-side with the Goddess and show my support but it's not the only reason.'

'It is my privilege to introduce the team of people who have been assigned the task of helping us to change our ways.'

'Milton Swizzer and his brother, Connor Burnett, have agreed to assist this extraordinary group of people. But what you really want is to see the face of the man responsible for this undertaking.'

'I have met Addric in person, and I know for a fact that he is a good and honest soul.'

'Addric loves Planet Earth as much as we do. But the last thing he wants is to see it destroyed by a natural catastrophe.'

'It could happen; the forces of nature could remove everything in an instant, but I don't think you want that to happen, and I certainly do not.'

'Addric is about to make an appearance, and when he does so, please listen to what he has to say, and please, please, just do as he asks.'

'Friends, brothers, and sisters, I know that you will find it in your hearts to say yes. I know that you will say loudly and clearly that you want to survive, that you want to be custodians of this beautiful world until the end of time.'

'And more importantly, you want your children to have a future here on this planet that we call home.'

Nicholas raises his snow dome into the air and says, 'Let this be your reason to live because it is certainly mine.'

'Thank you, your Holiness, for those encouraging and powerful words of support,' Milton says.

'And it is true what the Pope has just said. Our days may be numbered, but we can change that. We can change our future, and we have the power to do so, but it is only together that we will triumph.'

'Addric and his team have agreed to accept this task on our behalf, but they are not working alone. There is always someone behind the scenes, and in this case, Addric has the support of a special group of nature spirits called the Krugwah.'

'The Krugwah are residents of Addric's home world, the Khavala, a galaxy on the outer perimeter of the star system known as Alpha Centauri.'

'They are renowned for many things, and according to Addric, they are the star attraction at the Festival of the Skies on a little island called Kraga.'

'If you look to the sky, you will see what I mean. Their performance will commence with one of their signature pieces, an aerial ballet such as you have never seen before.'

Against the backdrop of a perfect blue sky, thousands of little Krugwah take their places at the outer edge of an imaginary circle. They have a variety of acts in their repertoire, but the most breathtaking of all is to see them weaving their way through the sky like synchronized swimmers in a waterless pool.

An aerial ballet is another crowd pleaser, and the Krugwah are obviously having the time of their lives. But one of their all-time favourites is an infamous battle between a ferocious queen and an evil and twisted villain.

This is an opportunity to have a bit of fun, and the Krugwah have everyone in stitches as they battle it out with energetic thunderbolts. But for the first time ever, the queen is triumphant, and the evil villain finally gets his just desserts.

The Krugwah receive a resounding round of applause, but they are not finished yet. They take their places as one component of an enormous heart, and for the next few minutes, it hovers in the sky above St. Peters and then dissolves into the ethers.

'My friends, that was a truly extraordinary performance,' Milton says. 'And I believe that the Krugwah deserve another round of applause.'

'But they have not finished yet. They are about to pave the way for the arrival of Addric and his team of Extra-Terrestrials.'

The Krugwah are equal to none when it comes to the fine art of transformation. And when a portal appears, they gather to create a guard of honour through which any monarch would be proud to walk.

Arrayed in a suit of white and gold, Addric appears at the door of a luminous gateway, and followed by his closest friends, he makes his way down a winding staircase.

Over 80,000 people are absolutely mesmerised, and the moment that the ETs step onto the podium, Milton and Connor take their places on the stage and bow respectfully to one and all.

CHAPTER 37

Addric steps forward points to the logo on his lapel, clicks his heels together, smiles, and nods. The Romans love it, and the applause is deafening. It's a routine that will catch on like wildfire and one that is likely to become the next biggest trend.

'Ladies and gentlemen, boys and girls, people of Planet Earth, people of Rome and Italy, did you like that?'

The response is an overwhelming yes.

'È buono, che è eccellenti, saluti,' he says.

'As you can see, I have been practicing my Italian as well. But that fancy little foot thing is in recognition of this grand old lady that we call Planet Earth.'

'She deserves a round of applause because she is a star in her own right. And I for one believe that she deserves our love and recognition for all of her efforts. Is that not so?'

The applause that follows is even more deafening, but it is well and truly overdue.

'Greetings and welcome my friends, I would like to thank you for being here today. And I especially want to thank everyone in every village, city, and town of this beautiful planet.'

'I am here to introduce myself and my team so that you can see the faces of the people working in your interests.'

'My name is Addric Sharano and I am a Yumi Master. That is actually my job, and that's what I do for a living.'

'Yumi Masters attend to jobs both big and small in any part of the universe. And that is why I am here today.'

'But I would not have achieved anything without the support of my friends, the illustrious Goddess of Wisdom, and of course, my wonderful friends, the Krugwah.'

'However, I would like to introduce the other members of my team. First of all, this handsome young man on my left is my son, Jatoo.'

'And believe it or not, I am a lot older than I look and a few years older than Jatoo.'

'This debonair fellow to my right is a good friend of mine, Reuben Ali Shah, and he is also a Yumi Master.'

'I am fortunate to have two special women on the team, Lady Felicity Originalis and her sister, Countess Demetra.'

'They are powerful women in their own right, but their skills and support are absolutely essential to the success of this campaign.'

'But that's not all. You will be pleased to know that we also have two Earthlings on our team.'

'As all good strategists know, it is essential to have inside information, especially in a situation like this, and that expertise is provided by two very capable young men.'

'I am sure you all know Milton Swizzer by now. I believe he is the most famous person on the planet. But we are also honoured to have his twin brother on our team as well, the equally handsome Connor Burnett.'

For the hundreds of television cameras from every country in the world, this is a moment to be savoured, and one that will never be forgotten.

But those few passing moments do not last long. Every head turns to the northern sky on hearing the stringent sound of Eenah's voice screeching through the heavens.

'Addric,' she cries. 'They're here.'

The ever-vigilant Eenah has been scanning the horizon and has every reason to be concerned. And when he realises that this is serious, Addric raises his arms, and within seconds, Vatican City is surrounded by a semi-transparent energy field.

'There is no need to be concerned,' he says to the now very worried spectators. 'You are safe.'

'What's going on?' Jatoo cries.

'It's an attack,' Addric says. 'That's no storm cloud on the horizon. That's an army of automated warriors.'

Even from a distance, it is possible to see their red sightless eyes flickering back and forth with metrical precision.

'I had a feeling that something like this would happen,' Addric says. 'Follow me boys, we have work to do.'

On a day in which many thousands have gathered to see the face of a man from outer space, a very different face has reared its ugly head.

Addric has chosen to serve and protect, but he is more than capable of handling an army of airborne drones. And he is about to send a very clear message as to what and who he is.

But it's on that day that one little Krugwah will cement her reputation as a stouthearted warrior. Who she is as yet, no one has any idea, but Eenah, as they will soon discover, is as fearless as any soldier on the battlefield.

A portal appears only seconds later, and a battalion of Krugwah warriors step into the fray. With Addric and Eenah in the lead, they move through the drone army and systematically destroy everything in their path.

The atmosphere is thick with a cloud of acrid black smoke and thousands of hearts are beating in unison. A profound and solemn silence follows, and an age seems to have passed before anyone even takes a breath. And when Addric is satisfied that they are no longer at risk, he returns to the podium.

Pope Nicholas steps up to his side a few minutes later.

'The people of Rome owe you a debt that we can never repay,' he says.

'Freedom is a precious commodity, Holiness, and one that we never want to lose.'

'Please tell that to these people, Addric. They are in dire need of a few comforting words.'

Addric steps up to the microphone and before he says anything at all, he raises his hand in recognition of the efforts of Eenah and her compatriots.

'We have a saying where I come from. Whatever you do, never mess with the Krugwah.'

'Believe it or not, they are the most placid creatures you could ever wish to meet, and their one and only joy in life is to make someone happy.'

'The Krugwah really are remarkable creatures. They are talented performers. They can sing, they can dance, and they are the best cooks in the universe, but they are also formidable warriors.'

'On behalf of everyone in Rome, I would like to thank you, my beautiful friends.'

'However, I just told the Holy Father that freedom is a commodity that we should never relinquish,' Addric says.

'I came here in peace, and I did so to protect the people of this planet from a fate too horrible to imagine. And if I am correct, that was an example of what we are up against.'

'But that was not the Hateful Army. That was an army of drones, and to my mind, that means they are a product of a computer program.'

'In other words, they were created by the technocrats who have gone out of their way to brainwash you over the last few decades.'

'These are faceless men with their own agenda, men who obviously do not care if this world survives.'

'But there are billions who do care, and I am one of them.'

'I had a feeling that we might be in danger today, and I planned for that eventuality.'

'But I have a message for the technocrats behind that assault. I am coming to get you. I will track you down, and I can assure you, whoever you are, that you will see the error of your ways.'

'You can take refuge wherever you want, but not for much longer. I will find you, of that you can be assured.'

'I am a Yumi Master and I have formidable power at my disposal, but I am only permitted to use them when lives are at risk.'

'A Yumi Master must abide by strict rules, and if they do not, they suffer the consequences immediately, and I mean immediately.'

'That is one way of assuring you that I am working in your interests, and even though I am an alien, I am a human being.'

'Earth may not be my natural home, but it is the place I have chosen to call home. And if I have anything to say about it, that's the way it will stay.'

'As a result, I have decided to do something I promised I would never do. I am going to show you what termination means.'

'Unfortunately, many of you will find this disturbing. However, it does have a point.'

'I ask my son Jatoo to forgive me because I know that he will find this very distressing.'

'This planet has a history that goes back 350 billion years, and it was inhabited by other civilisations long before you ever came along.'

'I am sure that you have heard of Atlantis, but you may not have heard of Lemuria. It was a beautiful civilisation, but it was wiped off the face of the Earth by a deluge of cosmic proportions.'

'That's how it happens and it's all over within seconds.'

'I was there on the day that Lemuria was targeted for termination, and I can assure you that it was a horrifying thing to experience.'

'Jatoo was born in Lemuria, and he would have perished along with millions of others if it had not been for me.'

'He is the only one who survived, but you may not be so lucky, especially it if happens again.'

'Now, as I have promised, I have something to show you.'

'Cameramen, please direct your cameras to the sky, and in a few minutes' time, you will see what I mean.'

'An aperture is about to open. It's a window onto the past and one that will show you what happens when a planet is targeted for reassignment.'

'I want this footage to be seen by the technocrats and the Heartless Army in particular.'

'I want it to be seen by those who choose to stand in the way of our future and those who choose to ignore the request of the Goddess.'

'And I especially want it to be seen by those who refuse to change their habits.'

'This is what I saw from the control deck of my ship, and that was only minutes after we made our escape from Lemuria,' Addric says.

Eighty thousand spectators turn to the northern sky and watch with bated breath as an enormous aperture opens. The ground rumbles beneath their feet, only to be followed by a sound such as a force of nature could make.

For a few horrifying seconds, they watch in disbelief as a massive ocean wave rolls towards the city of Lemuria and destroys everything in its path. Moments later, there is nothing to be seen, other than a vast ocean of angry water rolling back and forth.

'And that is all it takes,' Addric says. 'The destructive hand of nature has the capacity to transform the Earth into a ball of swirling water in a matter of minutes.'

'But that does not have to be our future, and it will not be, not if I have anything to say about it.'

'Lemuria was a beautiful place but it was also Jatoo's home. He lost his entire family, three wonderful people that I had the honour to call friends.'

Jatoo is sobbing uncontrollably and it's of interest to see that the person he turns to is Emphora.

'I am sorry I had to do that Jatoo.'

'This is what you signed up for,' Emphora says.

But their moment of introspection does not last long. For reasons of her own, Eenah decides to make an appearance on the podium as well. And with her hands perched on her hips, she wanders up and down glaring at a sea of stupefied faces.

'Peoples of Planet Earth,' she says. 'That was not a very nice thing to see, was it?'

'Something like that won't happen to good peoples because I like good peoples, mostly.'

'But I get very upset with bad peoples and I did not come all this way to see something that is not very nice. But that is what will happen because of bad peoples.'

There is no one quite like the inimitable Eenah. She may be small in stature, but she always speaks her mind. She can be vitriolic. She can be despotic. She has a reputation as a tyrant of the first order. And beyond anything else, she is someone to be respected.

When Eenah says jump, everyone jumps, everyone except Addric, that is. He was just a little different and Eenah had noticed that. Ever since then, she has made it her mission to help him out in whatever way she could.

'I think I should see what this is all about,' he says to Emphora.

'Please do so, as I am as curious as everyone else.'

'Eenah, what are you doing?'

'I had to say something, Addric, because I was very upset by that, you know, but now I have finished what I had to say.'

'But Addric, I be wanting to meet Him Holy Person. You be telling me I could.'

In all the confusion, Addric had forgotten his hastily made promise, but Eenah had not.

'In that case, it's the very least I can do. Please allow me to do the honours.'

He takes Eenah by the hand and escorts her up to the head of the Holy Roman Church.

'Your holiness, I would like to introduce Eenah. She is the most wonderful nature spirit that I have ever known and she is also the bravest.'

'Hello, Most Holy Person, I be liking you.'

'Thank you, Eenah,' he says. 'You are a very brave Krugwah, aren't you?'

'Sometimes Holy Person. I not be liking bad people.'

'And neither do I, but if I am not wrong, Eenah, I think you have a fan club.'

'What being that?' she says.

Eenah turns around, only to see a little girl in a white dress standing behind her.

'Hello, little human lady person. And what being your name?'

'I am Melita and I think you are very brave, Eenah.'

The people of Earth have always wondered if they would ever see an alien in the flesh, but Eenah is as close as it will come for the moment.

It might have been different if they had not seen her standing her ground in an effort to protect them from the drones, but because of that, she won a lot of hearts.

This little chat with Melita is about to make her a star in her own right. And as usual, Eenah speaks her mind and does so with an unusual touch of humour.

'You look like a very nice girl, Melita.'

'Oh, I am Eenah, but I have four brothers, and you know what they can be like.'

'These brothers of yours. They be here too?'

'Yes, they are, that's them down there.'

Eenah peers closely at four young boys who are doing their best to hide behind their father's coattails.

'Boys, come on up so I can see you for my own self,' Eenah says.

It takes a little persuasion from a responsive crowd, but four little boys creep hesitantly up onto the stage.

'Hello, human boy persons,' Eenah says. 'You be very handsome young boys, are you not?'

'And what being their names Melita?'

'This is Ronaldo, he is the youngest. And this is Angelo, Vincenzo, and Carlo. He is the eldest.'

'Are you good boy persons?' Eenah says as if she is interrogating a bunch of common criminals.

'We are, sometimes,' Carlo says. 'Why do you want to know?'

'Why I be wanting to know?' Eenah cries out in exasperation. 'Because I like good boy persons and not bad boy persons, and I just wanted to see for my own self.'

'But if I ever hear that you have been naughty boys, I will have to do something about that. Do you know what I mean?'

'We do,' says an almost petrified Carlo.

'Good, now be off with you.'

The boys scuttle off the stage, and for the first time in a long and illustrious career, Eenah receives her first public ovation. It is not as a peacemaker, but Eenah had a point to make.

She managed to do in a few minutes what it has taken Addric three weeks to achieve, but after an experience of that nature, it would be heartless to walk away and leave the world hanging in limbo. As Eenah knows, the Krugwah Choir is the last item on the agenda.

And on her command, several hundred Krugwah appear at a moment's notice. And in front of an enchanted audience, Eenah leads them through a rendition of three of the most stirring songs ever written.

As is her way, she saves the best until the last. The timeless and unforgettable Louis Armstrong classic, *What a Wonderful World*, is an opportunity to bring people together such as only Eenah can do.

CHAPTER 39

As Addric knows from experience, love is the most powerful force in the universe. He fell in love with Planet Earth from day one. He loved everything about it, the diversity of life, its vast continents, and its breathtaking landscapes. And unlike Vela-Rishan, which is a world of floating islands, Earth is seventy percent water, and Addric loved that more than anything else.

It was his reason for wanting to visit in the first place, and his dream finally came true, but it would never have happened if the chronometer on his ship had not malfunctioned. Accompanied by a few close friends, he spent two memorable weeks in Lemuria, but on the day that he finally saw the Indian Ocean, Addric was in Addric heaven.

'I have been waiting for this moment for the last two years,' he said. 'That is the most beautiful sight I have ever seen and it is just as I imagined it to be, shimmering like a jewel in the afternoon light.'

'Now I can boast that it was on a secluded beach, on the shores of a long-lost continent, that this dream of mine eventually came to pass.'

The water was much colder than they anticipated, and it was a shock to their system at first. They spent several happy hours on the beach, frolicking around in the chilly but crystal-clear waters of the Indian Ocean. Little Jatoo was somewhat hesitant and preferred to sit on the shore making sandcastles.

It was an exhilarating experience for four young men from the opposite side of the universe. After which, they sat back with a refreshing beverage under their very own marquee.

'To make your dreams come true,' Addric said, 'all you need is an opportunity, a place like this and good friends. Thank you, Planet Earth.'

Over the next few days, the classically beautiful image of Planet Earth becomes a marketing bonanza. It is visible on almost every digital billboard, on television, on T-shirts, and more importantly, it's at the forefront of everyone's mind.

'If the Earth is about to be destroyed by a deluge of cosmic proportions,' Yusef says, 'I think the people who live inside the planet should know about it.'

'You're joking, aren't you?' Connor says.

His learning curve has been like a rollercoaster ride over the last few weeks, and his eyes have been opened to things he never thought possible.

He is surprised to hear that a civilisation of highly advanced beings not only inhabit the inner Earthly realms they have done so for hundreds of thousands of years.

'No, I am not joking, Connor. We are not the only inhabitants of this planet. And a few of those who live in the inner Earthly realms are even friends of ours.'

'Now, you really have opened up a can of worms. Please enlighten us mere mortals.'

'Hyperborea is a civilisation deep inside the planet, but it's a well-kept secret and rarely mentioned in any of the existing historical documents,' Felicity says.

'You would never find it on a map, but it's been there from the beginning. Unfortunately, all evidence of its existence disappeared with the destruction of the Great Library of Alexandria.'

'Hyperborea exists with the permission of the celestial hierarchy, and in some respects, it is very similar to the outer world.'

'It was the inspiration for the first European civilisations, their gods and religions,' Addric says.

'And this is the part that just might do you head in Connor, they exist in the fifth-dimensional realm.'

'I should have guessed there would be a twist to this tale,' he said. 'So, could they do anything about Vengali and Scherle?'

'Probably not, but they survived the last deluge without a problem. And somehow or other, I don't think they have anything to worry about.'

'They, you mean that there's more than one civilisation.'

'There are at least three other races, or so I believe.'

'So, who are they?'

'Well, there's the Telosians and the Catharians and another race that live in the city of Shamballa.'

'And from what I have heard, they are regular visitors to the upper world. And I suspect they might be watching these developments very closely.'

'Like, how would they be doing that?'

'Well, they are a very highly developed race, for one thing, and are often mistaken for UFOs. That has something to do with the fact that they travel around in spaceships, but only at night, of course.'

Like everyone in the troposphere, Connor is stranded at ground level, but his education is on a fast track to the stratosphere. It is somewhat colder up there, and other than a bad case of windburn, the primary danger would be from low-flying aircraft.

'Now, we really have veered off the path,' Addric says. 'I call this meeting to order. Please try to stay focused. We were discussing Planet Earth if I remember correctly.'

'The grand old lady of the Solar System and a divinely inspired creation in her own right,' Emphora says. 'She deserves all the recognition that she can get. After all, most religions owe their origins to nature worship in one way or another.'

'In that case, pagans will be dancing in the street,' Felicity says, 'their beliefs vindicated after centuries of being outcasts and reprobates.'

'Talking about reprobates,' Addric says, 'I have a suspicion that Vengali and Scherle were behind that assault.'

'There is a way to find out,' Jatoo says.

'Ah yes, your ever-reliable magic mirror. Perhaps we should take a look, just to be sure.'

'And if they are the culprits, what will we do about them.'

'They should be publicly humiliated and exposed for the riffraff that they are,' Felicity says.

'May I borrow your mirror, please, Jatoo.'

Addric holds it up to his face with one clear question in mind.

'I am getting something. The fog is lifting, and I can see them, or at least I think it's them.'

'Ah ha. It appears that they have gone underground, literally, if I am correct.'

'Hiding away from you, no doubt,' Felicity says.

'But there's more. I can see a laboratory, possibly even a munitions factory.'

'Wow, that's serious,' Milton says. 'Can you see any evidence of those airborne machines?'

'Take a look for yourself. This is a major operation.'

'But where are they operating from?'

'It looks like an island in the Pacific Ocean.'

'Perhaps we should make a clandestine visit to this facility,' Felicity says. 'Check out what's going on and rattle a few chains while we're at it.'

'That sounds like fun,' Connor says. 'Can we come along too?'

'Why not make a day of it. After all, it has been ages since we spent some time on a deserted island in the Pacific Ocean.'

'In that case,' Emphora says, 'everyone should go, but we will be doing it in style.'

'Now you're talking, so when do we leave?'

'Within the hour, by portal, of course, very sneakily, in other words.'

'Where exactly is this facility?' Demetra says.

'Okay,' Milton says as he leaps into action. 'It looks as if it's somewhere off the coast of South America.'

'It is 650 kilometers west of Valparaiso on the coast of Chile, on an island called Más a Tierra. That's in the Juan Fernandez group of islands.'

'Now, that is interesting,' Felicity says. 'I just happen to know that is the very same island on which Alexander Selkirk was marooned in the 18th century.'

'And who was he?' Jatoo says.

'None other than the most famous castaway of all time, my boy, Robinson Crusoe, of course.'

'It's a volcanic island, which means that it probably has an underground cave system.'

'In that case, let's check it out. The weather should be very pleasant. However, we will probably need mosquito repellent and sunscreen.'

'Not on Emphora's ship,' Addric says.

CHAPTER 41

Emphora's idea of roughing it in the jungles of the South Pacific is nothing at all like Connor expected, but the next surprise of the day is their mode of transport.

'When you step through this doorway,' she says. 'You will be in a world of luxury.'

'What do you mean by that?' Connor says.

'Follow me and you will see for yourself.'

He steps through the portal, only to find himself in what appears to be the lobby of a five-star hotel.

'Wow, what is this?'

'This is my ship, a multi-dimensional environment which, as you can see, looks like a five-star hotel. But it's a ship nevertheless and it is also very well equipped.'

'Ah, we will be doing it in style.'

'What did you expect?'

'I thought we'd be doing it like the explorers of old, with a pith helmet and a canvas tent.'

'Never in a million years, Connor, besides there's a jungle out there, a hotbed of mosquitoes and venomous snakes, amongst other things.'

This is the very same ship on which Addric and his companions travelled to Lemuria forty years ago. And if the chronometer had not malfunctioned, they would have ended up in the year 2050.

Eenah is not about to be left out and heads straight for the kitchen. It's one place that she cannot redesign but she decided that she could live with that.

'A guided tour is an absolute necessity,' Addric says. 'Follow me, boys, and prepare to be amazed.'

Emphora's ship is like a palatial floating warehouse, but this is no ordinary ship as the boys can see. The Control Room looks like an imperial ballroom furnished with elegant but comfortable furniture.

'I am only going to show you the most essential areas,' Addric says. 'This ship is like a twisting maze. One corridor runs off another, and if you take a wrong turn, you could get lost for hours.'

'But the accommodation is excellent, and you even get a luxuriously appointed room with all mod cons.'

'When I come back in the next life,' Connor says, 'I want to be a Yumi Master.'

'You never know what can happen, especially with a friend like Emphora,' Addric says cryptically. 'A dream like that could come true much sooner than you think.'

'Sounds good to me,' he says.

Emphora's ship has the capacity to blend in with its environment and it is currently disguised as a tangle of jungle vines.

'The new password for the portal is *Open Sesame*,' Emphora says. 'But don't scream it out, just in case someone is listening,'

'Now, let's activate some of this rusty old equipment and see if we can get an aerial view of this island.'

When it becomes apparent that Emphora is a little lost, Addric volunteers his services.

'I remember what to do,' he says. 'Allow me, please.'

'It has been a long time since this old girl has had a workout.'

'And how long is that?'

'Um, let me think, the last time I used it was 1985.'

'That was over forty years ago, Emphora. What have you been doing since then?'

'Well, I had a child to raise, for one thing.'

'I wasn't that bad, was I?' Jatoo says.

'No, my darling, you were a treat and a delight in every way. That was an experience I would not have swapped for anything.'

'See, I told you so,' he says to Felicity.

'Hmm,' she says, pretending to be unconvinced.

'And what else do you do with your time.'

'Well, I had seven grandchildren to look after, at least for three days a week.'

'You told me you had nothing to do.'

'I stretched the truth a little, Addric. It's my prerogative. After all, I am a goddess, amongst other things.'

'You try responding to the prayers and supplications of twelve million people every day of the week and you'd be looking for a mental health break.'

'In that case, you are forgiven, Emphora. A mother's life is not an easy one.'

'So very true,' she says.

'So, let me see. I have an aerial view of the island, but it's a really old one, like 1985 vintage.'

'Let me have a look,' Milton says. 'Umm, this is an interesting system.'

'The controls are voice activated, Milton.'

'Easily fixed,' he says as he scrolls through one screen after another. 'Okay, we have three options, past, present and future.'

'Well, there's no point in checking out the future because it hasn't happened yet,' Emphora says. 'Try the present.'

'Ah ha, I've got it, and we now have a real-time view of the island, and there's a lot of activity at the southern end.'

'I believe we have found the entrance to Pirate's Cove.'

Accompanied by Reuben and Jatoo, Addric ventures down not long after. This is a reconnaissance mission, Yumi style, and hiding behind a veil of invisibility comes in very useful, especially where espionage is concerned.

A Yumi Master has to abide by a strict set of rules, and it is not advisable to cross the line in the sand, especially if they have no desire to spend the remainder of their lives in a domain called the Phantom Zone.

In this case, Addric's vows have been suspended. As a consequence, he can use whatever sneaky tactics he likes to resolve this situation.

Under normal circumstances, he would never torment another human being, but as far as he is concerned, Vengali and Scherle are criminals.

He made a public statement that he would track them down and see that justice is served. But before that happens, it's essential to take a closer look at this facility.

They get back to the ship an hour later, and it's obvious that they encountered more than they bargained for. Eenah is serving up a selection of pre-dinner nibbles, and like everyone else, she is waiting for a report.

'So, Addric, what you be finding out?'

'It's worse than we expected. I presume that you have heard of the secret government installation in the Nevada Desert called Area 51.'

'No, I haven't.'

'It's a subterranean facility established in the 1950s, and its purpose, apparently, was to develop defense technology for the US government.'

'It's been a favourite topic of conspiracy theorists for decades, but thanks to the internet, it's not much of a secret anymore.'

'So, what's that got to do with what you be finding?' she said.

'It's a very similar setup, one in which numerous multi-national companies obviously have a vested interest.'

'When we arrived, an emergency meeting was in session,' Reuben said. 'And most of those in attendance were the big players in the business.'

'The topic of discussion was Addric's threat to track them down. And most of those guys are worried sick about what he is planning to do.'

'It's an automated facility, and there is no such thing as a technician in sight, but this is where the airborne drones are manufactured.'

'So, what we saw in Rome wasn't the real thing,' Felicity says.

'Then, what are they?' Eenah says.

'Some form of remote-controlled hologram, which are obviously capable of mass destruction.'

'But they be looking so real,' she said.

'Yes, and they can be reactivated at the touch of a button.'

'So, do you have any thoughts on what we could do?'

'Well, you did promise to bring them down,' Demetra says.

'I did, but we have to make sure that everyone else knows about it as well.'

'In that case, I have a brilliant idea,' Connor says. 'We should make a documentary and expose them for what they are. We could upload it onto YouTube and send a copy to every media network in the world.'

'Do you have the skills to shoot and edit the finished product?' Felicity says.

'We certainly do,' Milton says. 'And I have the most up-to-date equipment as well.'

'Then, let's break open the bubbly and nut this thing out, shall we?'

As well as numerous lounge rooms and a fully automated kitchen, the control deck looks as if it was plundered from the set of a Star Trek movie. They work away late into the night, nutting out a screenplay, while Eenah occupies herself in the kitchen.

'It is essential to introduce the main characters first, and you, Addric, should be the narrator,' Connor says.

'A good report should include the back story, such as the appearance of the Goddess in Swizzer Plaza and, of course, that spectacular event in Rome.'

'Unfortunately, we have missed the boat on that one.'

'No, we haven't,' Addric says, 'We happen to know the secret of travelling back in time.'

'Now I really do want to become a Yumi Master.'

'Is that what you'd like?' Emphora says.

'Oh yes, please.'

'Well, that may be a possibility because I have been thinking of opening an academy on Earth as well.'

'Count me in,' he says.

'If that's the case, I will have to go with you, as I am the official photographer.'

'No problem, just say when,' Addric says.

The purpose of the documentary is to expose a cabal of international terrorists and air it on prime-time television.

'It has to be handled delicately,' Connor says, 'but a touch of humour wouldn't go astray.'

'This is not a comedy,' Jatoo says. 'The idea is to expose a bunch of crooks, isn't it?'

'Leave the dialogue to me, Jatoo, and once you have read the script, you will approve it.'

Now that he knows that he can do whatever he likes, Connor's talents come flooding out of the woodwork.

He spent his formative years dallying in fast-paced repartee on the streets of San Francisco, and he knows all the best lines. And after two days of intensive revisions the script is finally approved.

'Now, boys and girls, it's rehearsal time.'

'An actor works closely with the director, and the script clearly states how you should deliver your lines and in what manner.'

'When I say *Action*, the cameras will roll. And if your lines are not word-perfect, then we will have to do it all over again. You will get the hang of it soon enough.'

Acting in a film is more fun than they were expecting, and Connor has them in hysterics most of the time, but Eenah has her own ideas on what she should do.

The most important scene is the boardroom, and that means going back in time and changing the course of history. Emphora is adamant that it has to be done.

'We have to do what we can. After all, the future of the Earth is at stake, and that is the only thing that matters.'

The boardroom scene is one for which they cannot rehearse, but the cameras are rolling when Vengali and Scherle disembark from a sixty-foot yacht in the bowels of Pirate's Cove.

They have no idea that they are the stars of a warts-and-all movie or that their every word is being documented.

'Our only hope of salvaging our investments is to dispose of that alien and his henchmen,' Vengali says.

Unbeknownst to Mr. Vengali, Addric just happens to be in the boardroom as well, and at that moment, he decides to make himself visible.

'And just how do you propose to do that?' he says, as he materialises in front of twenty astounded technocrats.

They are on their feet in an instant, and some of the more athletically inclined even make a mad dash for the door, but that's about as far as they get.

'Back to your seats,' Reuben says, 'or we will show you what Yumi Masters do for fun.'

'Gentlemen, you might as well take a seat because you are not going anywhere.' Addric says. 'You know who I am, so there is no need to introduce myself, is there.'

'Mr. Vengali, you are the brains behind this operation, aren't you?'

Pradak Vengali is an overweight, second-generation Indo-American with the sharp but beady eyes of a pack hound. His primary goal in life was to make a fortune and extract himself from a life of eternal poverty. Over time, he created a globally successful empire, but along the way, he lost touch with the most important element of his being.

He soon learnt that the pathway to glory is by foul means and not fair. He sold his soul to the only god who would listen and inched his way up the ladder using every spurious means at his disposal.

And when he eventually reached the top, there was nothing left of his soul at all. He always believed that his strategy for global domination was achievable. Ever since then, he has been quietly orchestrating his masterplan behind the scenes.

'Well, I am waiting, Mr. Vengali, and believe it or not, I can wait for an eternity.'

'Go back to where you came from, you freak of nature.'

'That is one thing which I am not, Mr. Vengali. For your information, I have an important role to play in the scheme of things. And I plan to bring you and your henchmen to justice.'

'Do what you will, spaceman, you will never succeed.'

'I will do what I have to, Mr. Vengali, and to prove my point, I am going to take you somewhere and show you something you may not like.'

Addric grabs Mr. Vengali by the arm and they simply vanish from sight. Connor immediately hits the stop button.

'Where'd they go?'

'To a place that no one would ever want to go,' Emphora says. 'Just relax, Connor. They'll be back in a few minutes.'

To Mr. Vengali's horror, he is soaring through time and space, and a few seconds later, he arrives at his destination.

'Where is this, and why have you brought me here?' he cries.

'This is a cosmic penitentiary, a domain that is surrounded by a highly sophisticated network of volatile electrostatic fields,' Addric says.

'In Christian mythology, it is known as Hell, but this is so much worse than that in every way.'

'So, are you planning to leave me here?' he says.

'I should, Mr. Vengali, considering what you have done. But I am not in a position to make that decision. What I will do is explain what happens to people like you.'

'You are just one of many self-obsessed sociopaths who think they can do whatever they like without suffering the consequences.'

'The universe is an intelligence system in its own right, Mr. Vengali and the force that operates behind the scenes.'

'And it gets a little upset when someone like you decides to take things into their own hands. In times like this, someone like me has to sort out the mess. And that's why I am here.'

'Mr. Vengali, can you see those glowing spheres floating around out there?'

'What are they?'

'They are people like you, Mr. Vengali, beings of many persuasions who have committed one unpardonable crime or another.'

'What did they do?'

'They lost contact with the very essence of who and what they are, Mr. Vengali. And they are now permanent residents of an intergalactic penal colony called the Phantom Zone, a place they will call home for the rest of eternity.'

'I was responsible for the fate of at least one of its inhabitants, and I am telling you, Mr. Vengali, this could be your fate as well.'

'You see, global domination is not on the agenda, not for you at any rate, and it never will be.'

'As I have stated on public record, that is not going to happen, not if I have anything to do with it.'

'Mr. Vengali, it would be in the interests of the entire planet if you shelved your plans, or this is where you will end up, and much sooner than you think.'

They return to the boardroom a few minutes later, and as his compatriots can see, Mr. Vengali looks as if he has just seen a ghost.

'They're back,' Milton says. 'Hit the start button, Connor.'

'Greetings, gentlemen,' Addric says. 'Mr. Vengali has just had an opportunity to see what his fate could be, and if he could speak, he would probably say that he would not wish something like that on his worst enemy.'

'But that could very easily be your fate as well, gentlemen. You see, justice comes swiftly when it is ordained by the powers that be.'

'But you will not be judged by the justice system of the United States, but by the Intergalactic Alliance, my current employers.'

'It is obvious that you took no notice of the Goddess of Wisdom simply because it didn't suit your needs.'

'But as Mr. Spock famously says in the Star Trek series, the needs of the many outweigh the needs of the few.'

Over the next few minutes, Addric explains that there is a system in place and then makes it patently clear that a cabal of technocratic moguls will never dominate life on Earth.

'You have broken every rule in the book, but everything that has happened over the last hour has been documented, and the finished product will be released within the week.'

'In other words, gentlemen, you are doomed. Your careers are ruined, and the control of your companies will no longer be your responsibility.'

'And that, as they say in the celestial realms is instant karma.'

'In a few moments, a portal will open. It's a one-way ticket to an intergalactic penal colony on the planet Jupiter. And that is where you will stay until you have been judged on your actions.'

Addric has just delivered the motherlode, and it's obvious that Mr. Vengali and his inner circle are speechless.

'You see, the future of this world is at stake and that's the issue. If you had not tried to brainwash everyone on the planet, we would not be in this mess, now, would we.'

Addric's final words are directed to the camera and not to Mr. Vengali and his cabal.

'So, good people of Planet Earth, we have notched up another milestone in this campaign. We are not finished yet, but we will succeed.'

'In a few days, I will assess the implants scattered across the Earth. And if they have turned white, that will be a clear indication that things have improved.'

'I know for a fact that the Hateful Army is still out there. And for those of you who don't care whether the Earth survives, consider this is a warning.'

'I care, and I am on a mission to see that it does. And I intend to succeed.'

'The implants will reveal the identity of every member of the Hateful Army, and if you are one of those, you will be given three chances to change your ways.'

'And if you do not, you will have to answer to me personally.'

'You now know what fate has in store for the technocrats responsible for this situation. Well, that could be your fate as well.'

'But just remember this, if you decide differently, then that's your choice, but in the final analysis, it's all up to you.'

Majura Krestovori and Seray Antropedes are in a state of rapturous bliss over Addric's success rate.

'You are doing brilliantly and getting better every day,' Majura says.

'So, what we can do for you, Oh Mighty One.'

Addric simply shakes his head. 'Ladies, I think I went a little too far.'

'Addric, think of the alternative. If you don't wield the big stick, the fate of our dear and beloved Earthlings really will be at risk.'

'You are doing exactly what you have been asked to do, and you are doing it brilliantly.'

'Take a walk through the corridors of power and see what sort of reception you get. That'll show you a thing or two.'

'As soon as this is over, you will have to front up to the powers that be, not to be chastised, but in recognition of your astounding achievement.'

'That is a relief,' he says. 'Now for issue number two, the implants.'

'Addric, you will be pleased to know that you will not have to gallivant all over the place and check them out one by one.'

We have been monitoring them closely, and the news is good, not perfect, but good.'

'I will show you what we've got.'

Majura waves her hands in the air, and a holographic image appears.

'Now here is the full readout, place by place, country by country, and in glorious technicolour.'

It is all too overwhelming to take in at a glance, but it is really good news. The primary result indicates that 78% of the population are on track and doing their best to change their habits.

'But the others, the Hateful Army as they are now being called, those little scallywags, they still require a little work, Addric.

'I had a feeling this would be the result,' Addric says. 'And I made a public statement that I would go looking for anyone who is holding back.'

'Yes, a bold statement that they have three opportunities to change their ways.'

'So how do you propose to do that?'

'Using a hell of a lot of old-fashioned imagination, ladies, how else?'

'Go get 'em buster.'

Addric so wants to say that they are wonderful, crazy women, but Majura's response would be yet another of her classic lines.

'Of course, Addric. That's why they gave this job to us and not some prissy little thing that doesn't have a clue.'

Governments around the world issue a proclamation to ensure that changes take place. And now, users of any product will have to answer a series of value laden questions before they can use a device for any purpose at all.

The personal communicator, or PECO, is commonly known as one of the most popular on the market. Advances in technology have long since pushed other devices aside, only to be replaced by an on-demand holographic screen.

Servers are now connected to satellites, but for a device to operate effectively, a user has to be programmed by a microchip implanted into a personal item such as a bracelet.

But Addric has the Zilmo Tag at his disposal and this is the device that he will use to analyse the implants.

'So,' he says as he prepares to address his trusty companions, 'you will be pleased to know that we are on target.'

'Congratulations, you have done a colossal job,' Reuben says. 'All hail Addric Sharano, wonder boy of the century.'

'You are a hero to millions of people worldwide,' Demetra says.

'Not to mention a pin-up boy to millions of gay men as well,' Connor says.

'That is something I can live without, Connor, but I appreciate the honour.'

'Which means that we have reached a hell of a lot of people in a very short time, even if it is not for the right reasons,' he says cryptically.

'So, we have gathered here to consider the results of our efforts, and the news is good.'

'It's not perfect, but with the assistance of this little device,' he says as he holds up a very slim, almost invisible slither of transparent plastic, 'we will be able to find out a lot more.'

'What is it?' Milton says.

'This is the Zilmo Tag.'

'And does it do something interesting?'

'Oh, indeed it does, Milton. This little beauty contains a vast reservoir of knowledge about almost every planetary system in the known universe.'

'I will take one,' he says. 'How much are they?'

'They are free if you have the right connections, but this one is mine, Milton.'

'However, I will allow you to take a little peek if you are inducted as a Yumi Master sometime in the next five years.'

'In that case, Emphora, today would be good,' Connor says.

'Perhaps we should get this over and done with first. There will be plenty of time for that later.'

'But thanks to the delightful if eccentric ambassadors of the Intergalactic Alliance, I now have a copy of the report on the implants.'

'Before we take a look, you boys will have to work out how to download it in some other format.'

'Addric, I love you dearly,' says a somewhat unenthusiastic Felicity, 'but if you had not told the Hatefuls that they have three opportunities, we could just gather them up, ship them off to that penal colony, and be out of here by now.'

Felicity is not the only one who is starting to fray around the edges. Everyone is tired and in need of a good break.

'Yes, it has been a testing time for us all,' Emphora says. 'And we are all a little weary after six weeks on the job.'

'However, if you are interested, I know of a way to fix that little problem.'

'If I may interrupt,' Addric says, 'I think that's an excellent idea Emphora. We all need to clear our heads.'

'I will vote for that,' Milton says. 'So, when do we leave?'

'As soon as you boys have worked out a way to transfer that information onto your PC's.'

'Well, you could leave the tag with me.'

'No deal, Milton. There are rules about that sort of thing. Besides, the Tag contains information that mere mortals are not allowed to know about just yet.'

'Whatever,' he says despondently, 'but it was worth a try.'

'So Emphora, should we pack a bag,' Connor says, 'like now, for example?'

'By all means, but don't forget your toothbrush.'

'A mystery trip, I love that idea, but where are we going?'

'To Vela-Rishan, of course, and you have thirty minutes to get your act together.'

Up until a few weeks ago, Connor had no purpose in life, but the idea of becoming a Yumi Master is a dream that could come true. He wants to learn as much as he can, so he watches closely as Addric sets the coordinates on Emphora's ship.

'Unlike a starship that can monitor numerous factors related to long-distance travel, this ship doesn't have to worry about things like engine capability, fuel levels, gravity, or anything else.'

'So, I presume it's like a Krugwah portal,' Connor says.

'Yes, it is, and it does what you tell it to, mostly.'

Connor is mesmerised by the interstellar phenomena that flash by in the blink of an eye. The average Earthling would give their eye teeth to get a close look at bands of cascading colour, and vast clouds of cosmic dust engaged in some form of inexplicable symphony.

'So, that's what the universe looks like.'

'Don't ask me to explain what you're looking at, Connor, but it's pretty awesome, isn't it?'

'It sure is, Addric, but when you relocate, do you see any of this stuff?'

'No, you don't see anything at all other than a sort of black haze and a seriously odd whooshing sound. But physical relocation has one annoying drawback.'

'And what's that.'

'It makes a mess of your hair, a really terrible mess.'

'You could wear a skull cap, you know.'

'That's a good idea, I might try that next time.'

'So, where exactly are we going?'

'The first stop on the itinerary is the Palazzo Della Emphora.'

'She lives in a palace?'

'Now, that's a tricky question, Connor, to which there are multiple answers.'

'First of all, the Goddess of Wisdom, as she is known on Planet Earth, is a goddess in her own right, and she is adored and venerated by her people.'

'And she is a rarity in every way, as you might have gathered.'

'That she is,' Connor says.

'Thirdly, she has two homes in Vela-Rishan that I know of. One of those is an inconspicuous villa on the outskirts of the Imperial City. And the other is on the very top of the highest mountain in the realm. That's the Askadera.'

'It's nothing fancy when seen from the outside, but like this ship, it is a multi-dimensional environment. Which means that it's bigger on the inside than it is on the outside.'

Connor was brave enough to venture down a few corridors and open a few doors, only to discover a treasure trove of some of the most remarkable artifacts that he had ever seen.

One room was filled to overflowing with the sort of treasures that you would only see in a museum, while others had garments, jewels, and furniture from different places and different eras in time.

'Emphora is a collector of just about everything, especially of good people,' Addric says cryptically.

'What do you mean by that?'

'You will see,' he says.

'Now, her mountaintop retreat has a breathtaking view of the entire realm. And any self-respecting antique dealer would give their eye teeth for just one of the things in her possession.'

'Like Yusef, for example.

'Yes, but more about him later because he has an equally interesting story.'

Addric is very aware of Connor's interest in this unexplored new world, but he has an advantage as a Yumi Master. He can see the energy field of another human being, and as he relates one story after another, Connor's is pumping away as if it has just been activated for the first time in ages.

'I was somewhat hesitant to introduce Jatoo to Emphora when we got back from Lemuria because I wasn't sure how she would react, but I should not have worried.'

'Why was that Addric?'

'Jatoo would have perished in Lemuria if it hadn't been for me. Emphora was the first person that I ever wanted him to meet, and the way she responded when she saw that beautiful face was an awakening experience in every way.'

'I presumed that Jatoo was just a little boy from Planet Earth, but Emphora could see so much more.'

'That's what she's like, Connor. She can see so much more than we do, and she knew immediately that Jatoo had a different heritage.'

'So, what are you saying, Addric?'

'I would not be surprised if she is having similar thoughts about you and Milton.'

'After all, you are not unlike your mother, are you?'

'Shanala has one foot in this world and one in the next.'

Poor old Connor is lost somewhere to the east and south of just about everywhere. His little chat with Addric rekindles old thoughts and memories. He wanders around aimlessly for a while, only to encounter Milton reclining on a couch in a sumptuously furnished alcove.

'What's up,' he says. 'You look as if you've seen a ghost.'

The idea of having a brother is a Godsend to Milton. Their lives may have changed over the last few weeks, but he is not about to complain.

'Tell me everything you know about Shanala and how she does what she does.'

'Okay, I will do my best, but you are asking for a reason, aren't you?'

'I am, mostly because Addric had a few interesting things to say and it has left me thinking.'

'About what?' Milton says.

'Like, have you ever felt that you are different, for example?'

'Well, Mum spent a fortune trying to find out what was wrong with me when I was a kid. A specialist told her that I was an autistic savant, but that's just what he thought.'

'It made Mum feel better knowing that, but it had no effect on me, but now I know differently.'

'And why is that?'

'Haven't you been following the plot Connor?'

'Just about every child born in the last sixty years excels at something in one way or another?'

'It's no secret that the kids of today have skills and talents way beyond that of any other generation.'

'I never got a chance to excel at anything,' Connor says. 'I went to a private boy's school, a cesspit of depravity where you had to negotiate with the offspring of the Hateful Army just to survive.'

'Those imbeciles made my life a misery and ruined it as well.'

'So, what did Addric say that threw you into a spin,' Milton says.

'It's what he didn't say.'

'Does Shanala have any special powers?' he says.

'Sort of, she can see things in other dimensions, and I should know because I can, too.'

'Really, like what?'

'Like those things out there in La-La land, fairies, glowing lights and strange-looking characters that pop in for a quick visit and disappear just as quickly.'

'You may not believe this, but so can I, sometimes. My life would have been so different if I had not spent ten years at that revolting school.'

People like Emphora and Shanala exist in a rarefied zone. That has something to do with the fact that they are programmed somewhat differently.

Most people are not aware of the multi-dimensional world that surrounds them but it's there all the same.

That doesn't mean they cannot use their innate faculties to perceive what lies beyond the invisible veil. Many do so, using one of the most useful faculties they have at their disposal.

Our imagination is a mystery. We can't touch it and we rarely ever talk about it, but it's just waiting for us to connect with something new, something different, and occasionally, something divinely inspired.

Your imagination is an essential component of your DNA, and it provides a direct link to the cosmos and the vast resources of the cosmic warehouse.

As a consequence, Emphora's hastily planned trip to Vela-Rishan is about to become an essential component of Connor's education.

This will be a mind-expanding adventure of the first order. And the first thing on the agenda is a sightseeing tour of the galaxy that she calls home, the mysterious domain known as the Khavala.

'So, I presume we will be flying?' Milton says.

'Of course we will, my boy. Follow me, and I will introduce you to one of my other forms of transport.'

Hidden away in the dungeons of her palatial floating warehouse, Emphora has a collection of transport vehicles from different periods in Earth's history.

Her vehicle of choice is a wine red, steampunk version of a Rolls Royce, vintage 1929, with decorative brass fittings, just to give it a surrealistic, retro modern look.

'That is totally awesome,' Milton says. 'An original I presume.'

'Not entirely, but it is a replica of a Rolls, courtesy of the fine art of energy manipulation, of course.'

'And what's that?'

'Yumi magic, of course, the only kind.'

The Rolls is a seriously beautiful vehicle that can accommodate three people in the front and at least six in the rear. It's been in quarantine for ages, and after it has been dusted off, Emphora invites everyone to take a seat.

'So, I presume that this is a flying car.' Connor says.

'Not normally, but today it will be.'

'But there's no room for me,' Eenah says.

'Yes, there is,' Addric says. 'You can sit on my lap.'

'Nope, I am going to sit on the roof.'

'Then hold on tight,' Emphora says.

The docking bay is a vast open area on the lower deck of the ship, and it's from here that the Rolls will depart.

'If you've got a problem with flying, boys, just close your eyes for the next few minutes.'

'Not a chance,' Connor says, 'I want to see absolutely everything.'

Emphora doesn't use a wand or wriggle her fingers in the air, she uses thought magic.

The doors of the docking bay open, and the Rolls move forward, and when it sails out into space, Eenah start to scream at the top of her voice.

Their destination is a multi-dimensional domain called the Khavala, and one of its treasures, the city of Arinyah is a magnificent city suspended in the vast ocean of nothingness known as the Abyss.

Many years ago, this is where Addric and his brother decided to go for a holiday. They were travelling on an interstellar vessel called the Silhouette and decided to play a game called Labyrinth, but what they didn't know is that it was an intuitive game, one which could recreate the thoughts in a player's mind.

For a period of time that felt more like three agonising days, but which was, in fact, only thirty minutes, they had one bizarre experience after another.

That was their first experience of the Khavala, and as they found out, it really is an amazing place, and now, Milton and Connor are about to find that out as well.

'One of the many interesting features of the Khavala are inter-dimensional highways,' Emphora says. 'And under normal circumstances, they are not visible to the naked eye, but they serve a useful purpose.'

'Inter-dimensional highways crisscross the Khavala from one end to the other, and if you are in a hurry, they are the perfect way to travel.'

As the car zooms across an almost invisible highway, Eenah is still screaming away on the top of the car.

'I wouldn't worry about her,' Emphora says.

'Now, the Khavala is an essential component of a unique and ancient galaxy. If you look out there, you will see an inter-dimensional bridge.'

'That is one of many that stand at the border of other realms, but if you look around, you will see many other barely visible structures, and there are literally hundreds of these things, some of which look like exotic temples and palaces.'

'Does anyone live there?' Connor says.

'Not anymore. They are relics of the past, the ghostly remains of the original Rishani Empire.'

'They were our ancestors, a powerful race of beings that are sometimes referred to as the Gods of Space and Time.'

'Now, I have decided to treat you to a meal at one of my favourite restaurants.'

'That's more like it,' Jatoo says. 'Where do you have in mind?'

'Well, we have several options to choose from, but I know of one particularly good restaurant in the floating food markets.'

'In fact, it's as good as any of the restaurants in Hong Kong Harbour and that's saying something.'

'That's an excellent idea,' Addric says. 'It will be worth the effort, folks. The food is to die for. I can assure you of that.'

As the car sails through the ghostly domain that is the Khavala, their destination is clearly visible in the distance.

'That there is the fabled city of Arinyah.'

'That is truly awesome,' Connor says.

Arinyah is one of the most beautiful places in Vela-Rishan, a city floating in the clouds and one that is as old as time. It was once a mountain fortress, but today, it's a holiday destination without equal.

Arinyah is a feat of craft and engineering on an unimaginable scale, layer upon ancient layer of beautifully ornamented pavilions, exotic marble temples and luxurious palaces.

'And do you have a home here as well?' Connor says.

'Of course, I do, but it's very well-concealed, for obvious reasons.'

'Is it a palace perhaps?'

'No, it's very modest, but I haven't been there for ages and it's likely to be very dusty.'

The Rolls heads towards the uppermost point of the mountain and disappears into a doorway camouflaged by an energy field.

'That was so cool,' Connor says.

Emphora's house is not as modest as she led them to believe. It really is a palace overflowing with treasures collected over a lifetime.

As the proprietor of numerous antique stores, Yusef is always on the lookout for a masterpiece or two, and this place is full of them.

'Is any of this for sale?' he says as he takes a quick look under one of the dust covers.

'Not really,' Emphora says. 'They are family heirlooms, ancient beyond measure in fact, as is everything in this house.'

She escorts them to the front balcony, and the view literally takes their breath away. From one horizon to another is a panorama of floating islands of every shape and size.

'Magnificent, is it not?'

Emphora's modest home sits side-by-side with many other equally splendid homes, all of which have a view of the fabled world that is Arinyah.

To Connor's amazement, the sky is alive with a multitude of airborne vessels, all of which are making their way to destinations unknown.

'So, you obviously travel by spaceship?'

'Normal people do,' Addric says, 'but we don't.'

'So, Connor, what do you think.'

'I love it, and I want to live in this very house.'

'It's in dire need of a little love and care, as I rarely come here anymore, but I will keep that thought in mind.'

'Now, if you look down there, you will see the floating markets, and that is our destination.'

Way down below is a world such as you would only see in a busy Asian harbour. Hundreds of floating restaurants jostle for space around the base of the floating mountain that was once known as Mt Arinyah.

'Wow, that's awesome,' Connor says, 'but it will take ages to get down there.'

'About twenty minutes if you take the scenic route,' Emphora says. 'Which means that you will get your first taste of life in Vela-Rishan, the old-fashioned way, of course.'

'You are about to see some of the most fascinating streets that you have ever seen in your life.'

'Are you ready to go?'

'I can't wait,' he says. 'Come on folks, this is going to be good.'

'What happened to Eenah,' Addric says.

'I have no idea,' Emphora says. 'But I wouldn't worry. She can take care of herself.'

CHAPTER 46

For reasons of her own, Eenah decided to go back to Dragonshead, and to everyone's surprise she even took up an offer to appear in the newly revived Disneyland in Tokyo.

'We be watching that television thing, and those little Japan people, they were saying, Eenah, we love you. So, we go to this Disneyland place, and you know what Empora, it be a very exciting place.'

'And they want us to come back again.'

'That's so wonderful,' Emphora says.

'But it's not all good news. Some very bad men are saying not-so-nice things about you, Addric.'

'Who were they, and what did they say?'

'That be them Hateful types, and they even be saying awful things about Him Holy Person too.'

'Ah,' Felicity says. 'They're alive and well and getting a little too big for their boots.'

'The fact that they have the nerve to speak their mind so openly is a bit of a worry,' Yusef says.

'Well, we warned them that we are coming to get them,' Addric says. 'Unfortunately, we have to work out a way to identify them first.'

'Has anyone got any ideas on what we could do?'

'Strategies,' Felicity says. 'We play a game of cat and mouse and draw them into our net?'

'And how do we do that?'

'We tell them a barefaced lie, obviously, that we now have the names of over five million recalcitrants, all of whom have been identified by the implants.'

'That could work,' Reuben says. 'We just remind them of the three chances thing and that there's a deadline.'

'And if they refuse to comply, everyone on an alphabetical list will receive a visit from a portal in the middle of the night.'

'Ah, the pathway to the penal colony routine,' Felicity says. 'That would be enough to scare the pants off anyone.'

'However, it would be even more effective if the message was delivered as a sixty-second commercial, a community announcement, so to speak,' Connor says.

'And with special effects thrown in for good measure, we could create a graphically horrible video showing a Krugwah portal visiting someone in the dead of night,' Felicity says.

'It plucks them from their bed and drops them off at that hell-hole of a penal colony on Jupiter.'

'That's sort of unethical, isn't it?' Addric says.

'It's either that boyo or goodbye Planet Earth. Take your pick.'

'Okay, let's do it,' he says. 'We have nothing to lose, but they do.'

The campaign to save the Earth is gathering momentum, but it's a race against time. The media has gone out of their way to keep it in the public gaze and they are even presenting the statistics in a similar fashion to the daily weather report.

But Milton and Connor have the most tedious job of all. They have to itemise the ever-changing results from the Zilmo Tag and transfer them to a spreadsheet program.

'You may not believe this,' Emphora says, 'but Disneyland has invited Eenah and the Krugwah to perform at a special one-off spectacular.'

'Why?' Addric says.

'To celebrate Earth Day on the 22nd of April, no less.'

'We could use that to our advantage, couldn't we?

'Earth Day is an International Day of Peace and celebration and the one day of the year dedicated to Planet Earth.'

According to the news report, Eenah has won hearts all over the world. And it did not go un-noticed by Disney executives that she resembles Lena, the star of an animated movie called *Escape from Planet Earth*.

'*Lena the Astro Diva* is a space adventure in which a little astronaut responds to a mysterious message to save Earthlings from a tyrannical alien,' a news reporter says.

'Eenah is now a world-famous celebrity, but it would not be spectacular unless Addric and the Extra-Terrestrials make an appearance as well.'

'Why not,' he says. 'That will be the perfect way to send a message to the Hateful Army as well.'

'They are not a collective but people from all walks of life, and they have a long and recognisable history,' Felicity says.

'They are the ruthless, the desperate, and the dangerous, social outcasts in other words, and most of them are as mean-spirited as you can get.'

'They are the sort of people who would steal a handbag from an old lady or abuse a passing stranger for no reason at all.'

'They have been with us since the beginning of time,' Yusef says. 'Life in ages past wasn't just difficult. It was deplorable in every way, and it wasn't just poverty that people had to endure.'

'People lived in filth and squalor. There was no such thing as sanitation or medical facilities, and hygiene was virtually unknown.'

'For some people, this is a dog-eat-dog world, and everyone is a potential enemy.'

'Today, they are not as visible, but in the past, the Hateful Army was everywhere, and anything could set them off.'

'Women were constantly being abused and had no recourse to justice. For some people, nothing has changed at all.'

'Which means that the Hateful Army are not just the mean-spirited,' Emphora says, 'but those for whom life has been one horrible experience after another.'

'I never really understood who they were,' Connor says, 'but it would be heartless to hunt them down and terrorise them just because of that.'

'I have spent years battling the generals of the Hateful Army,' Felicity says.

'And how did you do that?'

'I figured out a way to travel back in time so that I could explore the history of the Earth.'

'The so-called leaders of past ages, the, kings, generals and military crusaders, were the Hateful Army in disguise.'

'Felicity is a collector, not of precious objects, but of battles that she has fought with the likes of Zeus,' Addric says.

'And wasn't he a treat and a half, but most of his family was just as bad. I soon learnt that strategy meant psyching out the enemy, but what those monsters got away with was abominable.'

'A modern woman would not tolerate the way they treated women in those days.'

'So, when I feel like a little diversion, Connor, I pop back to a period in Earth's history and play a few little games of my own.'

'You will be interested to know that Felicity's house is decorated with the trophies of her conquests,' Addric says.

'What do you mean, like the private parts of Attila the Hun or something like that.'

'Not likely, Connor, my house is a gallery of paintings and murals, real scenes that have been frozen in time.'

'I made a hit list of the top ten tyrants of the Ancient World and decided to visit them one by one.'

'My sole purpose was to see if they could outsmart me at one thing or another. My exploits were never recorded, but they should have been.'

'Even Vlad the Impaler found out what it was like to be on the receiving end of his own medicine.'

'His claim to fame was that he disposed of his enemies by impaling them through the heart with a pointed stake. So, I decided to give him a taste of what that was like.'

'One day, I invited him to go horse-riding. Unfortunately, Vlad's horse stumbled, and he ended up at the bottom of a pit, one that had an artful arrangement of greased and sharpened spikes.'

'And then what happened to him?' Connor says.

'I didn't wait around to find out, but when he was found two days later, he was a babbling mess.'

'Then there was that deranged idiot Caligula, whose favourite pastime was torturing innocent people while he entertained his friends at a banquet.'

'That was the very same Roman Emperor who promoted his horse to a Consul of Rome.'

'And what did you do to him?'

'I lured him to my villa on the outskirts of Rome and suspended him over a vat full of snakes. Not the poisonous variety, of course, but he didn't know that. I was hoping to re-educate the little ratbag.'

'And did it work?'

'Of course not, but after that, I realised that most tyrants had mental issues of one sort or another.'

'According to modern scholars, Caligula probably had schizophrenia or something like that.'

'That's an insight into the mindset of the people that we are dealing with,' she says. 'The Hateful Army has always been with us in one form or another. And they are still here and hiding away in the shadows.'

'Unfortunately, they have never changed. Some are patently obvious, while others manage to fly under the radar. But as we now know, they can also be the managing director of an international conglomerate.'

'But Connor, you will be pleased to hear that the Countess of Farago is actually a humanitarian at heart,' Addric says.

'You are a dear and beloved friend, Addric, but I pale into insignificance compared to you.'

'You are a great asset to this campaign, Felicity, and the people of planet Earth will one day thank you for that.'

'There is nothing more inspirational than listening to stories from like-minded souls, is there?' Yusef says.

'Gruesome stories if you ask me,' Connor says. 'But how will we identify these people?'

'A few more educational campaigns will help,' Addric says, 'but it will probably mean a face-to-face confrontation before it's all over.'

'And how will that happen?'

'Through a little bit of universal magic, of course. What other way is there?'

'Addric, stop teasing us,' Felicity says. 'Spit it out, for goodness sake.'

'Haven't you noticed anything about the Zilmo Tag yet?'

'Like what?' Milton says.

'Well, you sit in front of it every day, and the statistics change from one place to another. How do you think that happens?'

'How does it happen, Addric?'

'The stats are automatically connected to the consciousness of every person on the planet. In other words, they are hot-wired to identify changes in the human consciousness index.'

'And that means what?'

'Globally, the statistics are improving, and they will eventually reveal the location of the Hatefuls, but if we play our cards right, we can help that along a bit.'

'By doing what,' Demetra says.

'Firstly, by advertising the fact that everything is going brilliantly. It's essential to get the stats down to zero, or else, it's sayonara Planet Earth.'

'You clever boy Addric, I thought I was pretty good at old-fashioned trickery, but you're not too bad yourself,' Felicity says.

'Well, I have had the opportunity to observe a master in action.'

'Flattery will get you everywhere Addric, but now, we really will have to go to the next level, but how?'

'Well, our delightful friends, the Krugwah will be the star attraction at the Planet Earth Day celebrations at Disneyland next week.'

'And the ETs will be making an appearance as well, and of course, and we will be expected to say something important.'

'Every media network in the world will be watching, and that's where we slap everyone on the back and tell them that they're doing a wonderful job.'

'But we also alert them to the fact that every implant in the world has to turn white or else.'

'What do you think of that idea?'

'That will probably work,' Jatoo says, 'but don't scare them too much, or it could backfire.'

'So, now for the good news,' Addric says. 'You may not believe it, but you have a whole week in which to do whatever you like.'

'Well, in that case,' Milton says. 'I have a suggestion. I have a magnificent house overlooking San Francisco Bay and a yacht that hasn't been used for ages.'

'If you are interested, perhaps we could chill out for a few days, sail around San Francisco Bay, and maybe we could have lunch at one of my favourite restaurants.'

'Count me in,' Felicity says.

'And me too,' Emphora says. 'But if that's an open invitation, Eenah would love to come along as well.'

'Of course, she can, but I have a cat and a dog.'

'I don't think Eenah knows about anything about our beloved animals. Will that be a problem?'

'Well, not for Jezebel, nothing scares her.'

'Is she the cat or the dog?'

'She's a cat who appeared on my doorstep about ten years ago, but Frodo, he is absolutely adorable.'

'You called your dog after Frodo Baggins?' Felicity says.

'Well, he reminded me of Frodo when I first saw him, but you will love him, Felicity.'

'He's a golden Labrador, but I must warn you that Jezebel has a history.'

'I have a suspicion that she was once a woman of the night until she discovered that it was a much better idea to laze around in luxury and be pampered by my lady friends.'

'What lady friends,' Reuben says. 'You don't run a house of ill repute, do you?'

'No, Reuben, they're my housekeepers, seven lovely old Chinese ladies who have lived with me for the last ten years.'

'Minnie was seventy-eight when she applied for the job, and when I realised that she was having a hard time, I offered it to her and she moved in.'

'It was the best thing I ever did. I have three houses on my property. My chauffeur, Cedric, lives in a cottage on one side, and Minnie and her friends live in the guest house on the other.'

'Minnie is so beautiful, and she even reads tea leaves for a hobby.'

'And why does she do that?' Jatoo says.

'It's like fortune telling. Minnie has been doing it forever, and she's pretty good at it too.'

'But Friday is their day off, and they usually chill out, play Mahjong, gossip, and have a bit of fun.'

'But that's today, Milton.'

'Well, I'll give them a call and let them know that we're on our way.'

'They will be over the moon when they find out that they are about to meet the Eenah and the Extra-Terrestrials.'

'Now, the thing about my house is that it's not a traditional house. It's Japanese.'

'Which means what?' Jatoo says.

'Well, it's based on the design of a typical Japanese house. And for someone with a job like mine, it's just perfect. It is also very quiet and very relaxing, as you will see.'

'It sounds absolutely magnificent,' Felicity says.

'It is, and I know that you will love it.'

****

As to whether they would warn Eenah about Frodo or Jezebel prior to their arrival, they could not decide. Her response is likely to be nothing if not interesting.

As soon as she steps out of the portal, Eenah glances around suspiciously, and the moment that she sees Frodo, she is on Krugwah alert.

'Stay where you are. There's a monster on the loose.'

'That's no monster,' Milton says. 'That's my baby.'

'Him a very ugly baby, then. What is it?'

'It's a dog, Eenah, a very friendly and playful animal that loves people.'

'Will him be liking Krugwah too?'

'Allow me to introduce you.'

This really is going to be an interesting day, and for Eenah, it will be very educational as well. Milton hasn't seen Frodo for two months and it's a touching reunion that even brings a tear to Eenah's world-weary eyes.

After she gets used to the idea that Frodo isn't a threat, Eenah settles down for the first few minutes. But like all dogs, Frodo has to check her out. To be sniffed by a hairy animal is the next learning curve of the day and Eenah is doing her best not to laugh.

'Him a very nice baby, really, but why he so hairy?'

'All dogs are hairy, Eenah and so is my cat.'

'And what being dat?'

'Another animal that likes human companionship. But Jezebel is a bit like you, Eenah, which means that you two should get on like a house on fire.'

'Maybe we will and maybe we won't.'

A few moments later, seven elderly Chinese ladies dressed in their finest clothes appear at the door.

Minnie would love to rush over and take Milton in her arms, but time has taken its toll, and she just stands there quietly, with a few solitary tears glistening in her rheumy old eyes.

'Oh ladies, it's so wonderful to see you again,' he says.

'Our beautiful boy is home at long last,' Minnie says. 'How we have missed you, young man.'

Milton introduces each lady in turn, and some are as old if not older than Minnie, but each of them is a testament to the beauty and wisdom of old age.

Over the last ten years, their lifestyle has changed dramatically, and today, they live a life of luxury. Every now and then, Cedric takes them for a drive and treats them to the sights of San Francisco. But their favourite pastime is shopping, and the ladies love nothing better than to browse through one Chinese emporium or another.

'But a guided tour is an absolute necessity,' Milton says.

'I will show you to your rooms, after which we will be treated to a Chinese banquet such as only the experts can make.'

When the ladies realised that Milton was bringing his famous friends to stay for a few days, they leapt into action and rustled up a banquet fit for the Emperor of China himself.

The house is a masterpiece of modern design, based on a traditional Japanese house of the early 20th century. Situated on a high ridge, and surrounded by an extensive garden, it is concealed from the public gaze. But it does have a panoramic view of San Francisco Bay, and clearly visible in the distance is the unmistakable Golden Gate Bridge.

Milton's house is a superb example of the art of the traditional Japanese craftsman, with a floor and ceiling of beautifully finished Californian timber, but the highlight is a Japanese rock garden that weaves its way around the house.

'And the best part of all is the view of the Bay.'

'That really is beautiful,' Addric says.

'However, you will be pleased to know that it has every modern convenience you can think of, but most of the controls are concealed behind bamboo screens and doors.'

CHAPTER 48

The first course for lunch is a selection of homemade spring rolls, steamed wontons, and prawn dumplings, and every mouthful is a delicate combination of the subtle flavours of the Orient.

This is a new taste sensation, especially for Eenah, and she scrutinises everything closely, but she has to draw the line at one dish in particular.

'Whose hands are they?' she cries.

'They're not hands. That's chicken feet in black bean sauce,' Milton says.

'So, how is the chicken going to walk without any feet?'

'I don't think those poor little things will ever walk again,' Emphora says as delicately as she can. 'They are in chicken heaven now.'

'That being so very sad, to die without your feet.'

The main course is several platters piled high with a galaxy of culinary brilliance, crispy-skinned duck, Chinese vegetables, fresh lobster marinated in chili, ginger and shallots, sea cucumber and abalone, and a blazing platter of Mongolian lamb.

'Ladies, this is absolutely beautiful,' Milton says. 'Thank you.'

Milton is obviously the love of their life and his approval is more than enough.

'Have I died and gone to heaven?' Reuben says.

'Not yct,' Ecnah says. 'You're still breathing.'

'Milton, do you eat like this every day?' Connor says.

'I sure do. It's good, isn't it?'

'It's enough to make a person green with envy.'

'You're welcome to move in if you wish.'

'Truly, do you mean that?'

'Of course, the ladies will love you and I will be able to say that my brother lives with us as well.'

'I would take up that offer if I was you,' Felicity says, 'because if you don't, I will.'

'I accept. Thank you, Milton. That's very generous.'

'It's the least I can do.

'But the ladies won't know who's who,' Connor says.

'That problem is easily fixed,' Felicity says. 'You could always grow a Rhett Butler moustache.'

'Nah, not tall enough for one thing.'

A typical Chinese breakfast is the norm in Milton's house, and it's another educational experience.

A huge platter of Egg Foo Yong disappears within minutes, as does a Pan-Fried Turnip Cake, but no one other than Milton is game to sample one very strange-looking dish.

'What's that?' Reuben says.

'It's Congee, a combination of offal, liver and kidney in a thick rice porridge.'

'Okay, I think I'll pass on that one.'

Even the green tea is a little too stringent for Reuben's delicate taste buds, but to his relief, a pot of freshly brewed coffee is also on the menu.

'So, folks, are you ready for the treat of the day,' Milton says.

'You betcha,' Addric says.

'Okay, we'll meet back here in thirty minutes, but hats and sun cream are essential.'

'And what being a hat?' Eenah says.

'You wear them on your head, so that you don't get sunburnt.'

'But worry not, Eenah. I have hats to fit all shapes and sizes.'

'What about this one,' he says as he rummages around in a cupboard and presents her with a pink bucket hat.

'I think that's just you, Eenah.'

She plops it on her head, checks herself out in the mirror, and says, 'We will need a few more.'

'Okay, I'll be back in a few minutes, Eenah, as I have to change.'

When Milton reappears, he is dressed in a pair of white navy shorts and a shirt with a nautical design. He didn't specify the dress code, but he didn't have to.

Demetra and Felicity look like glamorous fashion models in colourful sarongs, broad-brimmed picture hats and oversized sunglasses.

'You ladies know how to dress for the occasion,' he says.

'Did you have your doubts,' Felicity says.

'No, not in the least. I think I know you well enough by now.'

'And so, you should, young man. After all, we have been living in the same house for the last two months.'

There is every possibility that they are wearing very skimpy bathing costumes as well, but all will be revealed.

The boys look very festive in multi-coloured board shorts and overly large straw hats. But Emphora looks radiant in a stylish red caftan decorated with a motif of miniature flowers.

Her accessories have been equally well thought out, a French designer sunhat, fabulous Italian sunglasses ornamented with sparkling diamantes, and a woven handbag draped casually over one arm.

'You were a model in a previous life,' Milton says.

'I have never had a previous life, Milton. This is as good as it gets.'

'Okay folks, are we ready for the adventure of a lifetime?'

'Lead the way Captain,' Connor says.

They wander down the steps to the jetty, and as everyone is delighted to see, they really will be sailing in style.

'I am the proud owner of a fifty-three-foot motor yacht,' Milton says. 'This is the MSS Enterprise, and it's my very own creation.'

The Enterprise is the quintessence of luxury, a vessel designed for a pleasurable outing on the Bay.

'So, Milton, who's driving?' Eenah says.

'I am, of course. After all, I do have a pilot's license.'

They presumed that their presence in the upper echelons of Marin County was a well-kept secret but that is not the case at all.

'The grapevine is obviously alive and well,' Felicity says.

A few of Milton's neighbours have gathered to see them off. Luckily, they don't try to clamber over the fence, and the only sensible thing to do is smile and wave and assure their devoted public that everything is going to plan.

'I wonder how that news got around.'

'Your beloved domestic staff probably had something to do with that,' Connor says.

'The little darlings. Nothing is sacred anymore.'

'It could have been worse.'

A guided tour of the upper and lower deck is proof of the extent of Milton's wealth and everyone is seriously impressed.

'Ladies and gentlemen, please take your seats. 'The MSS Enterprise is about to set sail.'

'Captain Kirk is at the Con, and we are about to go where no alien life form has been before.'

'What's he talking about?' Jatoo says.

'He is talking about one of the most famous science fiction shows of all times,' Felicity says.

'Milton obviously thinks that he is Captain Kirk.'

'And who was he?'

'He was a spunk and a lady's man in his spare time, but he was the captain of a starship called the U.S.S. Enterprise.'

'Their primary purpose was to go where no man had ever been before.'

'And did they get there?'

'They did Jatoo, on numerous occasions, if you are to believe what you see in the movies.'

'I am now ready for my first champagne of the day,' she says. 'Who's on bar duty?'

'I will do the honours,' Addric says.

'Wow, this is a well-stocked fridge. Would you like a local brew or something foreign? There's quite a lot to choose from.'

'Anything will do, Addric.'

As they sail along the coastline, they have an uninterrupted view of the magnificent homes that overlook the Bay, but the biggest thrill of all is to sail under the Golden Gate Bridge.

'This is where the adventure began,' Addric says. 'This is where Milton did a nosedive into infamy and the world beyond.'

'And he has proved himself to be a very amenable young man ever since,' Emphora says. 'But he is also a very generous host and a competent pilot as well.'

'That he is,' Connor says.

'Uh oh,' I think we have company,' Jatoo says. 'I can hear a helicopter.'

'Good morning, Extra-Terrestrials and welcome to San Francisco,' says a voice over a loudspeaker.

'Go away, you little pest,' Felicity says. 'I could dispose of him in a flash, and no one would ever know about it.'

'That would look really good,' Reuben says. 'We would be tried as criminals and all of our hard work would go down the gurgler.'

'It's thinking time,' Demetra says, 'otherwise our lovely day will be ruined.'

'This is the Coast Guard, and we will do our best to keep everyone as far away from you as possible.'

'Ah,' Emphora sighs. 'What a lovely man. He had no idea how close he came.'

'To what,' Addric says.

'I hadn't got that far in my thinking, but I would not have done too much damage.'

Milton moors the boat at a little jetty in an isolated cove, and as everyone is delighted to see, there is not another soul in sight.

'It can't be a very popular restaurant,' Jatoo says. 'There's no one else around.'

'This isn't a restaurant,' Milton says. 'But I don't think you will have any complaints about the food at my mother's table.'

'How clever is that,' Connor says. 'I am definitely looking forward to lunch now.'

'And we will not be harassed by those pesky reporters either.'

CHAPTER 49

After a delicious lunch, the boys laze around in the pool for an hour or so while the ladies relax under a pergola and soak up the classic view that is San Francisco Bay.

It is the second week of summer, they are in the company of friends, and it's a beautiful day to be alive. But what they don't know is that an intrepid reporter and his trusty photographer are hiding away in the bushes on the opposite side of the Bay. They are about to scoop the pools, and the whole world will get to see what the ETs do in their spare time.

The garden is the perfect place to idle away the day, and after a refreshing swim, Addric has an inspired idea.

'Let's play a game of Hot Potato.'

'How does that go?' Connor says.

'It's sort of like Catch Me If You Can.'

'The field of play will be the air and not the ground.'

'Sounds interesting. So, what else is involved?'

'This will be a variation of Bubble Ball, but instead of playing with bubbles, we will be using plastic balls.'

'You will be playing with a blue ball, but the trophy will be a yellow ball.'

'That's the ball you will have to apprehend. And if you do catch it, your ball will change to ycllow.'

'And this is where the game gets serious. That's the ball that everyone else wants.'

'How does that sound?'

'Maybe a practice session would be a good idea,' Connor says.

Addric conjures up a selection of plastic balls with handles attached.

'Now, these are not regular balls, as they have been infused with a simple spell.'

'Like, what sort of spell would that be?' Connor says as he rises off the ground.

'That sort of spell. The idea is to leap around the field and apprehend the yellow ball before anyone else does.'

'So, we won't be playing in teams then.'

'No, you'll be on your own.'

'The yellow ball is programmed to move about in a random fashion, and the idea is to apprehend it before anyone else does.'

'And that's when things get a little on the hairy side.'

They soon work out what Addric means, and a few minutes later, they are leaping about all over the place. Eenah is having more fun than she has had in ages, but there are rules to be followed, and Addric is adamant that flying is not one of them.

'Okay, let's get this show on the road, and just to make things interesting, we will play three rounds of ten minutes each.'

Once they get the hang of this idea, it is time to play in earnest. The general idea is not to demolish the opposition but to get hold of the yellow ball, and that is not as easy as it looks.

The yellow ball darts about all over the place, but Eenah is relentless and has it in her sights from the moment the game starts. By the end of round one, it is touch and go, Addric and Jatoo against little old Eenah. The last few moments are hair-raising, but Eenah has a fan club and they are rooting for her.

'Go, Eenah, go,' Felicity cries.

The bell is about to ring and time is almost up. Addric has the yellow ball in his sights but so does Eenah. And just as she is about to take possession, the yellow ball does a swift about-turn.

But Eenah is like a dog on a bone and she is not about to be outsmarted by a yellow plastic ball.

'I got it,' she cries triumphantly.

'Let's get her boys,' Addric says.

They find out sometime later that their few hours of fun is the news of the day, broadcast on every television station around the world.

'And that's how the ETs spent a beautiful Saturday afternoon,' the reporter says. 'Eenah was the star of the show, and she would scream and shout and leap about all over the place, especially if the boys got anywhere near her precious yellow ball.'

'If you have any reservations about the ETs, then this report might be the very thing to change your mind.'

'That could have been a disaster as an exposé of our private lives,' Felicity says. 'But that sneaky little reporter did a lovely job.'

'And in terms of free advertising,' Emphora says, 'it can only enhance the cause.'

'So true,' Addric says, 'but tomorrow will be a very big day, especially for the Krugwah.'

'Yay,' Eenah says. 'We be going to Disneyland.'

'The toughest part of the day will be the meet and greet, and we will be expected to chatter away with thousands of excited visitors.'

'Just like the Royal family,' Felicity says.

'Not quite so formal, but the highlight of the day will be another aerial spectacular.'

'That's all organised, isn't it, Eenah?'

'There's nothing to plan, Addric. We just do our thing as usual because we love Disney stories.'

'You do?' says a surprised Felicity.

'Oh yes, Felicity, we have our own version of Disney movies and we watch them every night.'

'Like at a movie theatre or something?'

'No, our screen be a big Krugwah portal in the sky. Our movies be the real thing with real Krugwah actors. We have lots of them you know.'

'We love Disney movies, but we not be liking some of those naughty bad people.'

'Like the evil queen for example.'

'We boo and hiss when we see bad persons trying to hurt our very special friends. Krugwah don't like bad persons you know.'

'I know that now,' Felicity says. 'So, what are you going to do?'

'That being a very big surprise, and I can't tell you Felicity, but we be going to do one of our very favourite stories.'

'Eenah, that is so beautiful,' Addric says. 'I have never asked about your life and I would love to visit Krugwah Land one day.'

'Oh, that would be wonderful Addric. Krugwah Land is just like a Disney movie.'

'In that case, we can sleep peacefully, because tomorrow the Krugwah are going to wow Disneyland with yet another extravaganza.'

'We certainly are,' Eenah says.

CHAPTER 50

It is the last week of May. It's a beautiful day and there is not a cloud in the sky. Thousands of people have gathered in Disneyland Park, and the fashion statement of the day is an *I Love Planet Earth T-Shirt*.

The air is aflutter with self-propelled balloons. The clock is ticking and everyone is waiting for a once-in-a-lifetime spectacular. And the stars of the show will be a species of little nature spirits doing what they do best.

Somewhere up above, an invisible Krugwah orchestra is playing a stirring rendition of the celebrated Disney theme song, the music that has introduced hundreds of Buena Vista movies for decades.

Thousands of children are waiting eagerly, and they gasp in amazement when an enormous Krugwah portal appears in the sky, a shimmering blue halo with golden starbursts, just for added effect.

The show starts with one little Krugwah wandering through an enchanted forest whistling away to himself. Everyone realises that they are about to do a Krugwah version of one of the most beloved stories of all time, *Snow White and the Seven Dwarves,* Disney's first major success as an animated film.

Eenah makes an appearance supported by a Krugwah choir and encourages everyone in every town, village, and city on Planet Earth to sing along as she leads them through an exhilarating version of *Whistle While You Work*.

The Krugwah really do know how to put on a good show, but they are not about to slip away quietly. There is so much more to come, and the stage is set for the guests of honour.

A voice over the loudspeaker alerts everyone to the fact that the main event is about to begin.

'Ladies and gentlemen, boys and girls, the Extra-Terrestrials are on the way.'

The Krugwah have been pecking away at another airborne creation, and to the delight of the crowd, it's an enormous bubble in vivid blues and vibrant greens. But this is no ordinary bubble, this is the portal through which the stars of the show will make an appearance.

'We are going for the big one,' Addric says. 'Take a deep breath and get ready to do your stuff.'

The spectators roar with excitement when they realise that the ETs are going to make an entrance in transparent bubbles, a form of transport inspired by a game that Addric concocted to while away a pleasant afternoon. And the moment they make a touchdown, they are besieged by fans both young and old.

The familiar faces of well-known Disney characters are a common sight on Main Street in Disneyland. And the young people on fairytale duty will be able to say that they touched the hands of the Goddess of Wisdom, the Extra-Terrestrials, and a few of their favourite Krugwah companions.

What they don't know is that the Hateful Army is also out in force, and if they did know, they would have given them a service of old-fashioned Californian hospitality.

Most people wouldn't recognise a Hateful if they saw one, not unless they come from a close-knit community in which everyone knows everyone else.

In places like that, a Hateful has a history and a reputation, and as Felicity was keen to point out, the Hatefuls of the modern age have one thing in common, they all have a deeply ingrained mean streak.

Like the dictators of days gone by, they are masters of intimidation, and the most effective weapon in their armoury is fear and the power of the gun.

Violence has always existed in one form or another, and as the Hatefuls know, it's a tonic that is best served under the cover of darkness.

Addric gave them fair warning that they are on his radar, and as far as the Hatefuls are concerned, this will be a perfect opportunity to dispose of the ETs once and for all. Word has passed around that this will be an opportunity to do what they do best.

CHAPTER 51

Addric insisted that everyone keep their eyes peeled for any problems, and under no circumstances were they ever to forget that they are potential targets.

'According to the data from the Zilmo Tag, at least six hundred Hatefuls live in the local area., and they have probably dusted off their guns.'

'So Addric, what's the plan if that happens?' Felicity says.

'Emphora and I have it all worked out. Subtlety is the best way to deal with a situation like that.'

A few hours later, they finally make it to the central stage, and while Addric prepares to address his adoring fans, Emphora scans the crowd as only she can do.

'People of Planet Earth, here we are again, friends and allies from a distant galaxy, and as you know, we are here for a purpose,' he says.

'Human beings are remarkable creatures. We have one foot in this world and one in the next, and even though it may not be visible, it is there all the same.'

'The inhabitants of this planet are an important part of this extraordinary universe, but you, my friends, have a future that really is very special.

'And if it had not been for the esteem in which you are held in the celestial realms, you could be deprived of that future in an instant.'

'The Extra-Terrestrials were sent here for just that reason. We were assigned the task of dragging you back from the brink.'

'And I am happy to report that you are almost there, but it's not all good news.'

'The only option is for complete and total agreement by the people of Planet Earth. But if you want to survive, you may have to fight for your freedom.'

'There are still five million members of the Hateful Army standing in your way, and I sincerely hope it never comes to a showdown between us and them.'

'As I told the technocrats who were determined to rule your lives, that is not an option.'

'The implants will reveal the identity of those who do not care less about the future of this planet, but we do, and I know that you do as well.'

Before Addric has an opportunity to say anything more, Emphora alerts him to the fact that trouble is brewing.

'A few members of the Hateful Army are here,' she whispers in his ear. 'Use your discretion, Addric or this could turn into a bloodbath.'

'Alert the Krugwah,' he says, 'and leave the rest to me.'

'The Goddess of Wisdom has just asked me to remind you that this is a day on which to celebrate this most extraordinary planet.'

'This is a day on which the people of Planet Earth have come together as one heart and one mind to be seen and heard.'

'We have just been treated to a delightful experience by our beautiful friends, the Krugwah. It was a tribute to the thing which they consider to be important and that is a quality called goodness.'

'Please give them another round of applause because that is the very least they deserve.'

During those few precious moments, Addric takes the opportunity to scan the environment for troublemakers.

'Did you know that the Krugwah can see everything,' he says. 'They can even see what you've got stashed away in your pocket or in your handbag.'

'Now, as you have probably worked out, Eenah does not like bad persons, and neither do we.'

'And before this day is over, I am going to show you something very interesting.'

'I am going to show you exactly what a member of the Hateful Army looks like.'

'If you look around, you will see friends and family. However, if you see anyone who is surrounded by a shadowy haze, you will know that you are standing side-by-side with a member of the Hateful Army.'

'Addric, that was inspired brilliance,' Felicity says. 'It was truly phenomenal how you handled that situation.'

'But I don't understand how you did that,' Connor said.

'Spit it out,' Milton says. 'How did you know that there were thirty members of the Hateful Army in the crowd?'

'Well, as you know, Emphora is a goddess.'

'Yes, I think we all know that, but there is obviously more to this story.'

'See, and now this is the thing. When you are in the presence of the divine, your energy field resonates at a vastly enhanced frequency.'

'You have been as close to Emphora as anyone can be over the last few weeks, but if she enters your personal space, something major happens.'

'Your energy field becomes active, and I mean really active.'

'Ah ha, so when Emphora whispered in your ear, you went into Zippo Land,' Felicity says.

'I did, sort of. Emphora was monitoring the crowd, and when she saw the danger signs, she entered my personal space and I responded.'

'And I knew immediately what I was going to do.'

'So, you weren't speaking your own words,' Milton said.

'He definitely was,' Emphora says. 'But Addric is a Yumi Master and he is sensitive to things that most people are not even aware of.'

Only moments after the Hateful Army had been identified, the ever-reliable Krugwah Security Service appeared out of the blue. The crowd moved back immediately, and thirty very unsavoury characters were immobilised by a simple Yumi force field.

'There they are, but fear not, they are under my control,' Addric says. 'And I can assure you that they are not in a position to do anything at all.'

The Krugwah confiscate their weapons and escort the men to the front of the stage. And over the next half hour, the world watches closely as Addric demonstrates the method by which he intends to reprogram people such as this.

'Now, gentlemen, you are the first members of the Hateful Army ever to be identified, and I am going to explain your options.'

'I am not here to be your judge and jury, but I am going to offer you a chance to change your life.'

'You are probably wondering if I am going to send you to that penal colony on the planet Jupiter.'

'Well, you will be relieved to hear that I am not.'

'And I am not going to do to you what you were going to do to us. On the contrary, I am going to do something very different.'

Everyone is waiting to see what he has up his sleeve, but to their surprise, Addric does something that no one expected.

This is a rare opportunity to see the power of a Yumi Master in action. Addric clicks his fingers, and two glistening portals appear in front of the stage.

'Now, gentlemen, you have a choice of two doors. You can take the gateway to freedom, or the portal to that dreaded penal colony on the planet Jupiter.'

'The gateway on the left will rectify an imbalance in your energy field, and if you step through that door, your future will be assured.'

'Now, you may not be aware of this, but the human body is surrounded by an energy field, and to the eyes of a Yumi Master, it is clearly visible.'

'It serves a valuable purpose, and in one sense, it is not unlike a spiritual engine.'

'The energy field of any living being is quite spectacular and extends up to eight meters beyond the human body.'

The lives of thirty men are hanging in the balance. This is serious, and Addric is not about to mess it up.

'As I said, if you choose the gateway on the left, it will make a simple adjustment to the energy field around your body.'

'After that, you can walk away, none the wiser that anything has changed in your life.'

There is every possibility that five million members of Hateful Army are watching this performance, and Addric is very aware of that.

'Now, gentlemen, take your pick. You can take the door on the left or the one to the right.'

'If you choose the one on the left, you will continue to live a long and happy life.'

'But if that is not what you want, you are welcome to step through the one on the right.'

'And after that, you will spend the rest of your natural life in a penal colony on Jupiter.'

If this was the brainchild of an overpaid television executive, he would have hit the motherlode. It would have been the culmination of three agonising years of work, and a group of handpicked contestants would have to make the biggest decision of their lives.

But this is not a reality TV show. This is the real thing, and everyone knows it. The tension is mounting, and everyone is on tenterhooks. Their hearts are beating away as they wait to see what path these men will choose.

CHAPTER 53

Some people are cautious by nature, and others are overly cautious for a reason. If you were raised by a father who gave you a hiding at least once a week, anyone on two legs would be a potential enemy.

If Chad Chibley had not inherited his father's paranoia about anything and everything, his life might have been different.

Every night for the last two months, he has sat in front of the television watching as the world went mad, and he knew that he had to do something about it. His father had drummed it into his head that if the day ever came when they were invaded by aliens, he was to take them out.

When Chad realised that the Extra-Terrestrials would be making an appearance in Disneyland, he decided that this would be the perfect opportunity. But he didn't expect to be caught red-handed, along with thirty other men who had exactly the same idea.

Chad could barely read or write and dropped out of school at an early age. He spent most of his childhood locked in the woodshed, but things might have been different if it had not been for his mother. She would have left home years ago, but she stayed for Chad's sake.

Her husband was a cruel and violent man who had little tolerance for a boy who stuttered and couldn't speak his mind. Any little thing could send him into a rage, and if Chad didn't answer a question immediately, he would be carted off to the woodshed.

After her husband passed out in a drunken haze, Chad's mother would sneak out to the shed and slip some food under the door. But one day, she left a holy picture on Chad's plate and told him to pray to Our Lady of Sorrows and ask her for help.

To Chad's surprise, his father was killed in a vehicle accident several days later, and ever since then, he has kept that picture close to his heart. But the last thing he expected is to see Emphora coming to his rescue.

With the television cameras following along behind, she steps down from the stage and heads directly for Chad. Emphora had noticed the sadness in his heart, and this as she knows, is one very unhappy young man.

Chad looks up, only to the most beautiful eyes in the most beautiful face that he has ever seen.

'I noticed the tears in your eyes and the crumpled picture in your hands,' she says. 'Our Lady has been very good to you, hasn't she?'

'She has,' Chad says.

'Have you decided which door you are going to take?'

'I don't really care,' he says.

'If I were you, young man, I would take the door to the left. That's what Our Lady would want and that's what your mother would want as well, isn't it?'

'It is,' he said.

He had no idea that he was in the presence of a divine being, and if it had not been for Emphora, Chad would have stepped through the door on the right.

'After today, your life will be so much better, believe me, my boy. Now, off you go, as you have a lot more living to do.'

Before he stepped through the door, Chad turned around and gave Emphora a kiss on the cheek.

'Thank you, My Lady,' he said.

'It was a pleasure, my friend.'

'Emphora, that really was a beautiful gesture,' Connor says. 'How did you know that there was something was wrong with that guy?'

'That young man was not like the others. They really were mean-spirited, self-opinionated, know-it-alls.'

'While they were struggling like rats in a cage, that young man was transmitting on a number of different frequencies, and I was all too aware of it.'

'What do you mean by that?' Connor says.

'It is not difficult for me to work out what's going on in the lives of other people, Connor. That's the way I am.'

'People have many ways of transmitting their thoughts and feelings, and it is not just through body language.'

'Think of it this way. Everything in this world is energy, which means that we are all connected.'

'And to some degree, that explains how someone like your mother knows things that other people don't.'

'She's a clairvoyant,' Connor says. 'She can see things in her mind's eye.'

'Yes, that's the gift of inner sight, but people receive and transmit information in other ways as well, all of which have names.'

'Clairaudience and clairempathy,' he says.

'Chad Chibley was broadcasting very clearly on at least two of my frequencies, and because of that I noticed the distress in his energy field.'

'So, what exactly was he transmitting?'

'Chad had lost the will to live, and if I had not intervened, he would have chosen the path to the penal colony.'

'But once I stepped into his personal space, I knew exactly what I had to say.'

'And it meant a lot to that boy. However, it did help that I just happened to look like the only saviour he has ever known.'

'And who is that?' Connor says.

'Our Lady of Sorrows, of course, Mother Mary, the mother of Jesus.'

'Chad's mother gave him a holy picture many years ago when she had no idea what else to do.'

'You see, Chad's father was a very mean man, the meanest of the mean, and he used his fists quite freely on his son.'

'Love is what that young man needed, and he never got that from his father.'

'You can rest assured that Chad will be a lot better off from now on.'

'Your gesture did not go un-noticed by the cameras,' Felicity says. 'That was good to see.'

'That's what I do, my dear, I have been responding to the prayers of my people for longer than I care to remember.'

'I hear the cries of the afflicted and I do my best to give them hope and occasionally a little bit of help.'

'I agree, that really was a wonderful gesture,' Addric says. 'And thank you, Emphora.'

'However, friends and associates, I have a secret that I have not shared with you as yet.'

'And what sort of secret might that be?' says a very worried Felicity.

'Unfortunately, there is a time limit on this deal. We have just over a month to succeed at this task, or the worst of all possible scenarios really will be set in place.'

'So how long have we got?' Felicity cries.

'Until the 30th of June, and if we cannot resolve this situation before then, that will be it.'

'One month, but why haven't you mentioned this before, Addric?'

'As far as I was concerned, we had enough on our plates as it was. Knowing that would have caused even more pressure.'

'But you have rallied to the cause, and you have been absolutely brilliant. Look at what we have achieved and in record time.'

'Oh my God,' Felicity says. 'In that case, we will need all the help we can get. We can't do this by ourselves.'

'If it had not been for the Zilmo Tag, we would never have known that there were so many Hatefuls in the local area,' Milton says.

'Changing the minds of thirty men was a drop in the ocean, Milton. There are five million more out there.'

'Which means that we really will need all the help we can get,' Felicity says. 'But the Zilmo Tag has to be our first port of call because it contains all the data on the Hatefuls.'

'Now, we really do have to put our thinking hats on,' Milton says. 'If we are to succeed, this has to become a global campaign and not just our responsibility.'

'We have to come up with a brilliant idea that involves everyone on the planet.'

'But what else can we do?' Jatoo says.

'Let's make a list of our options,' Milton says.

It is now the 1st of June, and the clock is ticking. Of all the options they have at their disposal, the Krugwah is one of the most effective.

Every television network in the world is keeping this issue in the limelight, and they would jump at the opportunity to go another mile.

'Should we advise the media that D-Day is imminent,' Felicity says.

'If people knew that a global catastrophe was about to wipe them off the face of the Earth, they would be freaking out big time,' Jatoo says.

'Well, I am a little freaked out myself.'

'Now that you put it like that, Jatoo, I don't think that was one of my better ideas.'

'Global hysteria is the last thing we want. Otherwise, our good work really will go down the gurgler.'

The Zilmo Tag has secrets that even Google doesn't know about and Milton would give his right arm to own it, but unfortunately, that is not possible. Until further notice, his window to another world is limited to the data related to the implants.

The Tag is Addric's property, and Milton can look but not touch. The fact that it can update data related to thousands of implants is a little on the creepy side.

'Ah ha, I have it at last,' he says, 'an itemized list of all five million members of the Hateful Army.'

'We now have their names. This thing is so cool, a program with a mind of its own.'

'Now that the data has been indexed and cross-referenced,' Addric says, 'we should, hopefully, be able to undertake a more in-depth investigation.'

'What genius created this thing?' Milton says.

'Someone called Zilmo, I presume, but while we have one at our disposal, let's see what we have got.'

The Tag is the product of a higher intelligence, and in Milton's mind that's about as incomprehensible as it is exciting.

'So, based on what we have here, it looks as if the Hatefuls are scattered all over the globe, but there is something irregular about this list.'

'What do you mean?' Addric says.

'Well, there are millions of blanks, for one thing, people with no names and no identifiable location.'

'How could that be?'

'I have no idea,' Addric says.

'Maybe they are aliens,' Yusef says. 'Activate one and see what happens.'

Addric taps away at one cell after another but gets no response.

'No luck, but why, I wonder.'

'Why don't you try another approach,' Felicity says, 'check out someone in particular, just to see what you get.'

'Okay, show me Felicity Originalis.'

'Addric, that's not fair.'

A moment later, an itemised list documenting the details of Felicity's life appears on the screen.

'And from the very day you were born,' he says.

'Now, that's just a little too scary. Perhaps we can check that out some other time. I have no interest in seeing my life in retrospect, nor do I want anyone else to see it either.'

Jatoo zooms in to investigate. This is an opportunity too good to be true.

'You were born in the village of Ditafarago in the year…'

'Okay, that's enough, Jatoo, that's my private life, young man.'

'Do you have secrets Lady Felicity?'

'Of course, I do, Jatoo, lots of them. So, stop leering at me like that or else.'

'Or what,' he says.

'Or else I may have to teach you a lesson in good manners.'

'Now, children, stop bickering,' Emphora says. 'Let's see if we can get to the bottom of this puzzle.'

Another investigation reveals that at least ten percent of the people in question are those who inhabit the inner Earthly realms.

'Our friends in Hyperborea,' Yusef says, 'I think we can safely say that they are not a threat.'

'I propose that we work to a system, or we will be here forever,' Milton says.

'We should create a list, one for those in the Inner Earthly realms, and one for any others, as they are the mystery element in this scenario.'

To be in possession of a self-aware and intuitive item such as the Zilmo Tag is a stroke of luck. It makes their job so much easier, but it does have its secrets, even if it does not reveal everything at once.

'We have a list of the Hatefuls, but it keeps on changing,' Milton says. 'What's going on with this thing?'

'I think we can safely say that they have come to their senses,' Emphora said.

'You mean that they have changed their minds.'

'Yes, Milton, and it also means that our message is working its magic.'

'The television networks have been playing the footage from Disneyland for days. At least the Hatefuls know what fate has in store if they don't come around to our way of thinking.'

'The prospect of eternity in a penal colony would be enough to scare anyone into submission.'

'And if they continue to run that footage, we won't have to deal with as many we thought we would.'

'A few thousand maybe, but I am sure we can handle that.'

'So now, let's have a closer look at list number three and see what that's all about,' Milton says. 'Who could it possibly be?'

'Well, there are several possibilities such as the Illuminati, the dark brotherhood, the New World Order, secret societies, and of course, numerous immortals and the occasional vampire,' Yusef says.

'If you are to believe conspiracy theorists, some of those organisations have been around for a very long time and they have their hands in a lot of pies.'

'They are believed to control world affairs, and have even infiltrated the highest levels of power, including governments and big corporations.'

'Well, this could take forever,' Felicity says. 'Can you please use your magic powers on this magic mirror, Addric?'

'I am doing my best.'

'It sounds as if you have had enough,' Emphora says.

'Not just yet, but we are wasting time just pussy footing around the garden. We should be out there doing something constructive.'

'The data from the Zilmo Tag has nothing useful to reveal about any of those so-called secret societies,' Milton says.

'I bet it would if we knew what to look for,' Yusef says.

'The Tag is only programmed to identify individuals and not the attributes of a particular group,' Addric says.

'However, this looks very odd,' Milton says. 'It appears that one million people are unaccounted for.'

'Check out one of those files and see if you can work out who they are.'

'We tried that, and it didn't work.'

'Have another go, the Tag might have been thinking about something else at the time.'

Addric chooses a random file from the list and is hoping that the Tag delivers the goods.

'We have something and it's a visual image this time.'

'It appears to be a cave of some description, and I can hear someone breathing,' Felicity says. 'There is definitely someone there.'

'Zoom in a little closer,' Milton says.

Addric does so, and for the first couple of minutes, nothing happens. Whoever this is, they are well and truly concealed. A few seconds later, they hear the unmistakable sound of gunfire, and a deep but gravelly voice barking out orders.

'I have a very uncomfortable feeling about this,' Emphora says.

'That isn't all,' Milton says, 'There's an implant on the list that wasn't there before.'

'What you mean by that?' Addric says.

'Look for yourself, Addric. It's implant 10,001, but that can't be right. We only installed 10,000 implants, didn't we?'

'We did, so what's going on, I wonder.'

After numerous attempts to get access to the unidentified implant, Addric has no choice but to call on his old friends, the Venusian ambassadors.

This is a mystery that can only be solved by the joint controllers of the celestial body known as Universal Intelligence, two rather exotic women who once dallied in the world of witchcraft and wizardry.

'Addric, I had a feeling that we would be seeing you again,' Majura says. 'What can we do for you?'

'We have encountered a mystery, and I am hoping that you can shed some light on what it means.'

'I presume that you are referring to the implants.'

'Yes, I am. We have encountered an implant that wasn't there before. And the weird thing is that it has all the features of an embedded code from an unknown source.'

'That is unusual,' Majura says. 'So, let's take a closer look at this mystery shall we.'

Mega-Google, the cosmic search engine appears once again as a ripple in time and space. Majura works her way through a constellation of flickering lights until the data from the implants appear in glorious technicolour.

'Implant 10,001,' she says, 'reveal your hidden secrets.'

Addric is watching closely and expecting it to happen automatically, but the only thing it reveals is a list of blank cells.

'Ah ha, I know what this means,' Majura says. 'Now, if you look closely, you will see that each of these cells has one identifiable attribute.'

'Which is what?'

'They're pink, but they rarely show up, and when they do, it's for a reason.'

'So, who do they belong to Majura?'

'A select group of people that have been on Earth since the beginning,' she says. 'They were the original inhabitants of Lemuria, people who have incarnated in almost every civilisation, but they have chosen to come back at this period of time.'

'To do what,' Addric says.

'They hold the light in one place or another. Some of them know what they are doing and why, but others have no idea at all.'

'However, they are very highly evolved beings, and many were active participants in the New Age Movement of the last century.'

'They can, if they wish, come back for another round in human form, but not everyone chooses to do so.'

'So, are you saying that they never die?'

'They do, but these people know the secret of longevity. Not of immortality, Addric, but of maintaining their biological system in a state of health and balance.'

'However, they are not a problem, but someone else is, and I can see that there is mischief afoot.'

'Like what Majura?'

'Those dirty little rascals are gathering their forces, so I see.'

'What rascals are you talking about, Majura?'

'It seems that the Hateful Army now have a confirmed leader, and he has you in his sights.'

'And who would that be?'

'A renegade from the past, a difficult character and the worst of the worst,' Majura says.

'This is a man who should have been brought to justice a long time ago. He controls the underworld, and now it seems he has infiltrated the world of the Hatefuls.'

'A name would be good,' Addric says.

'This information is freely available on the Zilmo Tag, Addric. Keep that in mind.'

'That nifty little device will provide you with a wide range of information on anything and everything, but you will have to search for it.'

'Now, this man's mother was a low-level member of the Russian aristocracy who escaped to America after the Russian Revolution.'

'She spent most of her life in Chicago as a dance hall attendant, as a prostitute that is. And his father was a high-level member of the Italian Mafia.'

'Your man has been known by many names in his time, and one of those is the Jaguar, but his real name is Dragoman, Colonel Vladimir Dragoman.'

'He has had a chequered career and it seems that he operates from a secure facility off the coast of Libya.

'That's not far from where you live Addric.'

'However, he was born in 1928, and that makes him 104 years old.'

The following morning, newsreaders on every network are almost hysterical. They have every reason to look a lot more solemn than usual. An animated graphic was uploaded onto You Tube the night before, and it's obvious what it means.

'An unidentified organisation has finally shown its true colours, and even though the source has not yet been confirmed, it is believed to be the Hateful Army,' the newsreader says.

The graphic in question is that of a pirate's flag, a laughing skull, and cross bones, but emblazoned across the front in red flashing letters is the message, '*The clock is ticking...and your time has come.*'

'It has to be the Hateful Army,' Addric says, 'courtesy of their self-appointed leader, Dragoman.'

'Then we will have to draw him out into the open,' Felicity said. 'It's time to activate the big guns.'

'What do you mean by that?' Reuben says.

'This Dragoman character is out to get us and everyone else as well. I can smell fanatical written all over this situation.'

'In which case we should be well and truly prepared,' Addric says.

'We have more options at our disposal than Dragoman, and with the help of the Tag, we should be able to pinpoint any unusual activity.'

'So, let's see if we can come up with a plan of action.'

At that moment Milton receives a message on his communicator.

'It's from Charles Derringer, the Acting Head of Swizzer Industries,' he says.

'*Milton, we have just received a message on a secure channel from the Oval Office in Washington DC. It's from the Private Secretary of the President. We have checked and doubled checked to verify its authenticity. The message is attached. Charles.'*

'It's not for me Addric, it's for you.'

'Dear Mr. Sharano. This threat is very disturbing news indeed. Up until now, you have not asked for any assistance, but numerous world leaders have indicated to me, in my capacity as the President of the USA, that they are ready to assist the Extra Terrestrials in any way that they can.

You are welcome to discuss this development with us at any time that you choose. We would be happy to meet you at a time and place to be arranged. I am at your disposal in this most urgent of matters and I will do everything in my power to do anything you ask.'

'Constance Lambert, President of the United States of America.'

'I think we should front up to that meeting, Emphora says.' 'We are dealing with global terrorists now.'

'Think of what it would do for morale on a worldwide scale if everyone was involved. Think of how many more eyes and ears we would have at our disposal. People from all walks of life would do anything to help us out.'

'If you ask me, this is an opportunity not to be missed.'

'How do you pull off a stunt like that?' Connor says. 'How do you bring the leaders of every country in the world together for a one-off meeting?'

'That's where we call upon the Krugwah Transport Service,' Emphora says.

'In other words, Connor, we do it the fast way, by Krugwah portal of course.'

'You would need quite a few.'

'Every Krugwah has the ability to summon a portal at will, my boy, and they appear without fail.'

'But where would we hold such a meeting,' Demetra says.

'In the most isolated country in the world of course, as far from the eyes and ears of the paparazzi as possible.'

'I just happen to be a close friend of His Holiness, the Dalai Lama, and he would be happy to host such an illustrious gathering.'

'In Tibet, you mean.'

'Yes, of course, Connor, where else?'

CHAPTER 57

On an average summer day in the city of Lhasa, the temperature can often reach a maximum of 29 degrees, but it can drop to 16 during the night.

A few days later, 195 world leaders come together for an emergency meeting in the Potala, the palace of His Holiness, the 15th Dalai Lama, and it is here that Jampa Gyatso, one of a long line of Lamas holds the position of the spiritual leader of Tibet.

Monasteries can be found on deserted plains in the middle of nowhere, and a few are found on the summit of a high mountain range, but the most impressive monastery of all is in the capital city of Lhasa.

The Potala has survived quite a few tremors since 1649, but it is a sight to behold. At thirteen storeys high, it rises from a wide base and sits on powerful sloping walls. It soars 347 feet above the valley floor, and from a distance, it looks like a sentinel overlooking its domain.

This is a one-of-a-kind meeting that will never happen again, and immediately after they arrive, 195 world leaders are escorted by monks in red robes to the venue for this historic event.

The Great West Hall, the innermost sanctum of the Red Palace, consists of four chapels, each of which is decorated with murals depicting events in the life of the fifth Dalai Lama.

A deep and resonant sound of monks chanting away in the background permeates the very foundations of this ancient space.

Jampa's predecessor, His Holiness the 14th Dalai Lama, was a peacemaker renowned for his compassion and wisdom.

Jampa stepped into his role twenty years ago, and as the first speaker of the day, he opens the meeting with a pertinent but reflective comment about the sanctity of human life.

The second speaker is the President of the USA, Constance Lambert, a 56-year-old woman from Wisconsin. Constance always knew that this would be her role in life. She was not a contender in the electoral race, but she edged her way to the top at a time when the American people had had enough of violence.

As the first female president of America, she changed the mindset and values of a nation that had grown tired of terrorism and warfare. Constance keeps her comments brief and to the point.

'This is a battle that we can win, but only if we pool our resources,' she says.

Addric declined the offer to speak and nominated Emphora instead. She steps up to the podium, and in her capacity as the Goddess of Wisdom, she receives a standing ovation.

Emphora is a consummate speaker, and a task of this calibre doesn't faze her in the least. She has less than an hour to get her message across and to fine-tune the details.

'We all know why we are here?' she says. 'The people of Earth are facing their darkest hour, but if Addric and his team had not accepted this task, it could have been much worse.'

'My friends, you have one chance to save this planet from destruction. Unfortunately, the Hateful Army is not the only problem that we have to contend with.'

'Another menace has appeared on the scene, a man called Vladimir Dragoman, who is also known as the Jaguar. He is a dangerous and powerful man with a history of violence.

'But he is also the leader of a worldwide terrorist organisation who not only has the Extra-Terrestrials in his sights, he is planning to destroy this campaign.'

'Do not even try to fathom the mind of a madman, for that is what he is, but we must, and we will defeat Dragoman by whatever means we can.''

'It is essential that we bring the Hateful Army into line as we did in Disneyland.'

'We can do this, of course, if we coordinate our efforts, but what you are not aware of is that there is a time limit on this routine.'

'That decision is not of our making. It comes from the highest of all celestial realms, and unfortunately, the bad news is that we only have twenty-six days to dispose of the Hateful Army, or the worst of all scenarios will become a reality.'

'Ladies and gentlemen, June the 31st is D-Day for this planet, but if we work together as one heart and one mind, we will succeed.'

'You are probably wondering how we can achieve the impossible at such short notice.'

'Firstly, you will have a major part to play over the next few weeks, but communication is the key.'

'That is the vital element which will keep everyone in the loop, but if you have any questions, please do not hesitate.'

'I do,' says the President of the Federated States of Malaysia.

'Addric and the Krugwah disposed of a major threat in Rome and did so with ease. They demonstrated that they really do have great power at their disposal.'

'What can we do in a situation like this, your Ladyship?'

'The Hateful Army is scattered throughout every country in the world, Mr. President. We know their names and where they are and we will provide you with the details before you leave this meeting.'

'Your task will be to track them down, and after that, they will become our responsibility. In other words, they will be given the same option as the men in Disneyland.'

'If you remember, Addric offered them the opportunity to choose life or spend the remainder of their days in a penal colony on the Planet Jupiter.'

'But our greatest allies in this campaign are our dear friends, the Krugwah, and they will be in charge of that task.'

'This is not just a battle against an aggressor, it is a battle against time,' Emphora says. 'But to succeed, everyone on this planet must be of the same mindset.

'However, whatever you do, please do not alert your people to the fact that their days might be numbered, as that would only cause mass hysteria.'

'What you can do is offer them an active role to play. Ask them to be vigilant, to keep a sharp eye posted for any unusual activity.'

'If Dragoman knows that everyone on the planet is monitoring his every move, that will have a decided effect on his actions.'

'Prepare your forces for evasive action just in case.'

'However, Dragoman is a dangerous opponent and we intend to do our utmost to stop him in his tracks.'

'And this is the most important thing of all, you must educate your people on the secret to success.'

'What do you mean by that?' the President says.

'Have you ever heard of a concept called human consciousness my friend?'

'Yes, I have, but I don't really understand what it is.'

'It's another term for people power, Mr. President.'

'Human consciousness is a powerful force in its own way and it has always been so. The power to bring about changes on a global scale comes from within, Mr. President.'

'And if everyone on this planet is thinking the same thing over a long period of time, magic can happen.'

'That is the key to success, Mr. President. The human race is not as helpless as they seem to think. They have power, real power, but they must understand what they have to do and why.'

'We have been monitoring the human consciousness index, and the data indicates that we are succeeding in this endeavour.'

'However, there are five million reprobates out there who could not care less about our future.'

'And over the next three weeks, we intend to track them down and see that justice is served.'

'As a consequence, every person on this planet must be working on the same page if we are to succeed.'

'We have to make sure that they are in possession of the same information, and thinking the same thing on a non-stop basis for the next twenty-six days.'

'Does that answer your question, Mr. President?'

'It certainly does, your Ladyship. It certainly does.'

'Before you leave today, you will be given a few useful resources, including messages from me, from Addric, and from Eenah.'

'But the message is essentially the same in all three cases. We want people to play an active role in this campaign.'

'You can contact us at any time via a secure communication system and we will respond with all immediacy.'

The Dalai Lama was not about to let them get away so quickly, so they spent a lot longer in Tibet than they were planning to.

Accompanied by an entourage of monks, he took them on a guided tour of the secret recesses of the Potala, an experience that few people have ever had before.

The Potala is thirteen storeys high, with over 1000 rooms and 20,000 statues. The White Palace is primarily the living quarters of His Holiness, whereas the Red Palace is a complex of libraries and galleries, a monastery devoted to religious pursuits, amongst other things.

The tour took a lot longer than they expected, and everyone agreed that it was worth the effort, but the treat of the day was a typical Tibetan meal with over 1000 monks in attendance.

'I can see why monks never get fat,' Felicity says. 'Everything was bite-size portions. A very sensible idea if you ask me. A little of this and a little less of that.'

'Very true,' Emphora says, 'but the Potala is a sacred site and another reason why we have to succeed at this mission.'

'It's just one of seven billion reasons,' Addric says. 'Planet Earth is a treasure that we cannot afford to lose.'

After a long and interesting day, the front terrace is the perfect place to sit back and relax. And from Felicity's perspective they have every reason to celebrate.

'That is what you call a coup, a victory of the first order, and in terms of our campaign, I agree, it was a masterstroke of inspired strategy, Emphora.'

'Thank you, my dear, and I have a feeling it will deliver the goods in terms of a global response.'

'In the meantime, we have a little breathing space before we venture onto the battlefield.'

'So, what are we going to do next?' Connor says.

'Brush your teeth and comb your hair,' Felicity says, 'because we are going to be busier than ever.'

'Doing what?'

'I have no doubt that we will be making guest appearances on just about every television show in the world, that's what.'

'Really, how can you be so sure?'

'Within twenty-four hours, everyone in the world will be talking about this.'

'The message of the Goddess will be the only topic of conversation on news bulletins, current affair shows, chat shows and the internet.'

'Have you ever wanted to be famous Connor?'

'No, not really.'

'Well, it's too bad buddy boy, because you are going to be busier than ever, but only for the next three weeks, of course.'

'And after that, you can retire on the royalties or join a monastery. Take your pick.'

'But what about the Hatefuls. They will be watching closely and if they know that we will be in Helsinki or Katmandu, they will be waiting for us.'

'Bad news for them. Good news for us,' Felicity says. 'Besides, you will probably have Eenah or Addric by your side. So, we will make it count.'

'Think of it like this, Connor. It will be another notch on your gun and one less Hateful to worry about. Mr. Dragoman's days as a terrorist are well and truly numbered.'

'In fact, Connor, you have just given me a brilliant idea.'

'And what's that?'

'As you know, one of my interests is terrorising the reprobates on my Hit List, so I am going to visit Mr. Dragoman myself.'

'You'd do that.'

'Oh yes indeed, I have taken on a lot worse than him. If anyone has any objections, speak now, or forever hold your piece.'

'That's a wonderful idea,' Emphora says. 'The sooner we trap Mr. Dragoman in our net, the easier it will be for everyone.'

'Excellent, I am looking forward to a showdown with this man. I have a short fuse for megalomaniacs of any description.'

Felicity's declaration was absolutely correct, and it took less than twenty-four hours before tongues started wagging in cyberspace. The reaction to Emphora's message was overwhelming.

For marketing gurus in the television industry, it was an opportunity to do what they did best.

Celebrities and politicians were happy to appear on one show or another, but what they really wanted were the stars of this campaign, the ETs, the Goddess of Wisdom and, of course, Eenah and the Krugwah.

Milton appears at the breakfast table the next morning, looking a little bleary-eyed.

'I have been up all night and you won't believe what has happened.'

'Someone has infiltrated your system,' Felicity says.

'How did you know?'

'The gossip vine doesn't understand rules and regulations, Milton, that's why. And it never has, not on this planet. So, how many got through?'

'We have hundreds of requests to appear in just about every place you can think of,' he said.

'Excellent. You take a seat. I will pour the coffee and you can spill the beans.'

'We have had requests from every major television network in Europe, America, Asia, Africa, Australia and even the Pacific Islands and there are just as many from radio stations as well.'

'However, there is a rather interesting message from Central Australia.'

'Really, that's one place I would love to visit,' Felicity says. 'Who is it from?'

'A young woman who operates her own radio station and has done so for the last seven years.

'She's an Australian aboriginal who was christened Philomena Gilbert, but is commonly known as Phizzy.'

'So, what does Phizzy have to say, Milton?'

'Take a look for yourself.'

'Addric, I encountered a man in a bar in Alice Springs recently. He had had a few drinks too many, but I was eavesdropping on his conversation, and he said that he had a list of every member of the Hateful Army.

I think his name is Jack Mastrick or something like that. If he is on your radar, he is here in Alice Springs. It's only a guess, but I would not be surprised if he is planning something.'

'Phizzy is my sort of girl,' Felicity says. 'And she definitely has her eye on the ball.'

'Milton, have you checked this fellow out yet?'

'There is no such person as Jack Mastrick, but there is someone called Jack Maastricht. He has a military background, and apparently, he is a resident of numerous countries, one of which is Libya.'

'You may not believe this,' Addric says, 'but according to Majura, Mr. Dragoman lives in Libya.'

'We should check this reprobate out,' Felicity says. 'I have always wanted to see Ayer's Rock.'

'It has reverted back to its traditional name,' Milton says, 'Ayer's Rock is now known as Uluru.'

CHAPTER 59

The midnight to dawn session, or the graveyard shift as it's also known is not the most popular timeslot for a radio announcer, but someone has to do it, and today it's Phizzy's turn.

It's almost six thirty in the morning and she is having a short break. In her case, that means a quick puff on a cigarette and a few moments to commune with the universe.

Philomena is a local girl from outback Australia, but everyone knows her as Phizzy, mostly because of her frizzy hair. She was born in an Aboriginal community in Central Australia, but she has lived in Alice Springs for most of her life.

Phizzy has always been a chatterbox and was planning to get a job in the tourist industry. But if it had not been for an opportunity to do a three-week job placement in a radio station her life would have been very different.

Big-Rock-Radio is an oversized hut on the outskirts of Alice Springs and other than a view of the desert, it's nothing to write home about.

BRR, as it is fondly known, was the love child of a local boy, Dibbles Bluestone, a Vietnam War veteran. Like most men in the area, Dibbles was the father of several local children, but Phizzy wasn't one of them.

On the day that she tuned up at his door, Dibbles was on his way out. He had been diagnosed with cancer and his days were numbered.

He had no time to waste, so he trained Phizzy for the job and transferred ownership of the station into her name.

Phizzy was a Godsend from day one. She had a knack for snappy repartee. She was a fast learner and knew exactly which buttons to push and when, and seven years later, the station has a much wider audience.

Most of Phizzy's listeners are avid country and western fans, especially the roadies, or the Delivery Boys, as they are fondly known.

They spend up to eighteen hours a day travelling all over the Northern Territory, delivering essential food items to the people of outback Australia. Phizzy went out of her way to draw them into her web and made a lot of friends in the process.

The Charley Pride song, *The Snakes Come Out at Night,* has one minute to go, and she just has time to make a mad dash to the bathroom.

Phizzy's shift is almost over, and her brother Martin is waiting to compere in the morning show.

Before she packs up for the day, Phizzy checks her phone, and to her amazement, she has a message from Milton Swizzer.

'Philomena, we would like to speak with you privately, if that's possible. Get back to me as soon as you can.' Milton.

'Milton Swizzer,' she cries. 'Oh my God, it got through. How awesome is that.'

The day that the Goddess of Wisdom made an appearance in Swizzer Plaza, life changed for millions of people in remote areas of the world.

Phizzy wasn't the only one who took her message to heart, and like everyone else, she hasn't stopped thinking about it.

On the day that the ETs made a public appearance in St. Peter's Square, life came to a standstill in Alice Springs. This was an opportunity to see real live aliens in the flesh, and people from all over the world gathered in public squares, shopping centers and schools. Something like this had never happened before, and it was definitely not a good idea to stay at home.

Until that day, Phizzy did not understand what was going on, but she was astounded to learn that a group of aliens from the opposite side of the universe were going out of their way to save the people of Earth from global annihilation.

If it had not been for an encounter with a man who sent chills up her spine, Phizzy would never have understood what they were up against.

And if she had not been eavesdropping on Jack Maastricht conversation, she may never have bothered to contact Addric at all.

She sends off a quick reply. 'Yes, Milton, just say where and when.'

Phizzy had never expected to get a reply from the ETs at all. They have enough on their hands as it is, but this must be important.

Why would they bother about a random text message from a radio announcer in Central Australia?

She is just about to leave when she receives another text message.

'It's from Milton.'

Philomena, pick a place, somewhere private and we will meet you there in an hour. Milton.

'Ho-lee, he's not wasting any time, but where can we meet so that no one will see us.'

'How about the Coolamon Café,' she says.

'Okay,' Milton says. 'We will meet you there at 8 AM, Central Australian Time.'

'I wonder if the Goddess will be with them. I would so love to meet her.'

The Coolamon Cafe is a popular place for lunch, and at this time of day, it is likely to be deserted.

'Some nosey tourist with a zoom lens will spot their spaceship a mile away.'

'Drat, I had better get there fast; otherwise this private meeting is not going to be very private at all.'

'I have been listening to Philomena's radio program,' Connor says. 'And she has a great sense of humour.'

'I think it would be a hoot to front up at the Coolamon Café and pretend to be someone else.'

'So, who do you have in mind?' Felicity says.

'I don't know. Maybe we could do the Blues Brothers thing with black sunglasses and a little black hat.'

'Just do it,' she says. 'Give the girl a thrill.'

After ten hours at work, Phizzy is in desperate need of a shower. That has something to do with the fact that it's always hot in Central Australia.

'I have met better-smelling koalas,' she groans as she takes a tentative sniff.

The Coolamon Café is a twenty-minute drive from the radio station, and Phizzy is relieved to see that there is not a tourist bus in sight.

She takes a seat at one of the empty tables out the front, but the aroma of freshly brewed coffee is wafting through the air.

She peers through the door, only to see the owner, Harry Grainger, working away behind the counter.

'Yoo hoo, Harry,' she says.

'Phizzy, what are you doing here at this hour.'

'I have a date, but Harry, I'd kill for a coffee.'

'Take a seat, my darling, and relax those weary vocal chords.'

Everyone in Alice Springs knows that Phizzy is a rising star. She has that extra special quality, but where it came from, no one actually knows.

Phizzy's family is a font of knowledge on Aboriginal traditions, and the history of the local area, and one of the most popular of all culinary pursuits, bush tucker.

Phizzy represents a new generation of Australian Aboriginals, but she would be the first to say that she is a self-created woman.

'Black or white,' Harry says as he places a coffee on the counter.

'White, I think,' Phizzy says. 'I haven't met him yet.'

Harry escaped from the Melbourne restaurant scene several years ago. He just happened to be having lunch at the Coolamon when the previous owner had a heart attack and died.

After numerous government agents had sorted out the mess, the Coolamon appeared on the market. Harry decided to settle down in Alice Springs, and ever since then, he has become a favourite of many of the local women.

'So, who is this mystery man? he says as he engineers his way just a little closer.

'Back off, Harry. His name is Milton.'

'Milton Swizzer, perhaps.'

'Harry Grainger, can you imagine someone like that being interested in someone like me?'

'Yes, I could.'

That was a compliment and Phizzy knows it. She is a good-looking young woman with a bright smile and a sense of humour. And over the years she has appeared as a guest presenter on one music program after another.

Milton is due in ten minutes and Phizzy has to go, but before she does, she reaches across the counter and gives Harry a light peck on the cheek.

'Don't be so bloody nosey.'

Harry bows respectfully. 'See you soon, Phizz.'

Like most men in Alice Springs, Harry is a lecher, a good man but a lecher.

'Bloody men. You're all the same.'

Now, where would an alien spacecraft land in a desolate place like this, Phizzy wonders. She has a suspicion that Milton has more finesse than to appear behind the old toilet down the back.

'Oh God,' she groans. 'What am I doing?'

She looks away for a moment, only to hear someone creeping up from behind.

'Excuse me, but are you Philomena Gilbert?'

The last thing she expected to see is two miniature versions of the Blues Brothers.

'Don't tell me that you are Milton Swizzer,' she says. 'If you are, you're wearing the wrong sort of hat.'

'Blame Connor for that,' Milton says.

'And who is that?'

'This young fellow here, my brother.'

Milton,' Phizzy cries. 'Oh my God, what are you up to?'

'Just a bit of fun, but we did have a date, didn't we?'

'We did Milton, but where is Addric and Eenah, and where is the Goddess?'

'One thing at a time, please, Philomena.'

'We can't talk here,' he says. 'How would you like to come back to our place for a while?'

'It's not in outer space, is it?'

'No, it's a villa on the coast of Spain. And yes, you will meet Eenah and the Goddess.'

'So, how long did it take to get here?'

'Twelve seconds to be precise,' Milton says.

'I don't want to meet the Goddess looking like this, I really need a shower and a change of clothes.'

'Is that a possibility?'

'Anything your heart desires,' Milton says. 'And if you are hungry Eenah will whip something up, especially if you ask nicely, of course.'

The next shock of the day is their mode of transport. A standard Krugwah portal looks nothing at all like the transporter on Star Trek.

The doorway is a glowing blue light, but trailing along behind is what appears to be a long deep throat. Phizzy is nothing if not hesitant.

'That looks positively dangerous?'

'It had the same effect on me when I first saw it,' Milton said.

'But it's perfectly harmless, and according to Addric, it doesn't have a taste for human flesh.'

'However, it is the fastest way to get from one place to another, and in record time.'

'But whatever you do, Philomena, don't open your eyes until we get there,' Connor says.

'I won't tell you why, just take my word for it.'

CHAPTER 60

Phizzy's first experience of a high-speed flight through space and time leaves her feeling a little disoriented. But when she steps out of the portal, it is only to find that she is in a beautifully appointed room.

'What is this?' she says.

'It's a room in Addric's house,' Milton says. 'And it's yours for as long as you are here.'

'Very nice, she says.

'Glad you like it, but Felicity will be here soon, and she will take care of everything.'

'Is she the housemaid?'

'Absolutely not,' Milton says. 'She is…well...anything but that.'

Felicity walks through the door a few seconds later, and she looks positively glamorous. She has a lithe physique, her soft silky hair is tied back in a loose bun, a pair of diamond earrings sparkle in each ear, and she is wearing a dress that probably came from an exclusive shop in Paris or Rome.

'Felicity,' Milton says, 'I would like you to meet Philomena Gilbert.'

'It's lovely to meet you,' she says. 'I am a friend of Addric's, just in case you were wondering.'

'You are one of the ETs, aren't you?'

'Hole in one, my dear, but don't tell everyone, at least not for a while.'

'But you are the brave one, accepting an invitation from Milton at a moment's notice.'

'It was a pretty wild thing to do, wasn't it?'

'It was, but I suspect that you are probably a weensy bit overwhelmed.'

As Phizzy is delighted to see, Felicity is not as stuck up as she looks. Beneath that glossy exterior is a totally different person.

'I can't believe this,' she says. 'Five minutes ago, I was in Alice Springs, and now, I am here in this splendid room.'

Under normal circumstances, she would have gone straight home, grabbed a couple of hours of sleep, had lunch with a girlfriend and then dropped by to see her mother.

'I don't even know why I'm here.'

'You are here because you identified a member of the Hateful Army,' Felicity says.

'We would never have known anything about Jack Mastricht if it hadn't been for you.'

'He is a mean piece of work if ever there was one,' Phizzy says.

'They're all like that, which is why we are out to get them.'

'If nothing else comes of this visit, at least you will be able to brag that you met the Goddess the ETs and even played a part in saving Planet Earth.'

'And that is no idle boast, is it?'

'Definitely not,' Phizzy says.

'So, my dear, you take a shower, and I will scout around and find some clothes. And after that, I will introduce you to the most famous people on the planet.'

'As you probably know, they are delightfully modest in every way.

On the day that a girl meets her very first goddess, she wants to look her best. Felicity returns ten minutes later with a selection of beautiful clothes, none of which have ever been worn.

Phizzy chooses a plum red jacket with a matching knee-length skirt, decorated with little golden studs.

'You look stunning,' Felicity says, 'but earrings are a must.'

Sartorially speaking, it's the most glamorous thing that Phizzy has ever worn. But she cannot resist a pair of platinum earrings with three brilliant cut diamonds dangling from either side.

'You look like a million dollars,' Felicity says. 'It's a pity we aren't going somewhere, but you never know. Crazy things happen around here.'

'Sometimes we pop off to a fancy restaurant in some out-of-the-way place just because we can.'

'But first things first. It's time to meet your fan club.'

Within the hour, Phizzy is the flavour of the month, but no one bothered to warn her about Eenah's sometimes volatile nature, but Phizzy has a few things in her favour. She is a beautiful young woman with a sense of humour and an infectious laugh as well.

Phizzy was a little nervous at the thought of meeting a real live goddess, but that mild state of hysteria did not last long.

Emphora is one of the loveliest people she has ever met, but this is not just a social call, Phizzy identified Dragoman's second in command, and this is one way of expressing their gratitude.

'However, we are looking forward to visiting Central Australia and to seeing Uluru,' Emphora says. 'It would be lovely if you could be our guide.'

'Just say when,' Phizzy says.

'And it would be great fun to be the guest of the week on your radio station as well, if you are interested.'

'If I am interested. Ho-lee Emphora, you bet your bottom dollar I am. That would be a great honour indeed.'

'Do you have any idea of the impact that you have had on everyone,' she says. 'Ever since you appeared on the scene, you have won hearts and changed lives.'

'This death threat thing has galvanized people all around the world, and it has given us something we have never had before.'

'People are thinking differently about who they are and where they belong in the world.'

'On an average day, I get about ten requests for a song, but now I get hundreds. And all they want to talk about is the ETs. You really have been inspirational.'

'I didn't know that. We don't hear from the man in the street. In fact, we rarely ever run into them.'

'Well, you should check it out for yourself,' Phizzy says. 'You might be surprised at the reaction.'

'We will, my dear, but before we do anything else, we have a job to take care of, starting in Australia.'

'We are about to process a few of the Hatefuls, starting with your man, Jack Maastricht.'

'Well, we know where he is,' Felicity says, 'and I think you should get it over and done with while you have the opportunity.'

'According to the Zilmo Tag, there are 8000 Hatefuls in Australia,' Addric says, 'and 2000 of those are currently in Central Australia.'

'Do we take them out under the cover of darkness or do we make it count.'

'We have to be seen to be delivering the goods, and that means doing it in front of the cameras,' Reuben says.

'In that case, I think we should contact the Australian media,' Emphora says. 'They will jump at the opportunity.'

'And as for you, my dear Philomena, this will be your chance to shine. If I was you, I would brush up on my reporting skills, because you are coming along for the ride.

CHAPTER 61

Milton has access to one of the most sophisticated pieces of technology ever invented. And until recently, the Zilmo Tag spent most of its time in Addric's pocket.

He would happily sign over the rights to his empire just to get his hands on it, but he is not about to jeopardise his friendship with Addric, not for anything, but he does have news, and he is excited.

'I have worked it out at last,' he says.

'The Tag is light years ahead of anything I have ever encountered before, but it only reveals fragments of data at a time.'

'In most cases, it's just endless reams of gobbledygook that makes no sense at all.

'Tell us more, Emphora says.

'Follow me, and I'll show you.'

He activates the Tag and a holographic screen appears in the middle of the room. Milton isn't known as a whiz kid for nothing and his ever-active mind is always in search mode.

'The first problem was to get past the implant data. After that, I was in no-man's land, until I realised that the data registers as pinpoints of light.'

'Say, for example you want info on frogs or something like that. All you have to do is concentrate on exactly what you want, select a sequence of lights, and hey presto, there it is.'

'So, boy genius,' Connor says. 'Show us something useful.'

'Your wish is my command,' Milton says as he activates his routine.

'I would like all the information you have on the green tree frog.'

With the speed of a megalomaniac on mind-altering drugs, the Zilmo Tag releases the motherlode, a never-ending display of information about everything it has on that particular topic.

'However, as I said, to negotiate your way through a minefield like this, you have to have a precise thought in mind.'

'In that case,' Felicity says, 'try something like this, Jack Mastricht, Central Australia, and see what comes up.'

'Okay, here goes,' he says.

'Well look at that, we even have a visual on the scoundrel, but where is here?'

'If I am correct, our man Jack is not far from Uluru,' Phizzy says. 'And that's the entrance to a subterranean tunnel system, or so it is said.'

Planet Earth is a self-sustaining ecosystem on an unbelievable scale, and there is every possibility that this grand old lady is at least 375 billion years old.

And if that's true, she has her secrets. Many civilsations have come and gone since the days of the great gods of yesteryear, and most left a reminder that they had passed this way at one point in time.

'That place isn't mentioned in local legends. It's more like an urban legend,' Phizzy says. 'But just about everyone has heard of it, and it's only two hundred miles from Uluru.'

'Several years ago, an archeologist unearthed a few artifacts, but he didn't have the backing to continue, so he gave up after a few months.'

'If he had, he would have discovered something that we know for certain,' Emphora says.

'And what's that?'

'Believe it or not, at least three civilisations have inhabited the inner Earthly realms for the last 350,000 years, and they all live in subterranean cities.'

'Really,' Phizzy says.

'However, an old friend told us about an underground tunnel system that's much closer to the surface.'

'Which means that Vladimir Dragoman probably knows about it as well?'

At that moment, Milton receives a message from Charles Derringer, the Acting President of Swizzer Enterprises.

'This should be interesting,' he says.

'Milton, we have received messages on our secure channel from over 190 government agencies all around the world.'

'Ah, that's good news,' Emphora says. 'What else does he have to say?'

'Every message is essentially the same, and according to our calculations, over 4,000,000 members of the Hateful Army have been located.'

'Government agencies are now waiting for the Krugwah to commence the task of reprogramming.'

'That is excellent news, and Eenah will be pleased, which means that you can zip off to Central Australia and round up Jack Maastricht and his conspirators.' Felicity says.

'However, I intend to track down Mr. Dragoman and give him a piece of my mind, amongst other things.'

'Now, be nice,' Addric says. 'He's an old man.'

'Not a chance, Addric. He's an extremist and always has been, and if he is 104 years old, then he has definitely passed his use-by date.'

'So, boys and girls, it's time to dust off your flight suits, polish your phasers, lasers, and Tasers, and get ready for a good old-fashioned skirmish. In other words, it's action stations.'

As to what Felicity is going to do, they have no idea, but the Krugwah are dispatched to every country in the world. Their task is relatively easy.

They are going to offer the Hatefuls the option of taking the portal on the right or the portal on the left.

'I have contacted four television networks in Australia, and they will meet us at Uluru in two hours,' Reuben says.

Phizzy's head is spinning at the speed at which things are happening, but she is itching to see how they plan to lure Jack Mastricht out into the open.

Two hours later, representatives from major Australian television channels are waiting for them at an appointed place.

Phase one is an interview in which Emphora briefs a gaggle of overly excited reporters on the current state of play.

'We believe that there is a cave system somewhere to the north of here, one that goes deep beneath the Earth.'

'Our intention is to venture in and see what's going on. And, of course, we are going to do our best to make a right old mess of things.'

'I presume the idea is to offer them the standard option, to repent or take an extended holiday on Jupiter?' Phizzy says.

She has one foot in the door, and that's what you call a scoop in the industry.

'That's it in a nutshell, Miss Gilbert. The ETs will do all the dirty work, but it will not be safe down there.'

'I do not recommend that you cameramen do anything stupid, and if you do, you will face the ire of the Krugwah.'

'They will be waiting for the Hatefuls when they emerge, and as we know, it is not a good idea to mess with the Krugwah.'

'That sounds pretty dangerous,' Phizzy says. 'But I believe that you are after one of the most dangerous terrorists of all time.'

'We are out to get them all,' Emphora says.

'Mr. Big is the one who pulls the strings. And at this moment, he is probably dangling over a cauldron of burning oil or something even worse.'

'And who is he?' Phizzy says.

'His name is Vladimir Dragoman, and I can assure you that if he is in the hands of Lady Felicity, he has not only met his match, he will regret the day that he was born.'

'So, who are you looking for? Phizzy says.

'His second-in-command, a man called Jack Mastricht, a ruthless man with a history of violence.'

'But there is nowhere to hide, and if Mr. Mastricht does find a place, it won't be for long, of that I can assure you.'

On Emphora's suggestion, the cameramen set themselves up around the perimeter, and in terms of a scoop, they will be in the perfect place to see the Krugwah machine in action.

CHAPTER 62

Felicity is looking forward to her one and only meeting with Vladimir Dragoman, a career criminal and a powerful man with connections to every major crime syndicate in the world.

'Just the sort of man that should be on my Hit List,' she says.

In his formative days, Mr. Dragoman operated from secure locations in many different countries. The power behind the throne was a stable of thugs who did his bidding without question. But the world has changed radically and in a short space of time.

The internet had a dramatic effect on the way in which people conducted business. And it soon became the breeding ground for scam artists and would-be criminals.

They have been there since the beginning, waiting in the wings for an opportunity to do what they do best, but now, they do it under the guise of a perfectly legitimate website.

The day that everything changed was the day that the world watched in horror as a force called terrorism reared its ugly head. The word terrorist soon became the name for extremists of every persuasion.

It also threw the spotlight onto millions of others as well, not just career criminals, thugs, and sociopaths, but a breed of faceless men in a thousand different places.

For reasons of their own, terrorists targeted innocent people. Some were lone wolves, while others operated behind the screen of a high-profile organisation.

When governments worldwide outlawed weapons, that situation changed as well. That was the day that they froze the assets of every career criminal and terrorist organisation on their books.

But the worst day of all was the day that the ETs came to town.

That was the day that the Hateful Army became a reality. It was also the day on which the ETs stated that there are five million members of the Hateful Army scattered across the globe.

As a consequence, Mr. Dragoman had no choice but to take a stand, or he would soon be listed as an endangered species.

At the age of ninety, Mr. Dragoman was determined to find the secret to longevity, so he scoured the world looking for the fountain of youth.

That discovery came from the website of a man called Morris Clayfield, who had an interesting post on longevity. Morris claimed that he was eighty and had the physique of a thirty-year-old man.

Morris and his website didn't last long after that, and before he took his last breath, he revealed the location of a series of subterranean tunnels deep beneath the Earth. And with a little more prompting, he also revealed the site of the fountain of youth.

This is Felicity's destination, a treacherous area off the coast of Libya. To the pirates of Tripoli, it was known as the Mouth of Hell, a graveyard of seagoing vessels and a place to be avoided at all costs.

And when seen from the air, it's a windswept escarpment surrounded by steep cliffs and bottomless chasms, but somewhere down below is a secret known only to a few.

Beyond the Mouth of Hell is the remains of an ancient city, a subterranean world in which darkness is not the only inhabitant. This prime piece of Libyan real estate has been Vladimir Dragoman's retreat for the last fourteen years.

Lady Felicity is disguised as one of his henchmen, and her black fatigues conceal a variety of weapons, none of which she has any intention of using.

She makes her way through a network of remote-controlled doors manned by armed security guards, and beyond that is Dragoman's private domain.

The Mouth of Hell is a secure facility protected by fifty men, each of whom is trained to kill. They are assassins of the worst kind, but Felicity isn't worried in the least.

She moves quietly past one guard after another and clicks her fingers, and before they realise it, they are clinging onto a precipice hundreds of feet above jagged rocks and a very angry ocean.

Dragoman's residence is on the lowest level of a facility that has been carved out of solid rock. And when Felicity eventually arrives at the last door of all, she stops to admire the view.

Mother Nature has carved out a subterranean paradise, an underground gorge with a quietly flowing subterranean river, and in the background, is the remains of an ancient city.

'Dragoman has obviously spent a fortune on this place,' she says.

Only one guard now stands between Felicity and Mr. Dragoman, a solidly built ruffian with nasty black eyes and big broad shoulders.

Being caught red-handed is the least of her problems. Sneaking around unseen is an art form that she long ago mastered to perfection.

Before doing anything else, Felicity disposes of this self-made monster, and seconds later, he is clutching onto the side of a perilous cliff.

Now that Dragoman's personal security force has been dealt with, she is ready for her first and last meeting with the man himself.

Dragoman is clearly visible through a solid glass wall but he certainly doesn't look his age.

'He looks fifty if that,' Felicity says.

'As to his secret, I will find out soon enough. But before anything else happens, it's time for a bit of light-hearted repartee.'

Dragoman's retreat is a sumptuously decorated and vast open space that has been carved out of solid bedrock. He has his eyes trained on a flat-screen television suspended from the ceiling, and he is seething.

'What is this?' he cries.

'I believe it is the latest news bulletin,' Felicity says. 'And it's coming directly from Central Australia.'

Dragoman turns around abruptly, barely able to believe his eyes.

'Who the hell are you,' he roars. 'And how did you get in here?'

'My name is Lady Felicity Originalis and I had to pass through at least ten remote-controlled doors to get here.'

'It wasn't too difficult, but I am one of those delightful little rascals affectionately known as the Extra-Terrestrials. Does that answer your question?'

'Where are my men,' Dragoman cries as he inspects the security monitors on each wall.

'Well, if they haven't scared themselves to death by now, they have probably plummeted into the ocean.'

'One or two may still be alive, but not for much longer. Don't bother trying to alert your security police, Mr. Dragoman. It would be a waste of your time and mine.'

'You take a seat and I will help myself to a glass of bubbly because I deserve a drink after what I have just been through.'

'Do you have any particular preference perhaps, wine or champagne?'

'No, nothing at all,' he says.

This is the first time in his life that Vladimir Dragoman has felt so helpless. He knows what the

ETs can do; everyone does, but the last thing he ever expected was to meet one.

'Mr. Dragoman, you stock the very best champagne, don't you?'

'I haven't had a glass of Dom Perignon for days, but I do love my champagne.'

'Now, you explain the secret of eternal youth, and I will tell you what I intend to do with you.'

'Whenever you are ready, just go for it.'

'There's nothing much to say,' he says. 'That underground river has the power to rejuvenate the human body, but I can't go anywhere near it anymore.'

'And why is that? Felicity says.

'It's cold, icy cold, and something I can no longer tolerate. I have a chest condition that I haven't been able to shake and I fear that my days are numbered.'

'They are Mr. Dragoman. That's why I am here, but if you had not vowed to eliminate us before we eliminated you, you may have survived a lot longer.'

'However, I am at a complete loss to understand why you would stand in the way of the future of this planet.'

'What were you hoping to achieve?'

'I was hoping to get rid of you lot, for one thing, so that the rest of us can get on with our business.'

'But no one will get an opportunity to do anything at all if we cannot sort this situation out,' Felicity says.

'The people of Earth have less than three weeks to prove that they are worthy custodians of this planet, or it's sayonara for absolutely ever and ever.'

'You have wasted your time and ours, Mr. Dragoman. You are obviously so self-possessed that you have lost contact with everything that's important in life, haven't you?'

Vladimir knows that he has met his match and has nothing more to say on the matter.

'Your days as a power-hungry mogul are over, Mr. Dragoman.'

'So, what happens now?' he says.

'Firstly, I will escort you to Central Australia so that you can catch up with your old friend Jack Maastricht.'

'The press will be interested in you as a story, but that's about all they'll be interested in.'

'After that, you will be given the choice to repent or you can trundle off to a penal colony on Jupiter, never to be seen again.'

'So, what's there?' he says.

'Nothing but dust. Jupiter is the penultimate dust bowl, but it's not the sort of dust that we have here on Earth.'

'How long will I be there?'

'Seconds at the very least. It's like a recycling plant in a way.'

'Sounds good to me,' he says. 'I need a change.'

'Well, in that case, there's no point in packing a bag is there.'

'I think this place would be an excellent site for a restaurant or maybe even an art gallery,' she says.

'Perhaps you could call it The Vladimir Dragoman Centre,' he says.'

'I will give that some serious consideration, but more than likely it will be a tiny little plaque in a dark corner with a-warts-and-all exposé of a man who spent his life doing all the wrong things.'

A Yumi Master is something like a double agent, and if you met one in the middle of the night, you wouldn't have a clue who they are. They make a brief appearance in one place or another for strategic reasons, mostly shuffle things around, sort out the mess and quietly take their leave.

But Addric has been in the spotlight for the last two months, and his every move has been documented by the media. Under normal circumstances, he would have to answer to the High Yumi Council, especially if his actions contravened Yumi law. And depending on the severity of the crime there would be consequences.

He could be sent into exile and never see his loved ones again, or if his crime was of an unpardonable nature, he would spend the remainder of his life in the Phantom Zone, a place that no one would ever want to go.

'However, it would have to be a serious offence for that to happen,' Emphora says. 'And so far, only two Yumi Masters have ever had to face the tribunal.'

'And what happened to them?' Connor says.

'The High Council chose the lesser of two evils. They were stripped of their Yumi powers, and returned back to a point in time prior to their induction ceremony, none the wiser that they had ever been a Yumi Master at all.'

'But an accomplice is essential, someone to remind you not to cross the line in the sand,' Addric says.

'But you did, Addric. You broke every rule in the book.'

'Yes, I did Connor, didn't I?'

'He certainly did,' Felicity says. 'That naughty bad Addric even revealed his identity to the entire world.'

'And for that alone, he would normally have to face the music,' Reuben says.

'This is a one-off situation and I was given a special dispensation by the Head of the High Yumi Council,' Addric says as he winks at Emphora.

'A nicer person you could never wish to meet, Connor.'

'But you wouldn't want to cross her on a bad day, that's for sure,' Jatoo says.

'Mean is she.'

'The worst, Connor, and I should know, because she's my grandmother.'

'So Addric, your mother is the Head of the High Yumi Council.'

'No, I am afraid not, Connor. She was a chef in a five-star restaurant.'

'They're talking about my mother,' Reuben says.

'But you're not…and he's not,' Connor splutters.

The penny suddenly drops, and he realises what's going on.

'Ah, I get it. You wait till Eenah hears about this,' he says with an evil Eenah-like look in his eyes. 'Your days will be numbered.'

'You are the Head of the High Yumi Council, aren't you, Emphora?'

'Well spotted my boy. I thought they had you cornered for a moment.'

They have every right to chill out and have a little bit of fun, even if it is at Connor's expense. It's not every day that you can say that you saved the world, but they can.

Jack Maastricht was just a little too cocky for his own good and believed he could hide out indefinitely, but he didn't count on Emphora.

'Jack had no idea who he was up against, but he found out soon enough,' Jatoo says.

On that day, over two thousand Hatefuls were rounded up in Central Australia and offered one of two choices, in the nicest possible way, of course.

Most chose to take the door on the left and a few, like Jack and Dragoman, took the one on the right, but it was the Krugwah who stole the limelight.

People in every country were fascinated as these extraordinary little creatures worked around the clock. For nearly twenty-four hours, they processed over four million members of the Hateful Army.

If these men had been convicts or Jews, they would have been treated very differently. But the Krugwah were not prison guards or Nazi storm troopers, and they were not planning to exterminate an entire race of people.

On that day, according to Majura Krestovori and Seray Antropedes, something extraordinary happened. The index that monitors human consciousness went through the roof.

'The thoughts of every single person on the planet were focused on one thing and one alone, and it was all because of the Krugwah.'

'Which means, Addric, that you have achieved a miracle,' Majura said. 'You saved an entire race from extinction, and for that you will go down in history.'

'I have a feeling that you will be invited to quite a few parties over the next few weeks and meet more people than you ever thought possible.'

CHAPTER 64

The 31st of June is a day worth celebrating, but it could have been Doomsday for the inhabitants of Planet Earth. It has been three months to the day since Addric agreed to this task, and it's on this day that thousands of adoring fans come from far and wide to say farewell to the people they have come to know and love.

This is a day to celebrate a great victory and a day that the people of Earth will never forget. The question on everyone's lips is how will the ETs appear this time? Will they arrive in big bubbles or will Addric come up with another ingenious idea?

This will be a grand celebration on a grand scale, but if it had not been for Prince George, the heir to the British throne, it would never have happened at all. George is a popular royal and he went out of his way to organise an extravaganza of global proportions.

As to what the ETs will do, no one has any idea, but the Krugwah will be executing another aerodynamic routine. Everyone is looking forward to a Krugwah version of yet another Disney story. And for the finale, Eenah will lead her choir in a performance of song, dance, and music such as only she can do.

An army of Krugwah engineers have activated thousands of portals around the world. And billions of people will get to see everything that happens.

Thousands of people have gathered in Green Park in the centre of London, and as soon as Prince George steps up to the microphone, the festivities will begin.

It is ten minutes to midday and the eyes of the world are trained on a very colourful stage, but this is no hi-tech stage. It's a Krugwah portal that flashes from red to blue and glistens with little golden lights.

Addric had no idea what he was going to do, but Prince George had a suggestion.

'Perhaps you could introduce famous people from the past,' he said. 'Is that possible, Addric?'

'That's an excellent idea, your Highness. I will think about that.'

Addric decided to discuss this idea with Felicity before doing anything at all.

'Prince George has come up with an idea.'

'And what would that be?' she says.

'Well, I haven't got my head around it yet, but he suggested a routine that includes resurrecting historical figures from the past, like Zeus, for example.'

'You want to resurrect the dead, Addric. Is that what you are saying?'

'Not exactly, Felicity, just open a portal to the past.'

Addric would never have considered such an idea if Felicity had not shown him the secret of stepping back in time. It was because of her that he and thirty like-minded souls had an opportunity to participate in a wedding in Ancient Greece.

Orpheus, the son of a Greek god was about to marry Eurydice, a beautiful young woman. And for a few unbelievable hours, they sang and danced and had the time of their lives with the residents of a little village somewhere in the Thracian hills.

'Not a good idea,' Felicity says. 'For one thing, most of those characters were nothing at all like they are in history books.'

'Unfortunately, children will be in attendance, at least three billion at a rough guess. And I think we should do something a little more family-friendly.'

'So, what do you suggest,' he says.

'See what you think of this idea Addric.'

To open a door onto the past would be a first in anyone's books, but Addric listens closely to Felicity's inspired idea and realises that she is onto a winner.

'That's clever,' he says.

It's a beautiful day, the sky is an azure blue and the very moment that the clock strikes twelve, Prince George appears on the podium.

'People of Planet Earth. Today could have been the very last time we ever saw the sun rise in this beautiful world of ours, but I am happy to say that it wasn't.'

'We are still here, and we are still the custodians of this planet, which means that somebody up there must like us.'

'We survived a catastrophe, but it could have been a lot worse, if it had not been for a man called Addric Sharano.'

'Three months ago, to this very day, Addric was offered the most challenging mission of his career. He was offered the task of saving an entire race of people from annihilation and he accepted.'

'He did so without a second thought, and not just because Earth is the place that he calls home, Addric did it for each and every one of us.'

'You see, Addric is a rarity, a unique man with a heart of gold. And if it had not been for he and his friends, it may never have happened at all.'

'We, the people of Earth, owe them a debt of gratitude that we can never repay, but what you can do is put your hands together and thank these wonderful people with all of your heart.'

'Today, my brothers and sisters of Planet Earth, the ETs and the Krugwah are going to treat us to a celebration such as only they can do.'

'Ladies and gentlemen, boys and girls, sit back and prepare for an experience such as you will never have again.'

Prince George makes a speedy exit from the stage, and the very instant he does so, the portal expands to several times its size.

Fiery little meteors whiz back and forth, leaving a trail of coloured lights across the sky, and it is then that Addric's familiar voice can be heard whispering a message through the corridors of space and time.

'People of Planet Earth, with your permission I would like to take you on a journey to the opposite side of the universe, beyond the borders of the Milky Way.'

'To get to NeverLand, Peter Pan had to take the first star to the right and keep going until morning. But our destination is not the constellation Centaurus, or the star system Alpha Centauri, we will be going even further than that.'

'For today and today only, you will have an opportunity to travel through space and time and see some of the wonders of our universe.'

'Words have the ability to bring things to life, but the words that I will be using are more like fairy dust. So, listen closely and prepare for the experience of a lifetime.'

'Before we get to our destination, we have to pass through clouds of cosmic dust. And they, as you can see, are infused with every colour of the rainbow.'

'The most famous constellations in the heavens are nothing but clouds of dust, composed of elements such as carbon, hydrogen, and helium.'

'But we are about to take a close look at one of the most famous cloud formations of all. And there it is, the constellation known as Orion's Nebula.'

'Orion claimed that he was the best hunter in ancient Greece, but a few of the other gods thought otherwise, and they decided to teach him a lesson.'

'As to whether he was poisoned or murdered will never be known for certain, but Orion ended up as a constellation of stars, accompanied by his dogs, Canis Minor and Canis Major.'

'Now, you may not know this, but stars come in three different colours. Our Sun is a yellow star, but a red star is about as hot as it gets, and that's pretty hot.'

'Whatever you do, never go anywhere near a star, because they are huge balls of exploding gas.'

'As you probably know, our Sun is enormous. In fact, it's thirteen million times bigger than the Earth.'

'But stars don't get any bigger than that one over there. That's Canis Major, a monster of a star if ever there was one. Canis Major is a hyper-giant, which means that it is almost two thousand times bigger than our Sun.'

'Betelgeuse is the star that represents Orion's right shoulder, and it is somewhat smaller in comparison. In fact, it's twenty times bigger than our Sun, and it has been around for a very long time.'

'But it's not going to be around for much longer. You see, Betelgeuse is about to supernova.'

'And when that happens, you will be able to see it from Jupiter to Mars, but we won't have to worry about that for quite a while.'

'Now, the next place on our journey is the star system, Alpha Centauri, and believe it or not, Alpha Centauri is 4.3 light years from Earth.'

'It is literally trillions of miles away, and even in a spaceship, it would take at least 80,000 years to get there.'

'But we will be travelling at the speed of light, and it won't take as long. Just in case I haven't said so yet, we will be travelling by Krugwah portal.'

'They are the most efficient form of transportation in the universe. And in a Krugwah portal, you can reach your destination in seconds.'

'But we will be going a little bit further than Alpha Centauri. We are going to the Khavala, the galaxy that we come from.'

'Unlike Planet Earth which exists in the third-dimensional realm, the Khavala is an inter-dimensional realm, and it is an unusual galaxy for many reasons as you will soon see.'

'If you look deep within, you will notice that it appears to be pulsating. That is the heart centre of our world, a domain called the Ocean of Infinite Mystery.'

'And it is also the home of the celestial being who looks after everyone in the Khavala.'

The Khavala is a place of astounding beauty, but where do people live, you might be wondering.'

'Unlike Earth, which is a planet of vast continents surrounded by oceans, the Khavala exists in a vast and waterless sea called the Abyss.'

'And the most prominent feature of the Khavala are floating islands, some of which are absolutely enormous, while others are relatively small.'

'And on some of those you will find civilisations as old as time,'

'The realm that I come from is known as Vela-Rishan, a civilisation that has its roots in the mists of time.'

'Vela-Rishan was once the home of a legendary race of beings called the Rishani. But they moved on a long time ago and are now known as the Gods of Space and Time.'

The Rishani left many legacies, one of which is The Imperial City of Vela-Rishan, an inspired creation that still exists to this very day.'

'Ladies and gentlemen, allow me to take you on a guided tour of my home, The Imperial City of Vela-Rishan.'

'As you can see, it's a sprawling complex of magnificent buildings, temples, and palaces, set amidst luxuriant gardens and long winding thoroughfares.'

'And in the very middle is the Holy Mountain, the Askadera, the birthplace of our ancestors, the ancient Rishani.'

'This, boys and girls, is the home of the Goddess of Wisdom, and it's our home as well.'

'Vela-Rishan is just one of many realms in the Khavala and the home of a wide variety of people.'

'Now, most people travel by one form of airborne vehicle or another, but a Yumi Master can take a portal if they're in a hurry.'

'One of the secrets of the Khavala is that you can travel from one place to another by an energetic highway.'

'They weave their way through the Khavala from one place to another, but these are not the sort of highways that you are familiar with.'

'An energy highway is a doorway to other realms, but to get anywhere at all, you have to cross one of many energetic bridges.'

'And that's one of them there. That's the famous Portal Bridge, a colossal structure bordered by two monumental pillars.'

'The secret of travelling by an energetic highway is to start out with a clear thought in mind, and if you don't, you could end up anywhere at all.'

'Now, allow me to show you what I mean.'

'We are going to do a quick tour of a couple of my favourite places, and the first of those is the Angelic Realm of Ra-Silonay.

'Ra-Silonay is a magical world floating in the clouds, but it is also the home of Prince Adartha, a man for whom I have the greatest respect.'

'And when the wind blows the clouds away, you can see grand houses from one horizon to the other. And if you are lucky enough, you will also see a legion of angelic warriors flying through the sky.'

'The angels of Ra-Silonay live on floating islands, but they are people just like everyone else. They can fly if they have to, but they use the power of thought to do most things.'

'However, angels love to have fun, and they have one of the best theme parks in the known world.'

'The Water Wheel is just about the most fun that you can possibly have, so let's take a closer look at it.'

'This magical thing is ten huge pools that move around at a moderate pace and it's very popular with little angels in particular.'

'The idea is to stay in one pool for as long as you can, but if you are on the wrong side when a pool tilts down, out you go. I can assure you that it's lots of fun because I have even done it.'

'Now, we are going to visit one more place, a beautiful little village called Ditafarago.'

'But before we go any further, I have a secret to share and one that not too many people know.'

'Ditafarago is the home of my dear friends, Lady Felicity and her sister, Countess Demetra.'

'But please, don't tell anyone whatever you do or I will never hear the end of it.'

'Ditafarago is not far from the Portal Bridge, but it is the home of many unique and wonderful people. And one of those is a strange but curious character called Slinkfoot Sam, or Slinky, as he is commonly known.'

The idea of resurrecting characters from Earth's history would have been fraught with danger. But the idea of telling a story accompanied by visuals and special effects was a much better idea all round.

'For one thing, you won't have to do any work, just tell a story,' Felicity said. 'In fact, just tell them a story about the place that we come from. After all, the people of Earth know nothing of other worlds, but you do Addric.'

For what felt like an eternity, but which was, in fact, less than an hour, Addric revealed one secret after another.

'I have just taken you somewhere and shown you something that you never knew before,' he said.

'And that's an experience you will never forget, but the show isn't over yet. In fact, it is just about to start.'

'However, before the ETs make an appearance, I think it would be a good idea if you got to your feet and stretched your legs.'

The sound of one of the most iconic pieces of music ever written reverberates through the heavens. *The Fanfare for the Common Man* is a stirring orchestral arrangement, and one in which trumpets predominate, but it's also a clear message that the moment has all but arrived.

Prince George races back to the microphone. 'If you look to the northern sky, you will see yet another amazing spectacle.'

The question as to how the ETs plan to make an appearance is answered a few minutes later.

'And there they are,' George says. 'But look at their mode of transportation this time. That is so awesome.'

To the sound of overwhelming applause, the ETs make their appearance, but this time, it is not on a golden staircase or in transparent bubbles. This time, they arrive by a very different form of transportation.

Addric decided to resurrect an idea he used many years before. It was one that he concocted for the battle during the last days of Lemuria, but today, that idea has no purpose other than to impress.

It was essential to practice beforehand, and the best place to do that was in the hills of Scotland, at the home of her Ladyship, the Countess of Farago.

The idea of flying through the air in winged chariots was something that Milton and Connor couldn't come to terms with at first.

'You won't come to any harm,' Addric said. 'Safety will be the least of your problems. You are not likely to come to grief, not in a magic chariot.'

'You will be strapped in with a harness. Your feet will be locked into place on the floor, and you also have a handrail to hold onto.'

That was issue number one, but Milton and Connor were relieved to hear they would also be wearing flight suits.

'The first time we did this, we were wearing the war crown of an Egyptian Pharaoh,' Addric said.

'Is that all,' said an astounded Connor.'

'No, it wasn't. We had a pleated tunic around our waist, a golden collar around our necks, and a pair of golden sandals.'

'I vote that we stick to flight suits. After all, we don't want to scare anyone, do we?'

The moment they leave the ground will be the scariest moment of all, but Addric straps them in just to make sure that they will be safe.

'Okay, boys, now, whatever you do, don't wet yourself, especially if things get a little rough.'

'That's easy for you to say,' Connor said.

'Flying solo is the best thing ever, as you will see for yourself.'

Milton and Connor have never been interested in extreme sports, but they have to do this. The moment that the chariots rise into the air, they have no idea whether to laugh or cry.

If Addric and Jatoo had not been flying alongside, they would have spat the dummy there and then.

'A bird with one wing could fly faster than you two,' Jatoo says. 'Come on, boys. Get this show on the road.'

A few seconds later, they are freewheeling through the air and circling around and around. To be up so high and see one valley after another whooshing by at the speed of light is all too much for Milton but Connor is almost ecstatic.

'How good was that,' he said as he stepped back onto solid ground.

'Well done, boys,' Addric said. 'But now for the hard part.'

'What hard part,' Milton cried. 'That was the hard part, wasn't it?'

'Nope, you only have a pilot's license for a winged chariot. Now we are going to play around with a couple of routines, just to start with.'

'It won't be anything fancy, just a few figure eights and maybe a couple of double loops. But the trickiest part of all will be the flyover, and that has to look really good.'

'Nothing fancy,' he groaned.

It is the last day of autumn, and as any skydiver will tell you, it can get pretty cold up there. Milton and Connor are happy not to be doing the Egyptian thing. Gallivanting half-naked through the sky on a self-aware chariot, wearing hardly any clothes at all is not their idea of fun.

If their taskmaster had been anyone other than Addric, they might have bailed out there and then, but they bit the dummy and persevered.

This routine was a lot more complicated than they expected, but the opportunity to fly through the sky in a winged chariot was an experience they would never have again, and they were determined to succeed.

Addric's plan for a display of aerial acrobatics works out beautifully. The sight of one winged chariot zooming through domestic airspace would have made headline news. But to see eight golden chariots looping the loop, doing figure eights, and freewheeling through the sky was absolutely awesome.

'That has to be the coolest thing I have ever seen, 'Prince George says.

When they finally hit the ground, the ETs are besieged by thousands of people desperate to get the autograph of the century. It's chaos for the first few minutes, and Felicity is doing her best to keep her cool.

'Addric, please do something about this.'

'Okay,' he says.

He rises up into the air and everyone steps back, uncertain as to what he is about to do.

'Ladies and gentlemen, boys and girls. We have to work to a system or we will be here all day.'

'Please line up in a single file, and we will be happy to sign your photos.'

'Good thinking,' Felicity says.

CHAPTER 66

Prince George isn't working to a timetable today, and he doesn't have to be in one place at 2 o'clock and somewhere else at 3.00. And he doesn't have to wander around shaking hands with complete strangers.

An intrepid reporter called Jasmine Darcy takes the opportunity to sneak up on stage to get a royal scoop but George doesn't mind in the least. The ETs are the news of the day and he is happy to pass the time with a pretty girl.

A few minutes later, he just happens to notice a little boy wearing a white leather flight suit.

'Look down there, Jasmine. That's a story if ever there was one.'

'He could be Addric's little brother,' she says.

'I would love to know what that's all about. Come on, your Highness. Let's check this out.'

If it hadn't been for eagle-eyed George, Jasmine might have missed the story of the day.

'Hello,' George says. 'Do you mind if we talk to you for a few minutes?'

'You can,' the boy says, 'but I have to speak to Addric.'

'And why is that?'

'I am going to be a Yumi Master too, that is why.'

'Ah ha, that explains the flight suit. Where did you get it?'

'Mama made it for me.'

'And is she here?' George says.

'She's over there, under that tree.'

'We will be back in a moment.'

Francesca Donatelli can hardly believe her eyes when she realises that Prince George is heading in her direction.

'Excuse me,' he says. 'Are you the mother of that little boy?'

'I am your Highness, I am Deodato's mother.'

Francesca is a beautifully dressed young woman in her mid-thirties with shoulder-length brown hair and gentle blue eyes.

'We would love to know Deodato's story if you would care to tell us.'

Deodato's interest in stars and planets was a little out of the ordinary for a seven-year-old boy from the back streets of Naples.

'Ever since he saw Addric in Rome, he has done nothing but watch him on TV.' Francesca says.

'Deodato is obsessed with the idea that he is going to be a Yumi Master, and he hasn't talked about anything else for weeks.'

'But when he heard that Addric was coming to London, he decided that he just had to meet him.'

'He said that if he saw him dressed in a flight suit, he would believe what he said.'

'He obviously believes that as well,' George says.

'Let's see what Addric thinks. Come on, Francesca, we have to see this for ourselves.'

Addric is surprised to see that the next person in line is a little boy with blue eyes and blond hair, and one who looks like him at that age.

'Hello, young man. You look very handsome in that outfit.'

'Thank you Addric, and so do you.'

'Now, what's your name, my friend and why are you wearing a flight suit?'

'My name is Deodato and I am going to be a Yumi Master just like you.'

Emphora has been watching closely and decides to step out of line and introduce herself.

'Deodato,' she says. 'That's a very special name, but where are you from, if I may ask.'

'I come from Napoli,' he says. 'That's in Sicilia.'

'Ah, and such a beautiful place it is, too, but do you mind if I hold your hands, Deodato?'

'You can, but why?'

'I once met another little boy who said that he was going to be a Yumi Master.'

'That's Jatoo, Addric's son, and I knew immediately that what he said was true. And today, he is a Yumi Master.'

'You see, Deodato, only special people know that they are destined to be a Yumi Master. And I believe you might be one of them.'

'Really,' he says.

'I am absolutely certain of it,' Emphora says.

'Mama, did you hear that,' he cries. 'The Goddess said so herself.'

'I did, my darling and I think you will make a wonderful Yumi Master.'

'So, it looks as if I really will have to establish a Yumi Academy on Earth,' Emphora says.

'You are the third person I have met in the last two months who has made that decision, Deodato. And I would not be surprised if there are a few more out there.'

An hour later, Emphora steps up onto the stage, accompanied by the ETs and a little boy in a white leather flight suit.

She looks out across a sea of faces, all of whom are aware that this is the last time that they will ever see these people again.

'My dear and beloved people of Planet Earth,' she says. 'This is both a sad and a happy occasion.'

'More than anything else, this is a day to celebrate because your future is no longer in jeopardy.'

'You have passed a very important test but it may never have happened at all if it had not been for this extraordinary team of people at my side.'

'They went out there, not knowing whether they would succeed, but they did. The odds were against them, but they persevered, and in the end, they were triumphant.'

'These are your new heroes, and it is their exploits that will live forever in your hearts and minds.'

'But they are not the only ones who came to your rescue. We cannot forget our beautiful friends, the Krugwah, can we?'

'They captured your hearts in the same way that they captured ours, simply because of what they are.'

'And I know you would agree, that when it comes to heroes, they don't come any better than the Krugwah.'

'However, we are here to celebrate your courage and your determination, in particular.'

'If you had not made fundamental changes in your life, your future could have been very different.'

'Unfortunately, this will be our last public appearance, but it may not be the last time you ever see us.'

'This is where the ETs have chosen to live, and the reason for that is obvious. Planet Earth is one of the most beautiful planets in the universe.'

'However, we are not going anywhere, not just yet.'

'It would not be a celebration without all of the good things of life, like music, song, dance, and of course, delicious homemade food.'

'As you know, the Krugwah are mighty warriors and talented entertainers, but they are also the best cooks in the universe.'

'Many years ago, Addric christened them the Krugwah Catering Service, and today, you are going to find out why.'

'If you can smell something wafting through the air, that's a clear sign that their invisible ovens are in business.'

'You see, they can make anything you can possibly imagine, and the best part of all is that the food never runs out.'

'You can eat as much as you like, but don't overdo it, because the entertainment starts at 3 PM sharp.'

'And after that, you can sit back and be entertained by some of the best performers in the world. However, that isn't all.'

'The final event of the day will be a performance by the talented members of the Krugwah Choir, but before that happens, Eenah will be making a special appearance.'

'You may not believe this, but she has a band called *The Very Lovely Krugwahs*.'

'And she is going to get you on your feet and teach you to dance, Krugwah style.'

'I can assure you that it's a lot of fun because we have done it before.'

The moment that Eenah steps onto the stage wearing a pair of cowboy boots and a cowboy hat, she gets a standing ovation.

'Thank you, peoples of Earth, I be liking you too,' she says. 'And because you are such very nice peoples, we are going to put on a very special show.'

'As you know, I only likes good peoples and not bad peoples.'

'But the good news is that all of those naughty bad peoples have gone back home to be good peoples again.'

'Now, I be having an announcement to make. We are going to sing a few special songs for all the good peoples, just to make you happy.'

'This here is my band and it is called *The Very Lovely Krugwahs.*'

'This is Wimple and he plays the guitar, and he is very good at that, you know.'

'This is Gwendo and he is a very talented musician too. He plays the triangle, and he knows how to make that little thing sing.'

'But what you maybe do not know is that this is Bootee, and he be a devil on the fiddle.'

'And what will you do, Eenah?' says someone from the audience.

'Who be saying that?' Eenah says as she scans the thousands of faces in Green Park.

'Come on, show yourself, or I be coming down to get you?'

A teenage boy rises tentatively to his feet and raises his hand.

'It's me, Eenah,' he says timidly.

He has every reason to be wary. As everyone knows, it is not wise to aggravate Eenah.

'You boy, come up here right now,' she says.

This kid has no idea what he is in for.

'And what being your name,' she says as she gives him the once over as only Eenah can do.

'Tristan, Mam,' he says nervously.

'Do you know what I do with naughty boys?'

'Nothing awful I hope.'

'Normally, I make them suffer, but I am thinking that I might even like you.'

Eenah turns back to the audience and says, 'Do you know why I am now liking Tristan?'

'No, Eenah,' they cry. 'Why is that?'

'Because he have the same hair style as we do.'

Things could have been a little different for Tristan if his hair has not been a natural shade of ginger. The most popular style for men and boys in the early 21st century was a style called a comb-over. But when the Krugwah appeared on the scene, the Krugwah curl became the flavour of the month.

'However, because of that, I am now in a very good mood,' Eenah says. 'But for being such a bad boy, Tristan, I am going to make you dance.'

'You can dance, can't you?'

'That depends on what you've got in mind.'

'I will sing and you will dance. I am sure you'll work something out.'

'As I was saying before, I was so rudely interrupted, I is a very good singer, as you will see for your own self.'

'But so too are my backup singers, Malila and Peedie and they have excellent voices as well.'

Gwendo taps his triangle, and Eenah coughs and splutters and pretends to clear her throat.

'Just to make sure my voices be in good shape, all three of them.'

Eenah might have a reputation as a firebrand, but she is not in the habit of taking prisoners. And even though humour has never been one of her strong points, she is a natural comedian.

It has been a tough couple of days, and after everything she has done, she still has the energy to get up on stage for one more performance.

'Okay, our first song is about a naughty boy called Tristan,' she says. 'Get ready to dance, young man.'

With one foot tapping out the beat, Eenah bursts into song with the skill of a seasoned performer, but this is no love song or stirring anthem.

It has the distinctive beat of a fast-paced country and western song, and luckily for Tristan, he knows what to do and gets into the swing of things.

Eenah really can sing and she has a remarkably versatile range. As to where the lyrics came from, no one knows but they are definitely original.

Eenah's on the spot lyrics about a wayward boy has everyone in hysterics. Tristan has no idea that he has just become a star, but not for the reasons he would have liked. And to his surprise, he even gets a wild ovation from the audience.

'More, more, more,' they shout.

'That was good huh?' Eenah says.

'Yes Eenah,' they cry.

'So, you want more?'

Yes, please Eenah.'

'However, I be thinking we need a few more dancers up on stage, but only peoples with the same coloured hair.'

Several overly excited boys race up to the stage and take their places beside Tristan.

'Where be the girl persons?' Eenah says. 'We need girl persons too.'

Five young girls dash up to the stage, but to Eenah's dismay, only three of them have ginger-coloured hair.

'You'll do,' she says. 'Get up there beside Tristan.'

'Okay, peoples of Planet Earth, this be one of the Krugwah's very favourite dances.'

'It's called The Krugwah Hop.'

'Now, get up on your feets and get ready to dance.'

'You will be liking this one very much, but you will be needing room to move.'

It's obvious that some people cannot understand instructions, so Eenah leaps off the stage and wanders around harassing one person after another in her usual militaristic fashion.

'Come on, spread out. You be needing more room, you know.'

'That be much better.'

'Now, I show you what to do and then you do as I say.'

'Can you wobble your backsides?' she cries.

'Yes Eenah, we can.'

'Okay, but you have to hop first and then wobble. Hop and wobble.'

'Why you not be understanding?' she barks at one unfortunate boy in the front row.

Eenah is not going any further, not until she is satisfied that he has mastered the fine art of wobbling.

'Good, that not be too difficult. Now, for the next bit, you have to wriggle your hips at the same time?'

'Okay, now we try it to music,' she says. 'Maestro, music please.'

'The music starts slowly at first, but after that it gets very fast moving, and then it be like riding a four-legged horse.'

'Now, do a little knee-bending thing.'

'Clap those hands and slap those thighs, move to the left and then to the right and wobble those hips from side to side. Yay, yay, yay.'

Eenah has twenty thousand delirious people in the palm of her hands as she belts out a bawdy ballad at the top of her voice.

The music starts out as a slow-moving canter and gradually builds up into a trot and then into an all-out whip-cracking gallop, and by the time it's over, everyone is exhausted.

'That be good, huh?' she says.

The response is not quite so overwhelming this time, but a few stalwarts have the energy to mumble, 'Yes Eenah, it was.'

'Very good, now sit down and Eenah and her lovely band will sing you a very beautiful song so that you can recover your healthiness.'

'After that, it be a very good idea if all you went home and got into bed.'

'Whatever you say, Eenah,' an old man groans.

CHAPTER 68

To say that the history of the Earth can only be found in libraries scattered across the world is not entirely true. It is usually the big stories that get top billing, but it's the other ones that people remember.

This was no footnote to history; it was history in the making. And if television networks around the world have anything to say about it, no one will forget this experience for a long time to come.

There is every possibility that it will change the future in ways that no one could imagine, but the habits of everyone on the planet has changed over the last three months.

The people of Earth were on a collision course with oblivion, and it might have happened if not for those old scoundrels Fate, Providence, and Destiny. Fortunately, the Earth survived, and the rest, as they say, is history.

'I like that, Addric says.

He has been sitting in front of the television watching yet another re-run of the highlights of their big day.

'What do you like?' Felicity says.

'What Prince George said. That somebody up there must like us.'

'Well, they do,' Emphora says. 'The big guys don't get all hysterical if someone goes off the rails. They find a way to sort things out.'

'The God that we know and love may have many faces, but it's the same God wherever you are, and she has never been the vindictive type.'

'Why do you think that God is a woman?' Jatoo says.

'It's obvious, my boy. We are one big family, and we not only need a loving mother; we have one.'

'Okay, I understand now.'

'But look at that,' Addric says, 'Deodato is on television again.'

'Oh, he's so beautiful, isn't he?' Emphora sighs.

Eenah is curious and appears from the kitchen wearing a frilly apron.

'And who being this Dato person?' she says in her usual fashion.

'That's him, the little boy in the white flight suit. Didn't you get to meet him?'

'I was in that India place, in some noisy city called Mum…something or other.'

'Mumbai,' Addric says.

'Yes, making very smelly foods for people in turbans.'

'I did not like that food at all. It burnt the hair off my tongue.'

'I don't think you have hair on your tongue,' Addric says. 'But curry is absolutely delicious Eenah.'

'Krugwah do not like that sort of food. So, tell me about this Dato person.'

'That's him there, the little boy talking to Emphora.'

Very few things have the capacity to touch a stonehearted creature like Eenah, but Deodato reminds her of another little boy who once stole her heart.

Addric was the first human being to whom she had ever given her wholehearted support, until the day that she set eyes on Jatoo.

After they made their escape from Lemuria, Addric wanted Emphora to be the first person that Jatoo had ever met. She took him by the hands, looked into his eyes, and said, 'Hello, my little friend.'

'Hello,' Jatoo replied in his own beautiful way.

'My name is Emphora, and I am pleased to meet you.'

She asked him how old he was, and then about the locket he was wearing around his neck.

'It's a picture of my mother,' he said. 'My grandfather gave it to me. I never knew my mother, but Addric gave me this mirror and every time I look at it, I can see her face.'

'Would you like to see her too?'

'I would love that,' Emphora said.

'That's her. She's very beautiful, isn't she?"

'She certainly is, and I am sure that she is very proud of her little boy.'

Addric heaved a sigh of relief and didn't even try to introduce Jatoo to anyone else. But Eenah had been watching closely and she did exactly as he predicted.

She waddled over, held out her hand, and said, 'Hello, Jatoo, my name is Eenah and we are going to be very good friends.'

Jatoo had never met a nature spirit before, but Eenah knew exactly what to say.

'I can do magic tricks and fly.'

'You can,' Jatoo gasped.

From that moment on, he was hooked.

'I am going to be a Yumi Master too one day, and I am going to fly all by myself. Addric took me for a ride on his golden chariot and we went up above the clouds.'

'Maybe we can find somewhere quiet so we can have a party,' Eenah said. 'What do you like to eat Jatoo? We can make anything, you know.'

If there was ever a moment when the most innocent of creatures stole their hearts, it was then. As Addric knows, the Krugwah are the most lovable and most adorable creatures in every way.

But from that day on, they would be Jatoo's friends as well, and Eenah would go out of her way to see that he wanted nothing.

'So, what be happening with Dato now?' she says.

'Well, we haven't worked that out yet,' Emphora said. 'But we will need someone to teach him our special ways.'

Diplomacy and sensitivity are the secret as Emphora knows from experience. She has never had to ask Eenah to do anything. Like all Krugwah, she does what she knows to be right.

'Him looks like a very nice little boy,' she says. 'But do Him have a mother and a father.'

'He has a mother,' Addric says, 'but I don't think he has a father.'

'That be so sad.'

'I was thinking it would be a good idea to establish a Yumi Academy here on Earth,' Emphora says.

'We have three students interested already, but they will need a teacher if they are to graduate.'

'Are you interested in the job perhaps?' she says hopefully.

'You be wanting me to be a teacher,' says an astounded Eenah.

'If you are worried about your candidacy,' Jatoo says, 'I will happily write a personal reference.'

'Thank you Jatoo, I be needing no words on paper to prove that I be the best Krugwah for the job.'

The festivities are not over yet. A few weeks later, they head for the convention centre at Station 51. And the audience, in this case, are ascended masters from every corner of the universe.

'These wonderful people have achieved the impossible,' Archangel Michael says. 'And tonight, they will be praised, applauded, celebrated, congratulated and rewarded for their efforts.'

'But they will not be leaving empty-handed. They will walk away with a show bag full of awards, one of which is this newly minted medal.'

'If you look closely, you can see that it's a winged chariot made of eighteen-carat gold. But they will also receive a celestial version of an Oscar.'

'Unlike the glitzy statue that you get in Hollywood, these are the walking talking version.'

'They are a tour-de-force of celestial wizardry that come to life at the push of a button. And they even recite the legendary tales of the ETs, from different points of view, of course.'

'As you know, the Krugwah are huge celebrities on Earth, but they're just as popular in the celestial realms.'

'And now for the good news. For one night and one night only, the *Krugwah Happiness Factory* will perform their version of Snow White and the Seven Dwarves.'

'But that isn't all. We will also be entertained by the one and only Eenah, who will be accompanied by her equally talented band, *The Very Lovely Krugwahs.*'

'And by special request, Eenah will do a whip cracking rendition of *Rawhide*, the theme song from a popular television series of the 1960s.'

To everyone's delight, Eenah appears in a cowboy hat and boots, and a suede vest decorated with frills that reach to the floor.

And for a few intoxicating minutes, she twirls around the stage and propels herself onto the lap of one ascended master after the other.

'That was good, huh?' she says.

'We could do better than that,' one brave soul in the audience calls out.

'And who be saying that?' Eenah says.

'It's me,' Addric says.

'Then you better be getting up here quick smart.'

'Not without backup and support, I'm not.'

'Just be getting up here, Addric, or I be coming down to get you.'

'Yes Eenah, whatever you say Eenah.'

'He be a very naught boy tonight. I think him had way too much Vosomor.'

Addric knows exactly what he is in for, and accompanied by the ETs, he scrambles up onto the stage under Eenah's leering gaze.

'So Eenah, what song are we going to do.'

'Dancing Queen,' she says, 'Krugwah style.

In front of an adoring crowd, Eenah pulls another rabbit out of the hat, and a few minutes later, hundreds of ascended masters are dancing around the room and having the time of their lives.

'So, what did you think of that,' she says.

'That was the best thing ever,' Addric says. 'So, how did we go?'

'I have seen better,' she says. 'Now get out of here, as I have things to do.'

'I love you, Eenah,' Addric says.

'Him has never been a bad boy. It must be the Vosomor.'

For the next hour, Eenah has everyone in hysterics as she does her version of some of the most popular country and western songs of all time.

'That was Miss Dolly Parton's song before I got hold of it,' she says. 'But now it's mine.'

After three months of selfless dedication, they have every right to chill out and enjoy the fun and games, but the festivities are not over yet.

Zubia Lembossa is hosting a gala party at her infamous establishment, the Cosmic Café. And it really is going to be a night to remember, especially for Milton and Connor.

On that night, they venture into outer space and get their first glimpse of the Milky Way. To see the Earth from a distance is a spectacular sight, but it pales into insignificance when compared to the mighty planet Jupiter.

Words such as immense and awesome are useless when it comes to describing a celestial body of such proportions. Jupiter is a Leviathan that can generate a level of atmospheric activity more powerful than a cosmic storm in the depths of outer space.

By three o'clock in the morning, their poor little brains are well and truly fried, and just before sunrise, they stumble into a Krugwah portal before they pass out altogether.

After a very big week and an even bigger day, an unusually wistful Eenah cuddles up beside Emphora and places a sleepy head on her lap.

'It be time to go home now,' she says. 'Our work is done.'

'This part is but we will be back soon.' Emphora says. 'A little boy called Deodato is waiting for us to show him how we do things, and I believe that there's a little girl as well.'

'And what being her name,' Eenah says
'Graziana, I think.'
'I be looking forward to that Empora.'
'So am I, my dear. So am I.'

THE END

The Gods of Space and Time
A series of fantasy fiction stories.

BOOK ONE
THE ETERNAL OPTIMIST

Unlike his brother who is cautious and irritable, Addric has a bit of a reputation. He not only believes in miracles; he also believes in the impossible.

Their holiday plans are sabotaged from the first day and they barely survive one life threatening situation after another. The stakes are high and they have to succeed.

A card-carrying member of the dark side is out to get his revenge, but they can't allow that to happen. Addric rises to the challenge and shows what he is made of.

He proves to everyone that he is both brilliant, and audacious. Fearless is a rollercoaster ride through an inter-dimensional realm, a place where unusual things can happen.

A drama set in motion long, long ago is about to unfold. All they wanted was a boy's own holiday. They had no idea what sort of holiday they were in for.

This story was selected as a finalist in, The 2020 Book Excellence Awards.

Allow your mind to roam further than it has ever done before, to the outer perimeter of Alpha Centauri. It is here you will find a galaxy called the Khavala, an inter-dimensional realm, where many worlds exist side-by-side, a world of strange beauty, hidden power, and wondrous mystery.

The Khavala is a self-conscious entity, but when danger threatens the most sacrosanct of all domains, she calls upon the assistance of her most powerful creations, an invincible task force that includes Yumi Masters and Warrior Angels.

To resolve this problem, they must travel deep into the heart centre of the Khavala, to a place of legend, to the domain known since time immemorial as The Ocean of Infinite Mystery.

BOOK THREE
THE LAST DAYS OF LEMURIA

Elisabeth Trundle's life changes on the day that she meets two young men in The Great Library of London, but these guys are not Earthlings.

Elisabeth has been having dreams about the lost continent of Lemuria ever since she was a child.

But the last thing she expected is that she would actually get an opportunity to go there. And that would never have happened if the chronometer of a passing spaceship had not malfunctioned.

Accompanied by four Yumi Masters, Elisabeth's dream comes true and she ends up in a civilisation that's about to be destroyed by a natural catastrophe. Over the next two weeks, they have to train an army, defeat the high priest at his own game and save a young boy's life.

But it's not all bad news, the people are wonderful and the food is even better. Before the dreaded day dawns, they discover how the Lemurians intend to survive.

BOOK FOUR
THE GOLDEN PHOENIX

Accompanied by a few feisty friends, Addric embarks on a mission to rescue his brother's girlfriend from the clutches of a necromancer with delusions of grandeur.

To save Elisabeth, they will have to battle it out in the Roman arena, cross the Arctic Ocean on a crystal powered boat, venture deep into the bowels of the Earth, and then brave the fires of hell on a volcanic planet on the verge of a major transformation.

It will take something more than sharp claws and attitude to defeat a necromancer at his own game, but these boys are Yumi Masters and they have a few tricks up their sleeve.

It is Tuesday, the 13th of May 2048 and it's almost D-Day. 80,000 people in St. Peter's Square are awaiting the arrival of a saviour. He appears at the door of a luminous gateway and makes his way down a winding staircase. He has the physique of a Spartan warrior and is dressed in a suit of white leather.

Addric Sharano is about to reveal his true identity to seven billion Earthlings. Addric is an alien, and he is on a mission. The people of Earth have lost touch with the very essence of who and what they are. They have been seduced by the allure of electronic devices. The big guys upstairs are willing to give them one more chance but only if they change their ways.

On that day, Addric became a global celebrity and he was going to use it to his advantage, but there's a time limit on this deal. If the people of Earth want to survive, they have to change their ways. Earth is his home as well and Addric is not about to fail, and he is definitely not interested in saying, "Sayonara Planet Earth"

BOOK SIX
Addric, Eenah and Lady Felicity
are the stars of book six of
QUIETLY, THEY CAME

The master of fun and games is back, and Addric is in fine form in this light-hearted adventure. His next mission is to rescue forty-two orphans from Pompeii, before they are incinerated by the volcano.

Accompanied by his best friends and glamorous offsiders, Lady Felicity, and her sister, Demetra, two exponents of the fine old art of subterfuge, and the modern version of sorcery, Addric comes up with a clever if not complicated plan.

However, there is one little catch. These kids have a greater purpose in life. They were born with a coded message in their DNA, and it's just waiting for an opportunity to be expressed.

Addric is not known as the master of spin for nothing, so, he takes them by the hand and they dive into the deep end. And when they come up for air, they hit the big time.

Addric is the man with golden touch, and when it comes to doing the impossible he delivers the goods in this rollicking romp of a story. Sit back and enjoy a ride that starts in Pompeii and ends on some of the great stages of the modern world.

The future of an inconspicuous village is threatened by an ungodly invader, but a prophecy states that a messiah will come to their rescue.

The first person on the scene is a Yumi Master with a history of battling the bad guys. And not long after, the real messiah appears in a blaze of glory.

Disposing of the invaders is a serious business, but they have quite a few tricks up their sleeve, and the most potent weapon in their armoury is the power of sound.

And when they are not doing that, they entertain the musically inclined villagers with a selection of inspirational songs from the 20th century. It's a tough call, but someone has to do it. A story to put a smile on your face.

KASHMIRA
The Snake Charmer's Wife

Part One. The Snake Charmer's Tale is a story about an orphan called Govinda who raises his children, Roshan and Kashmira, to become the most celebrated snake charmers of 19th century Ceylon.

Part Two. A Tale of a Modern-Day Holy Man is set in 21st century Melbourne.

After an untimely death, Kashmira embarks on the life of a time-travelling spirit and makes an appearance in the life of Jasper Powell, a young man from modern-day Melbourne.

Kashmira has unfinished business and she chooses Jasper and his girlfriend Sally to complete a task that she could not. This book was a finalist in, The 2019 Book Excellence Awards.

THE GODDESS OF GOOD FORTUNE
The Sequel

When she is offered the opportunity to dispose of a recalcitrant necromancer, the illustrious Lady Felicity Originalis jumps at the chance.

Lady Felicity is not your everyday detective. In fact, she is not a detective at all. She is an exponent of the fine old art of subterfuge, and the modern version of sorcery.

She and her partners in crime uses every trick in the book to protect a 9th century Arabian knight from the clutches of an evil Vizier.

Memphalut el Shakar is the quintessence of a self-obsessed despot with the sharp but beady eyes of a pack hound. As he is about to discover, he is no match for a woman loves a good challenge. Old-fashioned methods of torture are never on the agenda for Lady Felicity. She prefers to use other much more subtle forms of persuasion. And she goes all out in an effort to make sure that this old reprobate gets his just desserts.

ABOUT THE AUTHOR

Vincent Gilvarry is a writer from tropical North Queensland in Australia and one whose creative journey traverses the realms of imagination and of artistic expression.

With a foundation based in the visual arts, his transition into the realm of literature was sparked by a life-changing situation that inspired him to embark on a literary career and an odyssey that has lasted for over 25 years.

He boasts an eclectic repertoire that showcases his versatility across various genres and his fantasy fiction books in particular are a testament to his unparalleled imagination and his narrative prowess.

He is the author of a series of eight fantasy fiction books, a romance novel and a historical fiction based on an old family legend.